ILLEGAL AFFAIRS

ILLEGAL AFFAIRS

Shelia Dansby Harvey

Writer's Showcase
San Jose New York Lincoln Shanghai

Illegal Affairs

Writer's Showcase
an imprint of iUniverse, Inc.

For information address:
iUniverse, Inc.
5220 S. 16th St., Suite 200
Lincoln, NE 68512
www.iuniverse.com

This is a work of fiction. Names, characters, places and incidents either are the product of the author's imagination or are used ficticiously, and any resemblance to actual persons, living or dead, business establishments, events or locales is entirely coincidental.
Cover design by Carlfred Giles
Author's photograph by Henry F. Harvey III
www.sheliadansbyharvey.com

ISBN: 0-595-21535-1

Printed in the United States of America

To Henry, my rock.

And whosoever shall not receive you, nor hear you, when you depart thence, shake off the dust under your feet for a testimony against them.

—Jesus

Shake them haters off...

—Rap lyric

Acknowledgements

Lee Warren and Carol Taylor, thank you for your editorial comments; Lee, your infectious excitement inspired me. I couldn't have completed this book without you. Leslie Henderson and William July, thanks for being persistent and urging me to finish what I started. Marilyn "Miz' Ames and Mary Wanza, you were pressed into service, and, as usual, gave your best. Thank you. Sunday Brunch girlfriends, I can do without a lot of things, but I hope never to be without you! And to my family: Annie Bell, Kenneth Ray, Sharon Kaye, Jesse, Kendrick, and most of all, Henry—thanks for the love.

FINALE

*T*HE WOMAN STARED at the caller ID, but instead of answering the telephone, she walked to the bay window overlooking her backyard. She wasn't looking at anything in particular; rather she steeled herself to answer the telephone the next time it rang. The woman knew that the calls wouldn't stop until she answered. Might as well get it over with.

When the phone rang again, she answered it and launched into a tirade. "I've told you people not to call here! For over a year, you've harassed my family and tried to ruin my daughter's life," she said. Her voice was tight and hard.

"Ma'am, we need to talk to your daughter immediately. Do you know where she is?" the caller asked. The drill was as familiar for him as it was for the woman. Although there were two other people assigned to the case, somehow he always got stuck with making the calls.

"My daughter is on her honeymoon," the woman said. "You idiots tried, but you couldn't stop her from getting married, or from getting her law license. You're out of your league—haven't you figured that out by now? You'll *never* stop my daughter from doing any damn thing she pleases!"

Detective Coolidge smiled. Sometimes he felt sorry for the woman because the daughter used her as a shield. But not today. Today his team's hard work finally paid off, and he took pleasure in delivering the news. He uttered one last sentence and hung up in the woman's face.

The woman immediately picked up her cell phone and called her daughter.

"Where are you?" she demanded. Although the two women hadn't spoken since the wedding three weeks before, the mother didn't bother with niceties.

"We're on a cruise ship in the Mediterranean. I told you that we don't want to be disturbed, and I meant it," the young woman said.

"Detective Coolidge just called."

"So!" the daughter quipped. "He's been calling you every month for almost a year and a half. Don't whine to me—Coolidge is your problem, not mine."

That made the mother smile, just as Detective Coolidge smiled when he told her the news. In many ways, she and the detective were on the same side.

"I'm not whining, dear, and I'm not the one with the problem. Detective Coolidge said that they finally found the body. He can't wait to talk to you."

PRELUDE

THREE YEARS BEFORE Detective Coolidge made his telephone call, Callie Stephens surveyed a half-filled auditorium. New challenges always gave her a rush, and this was no exception. She wasn't the only one who was excited; the entire room felt electric as more and more people filed into Monroe Law Auditorium.

A statuesque woman, arms folded, stood near the front of the auditorium looking over the crowd. Clearly older than almost everyone in the room, she still managed to get double-takes from many of the men. She was honey-brown with clear skin; her face would be perfect but for a thin, half-moon scar just above her right brow. The scar didn't harm her looks; rather, it added something both interesting and off-putting. The woman had a good figure, not good for a woman obviously over forty, but good, bar none. She wore a pale green summer-weight wool suit and understated jewelry. Her hair was streaked with perfectly patterned gray, giving her an edgy, urbane look.

She glanced at her watch and said, "Good morning, first-year students, or 1-Ls, as we say around here, welcome to Monroe Law School. I'm Professor Adel Lenton. We'll be spending a lot of time together, starting now. Right now is also an excellent time for you to begin taking notes.

"Excuse me, sir. Who are you?" Professor Lenton said. Her abrupt shift caused the students, who had been scurrying for pen and paper, to follow her gaze, which was fixed coolly on a tall, deep-ebony guy with intense eyes doing his best to make an unobtrusive entrance.

"I'm Keith Dawson, Professor. I'm sorry I…"

"Mr. Dawson, no need to apologize," said Professor Lenton, as she interrupted him. "Class begins at eight, but I allow a grace period of exactly one minute." She paused, looked at her watch, and smiled at him. "If my watch is correct," she looked him in the eyes, "and it's *always correct*, you've missed the grace period by exactly a minute and a half. Leave the room, Mr. Dawson."

The woman seated next to Callie spoke just above a whisper, "Lenton's strictly business. I like that."

Always quick to take measure of a person, Callie looked at her neighbor and thought *sharp*. She looked to be in her early thirties, which would make her, like Callie, about a decade older than most of their classmates, who were straight out of undergraduate school. She was a shade or two darker than Callie, the color of unadulterated Hershey's cocoa, rich and smooth. She had the erect, confident posture of a model; Callie could tell that the woman was about three inches taller than Callie's height of five-foot-five.

"I'm Raven Holloway," said the woman, her voice still not quite low enough to suit Callie. As Raven returned Callie's silent hello with a direct look and conspiratorial smile, another thought came to Callie: *sexy*. Raven had what Callie's brother, Tyler, described as "that intangible thang." Her looks were impressive, but not what put her over the top in the attraction department. Raven Holloway's intangible thang, Callie suspected, was attitude.

Raven smiled again, wrote something on her note pad, and showed it to Callie. "We'll talk after class," it read.

The rest of the hour passed quickly as Professor Lenton lectured nonstop. She covered the first forty pages of their assigned text, *Cases and Materials on Property*, although most of the students, including Callie, hadn't found the time even to locate a bookstore.

After two months of feeling out of kilter, Callie was surprised at how satisfying it was to walk through the doors of Monroe and get right to work. She was glad that her mother talked her out of waiting another year before starting law school.

Professor Lenton closed her book. "I did most of the talking today but on Wednesday, that'll be your job. Be prepared to discuss the cases on pages forty-one through ninety." As soon as Professor Lenton closed the door behind her, everyone rushed to compare notes, study their class schedules and to figure out which of the three bookstores that serviced the university carried *Cases and Materials on Property*.

"Now I can introduce myself," said Callie as she turned toward Raven and extended her hand. "I'm Callie Stephens."

"Nice to meet you, Callie," said Raven. "Sorry about talking in class. It's going to take me awhile to get back into this professor-student thing."

"I know what you mean," Callie agreed. "Lenton had me reliving the first day of seventh grade, but I like it already. I thought that I'd feel out of place, you know. I figured everyone here would be about twenty-one, except for me."

"I knew there'd be lots of real adults; the days of having one career for life are over. People are working some, then going back to school, so you end up with lots of students who are already professionals. Late twenties, early thirties." said Raven, gesturing toward the students milling around the auditorium. Her glance toward a fiftish salt-and-pepper haired man finished the story.

Callie looking at her watch, said, "I've got an hour before my next class. Want to ride to the bookstore with me? We can get our property books before they're all gone."

"You must be from around here: known me for two minutes and already offering me a ride. I can't get over you Texans," Raven said.

Callie smiled. "We're friendly, and you don't look too dangerous. Besides, unless you're a loner, you're bound to meet new friends pretty quickly. They say law school does that to people; it's all that studying together, eating together, pulling all-nighters.

"All-nighters, huh?" Raven said as she watched a guy walk out of the auditorium. "What a way to learn." She leaned toward Callie and began, "Have you noticed–"

"Hard to miss." Callie said as she interrupted Raven and nodded. "I haven't seen this many good-looking men in one place since...ever." Although Callie said it, she wasn't feeling it; she was at Monroe to become a litigator, not a significant other.

If she changed her mind, Callie would have no problem meeting men. For her first day, she wore her hair pulled back from her face and pinned up—a style popular with professional women wanting to project a no-nonsense attitude. Not all men liked the style, especially not on a woman who had grabbable hair like Callie. But the simple hairstyle drew attention to her features. Her deep brown skin was flawless, as was the smooth, natural arch of her eyebrows. Callie didn't fit the classic American beauty category because her nose was more rounded than pointed and had a bit of a flair, yet many men, irrespective of color, thought that her nose was her sexiest feature. Her lips were full, and on that first day, a rosy color. Her perfect smile completed the package.

Callie got back to the subject. "So do you want a ride?"

Raven took a blue casebook from her leather satchel. "I already have my property book—all the other books, too. But I'll go with you. In fact, I'll drive."

"Let's go to Reese's Bookends," Raven said as she braked at the light in front of University Books Superstore. "It's a bit out of the way, but it's black-owned, so it gets my money."

"This looks just like the area around Howard," Raven commented as the tidy university boulevards abruptly gave way to littered streets and boarded up buildings; trademarks of communities that border urban black institutions.

"Did you go to school in D.C.?" Callie asked.

"I worked there and took a few graduate courses at Howard before moving here for law school, but I attended undergrad at Hampton

Institute in Virginia. So *you know* I'm prepared to deal with my people at Monroe. What I didn't expect to find is a school that's only half black."

"I know. I knew there'd be Hispanics, but so many whites and Asians? That surprised me."

They rode in silence until Callie asked, "So D.C. isn't home?"

"Home." Raven laughed. "No, it isn't. My parents are in San Diego, so I guess you could call that home."

"What sort of work did you do in D.C.?"

"Aren't you the interrogator?" asked Raven, making her first assessment of Callie. "What about you? What were you into before this?"

"I was a sales exec for Radnel Pharmaceuticals. Ten years I did that."

"Ahh Radnel, savior to the HIV infected," Raven commented.

Callie, looking out her window, said, "Yeah, unless you're poor, or a kid. God forbid you're both."

"Meaning?"

"Radnel pushes what's known as 'cocktail therapy,' which is when you combine–"

"I know what a cocktail is," Raven interrupted.

"Well anyway, Radnel's therapy is expensive and it's potent, too strong for children."

"So if you're poor, you're dead, and if you're a kid you get routine antiretroviral therapy because Radnel doesn't want to fund research focusing on kids," Raven said.

"How do you know so much, don't tell me you worked for Radnel, too?" asked Callie who wanted to put her time with the company behind her and didn't like the idea of taking up with another bitter Radnel refugee.

"Nah, I'm a physiologist, a researcher," Raven replied. "I worked on federal defense contracts in D.C."

"Physiology? Wow, you don't look like the pointy-headed type. Not to be sexist, but you look more like a model than a scientist."

"Yeah, and I like having the look." Raven wasn't bragging, just speaking the truth. "When I was a girl, I hated being called "cat eyes" and being told to stay out of the sun so I wouldn't get any blacker."

Callie's family worshipped the sun, but she understood what Raven meant.

"Now, everything's different, my lips are bee-stung sexy and chocolate is in. Thank God for Naomi Campbell and Robert DeNiro," Raven said.

"Still, I'll bet people misjudge you all the time, especially men."

"They do," Raven admitted. "I love the look in their eyes when they find out that I'm a little bit different on the inside."

$\mathcal{R}$AVEN PULLED INTO the driveway of what looked to Callie like an unoccupied building. The worn 'Open' sign on the inside of the building's glass door looked as though it hadn't been flipped for years.

"This is a bookstore?" Callie asked.

"The best," Raven responded. "Reese's Bookends has been around for more than thirty years. Once you meet the owner, you'll understand why."

Once inside, Callie was amazed by the bookstore's cozy atmosphere and by the rows and rows of books of all types. "Maybe for now I should just get the property book and come back this evening."

"No way," Raven said as she bobbed her head to the music of Monroe University's jazz radio station. "Let me see your class schedule," she said. She glanced at it for a moment, smiled at Callie and then began methodically pulling books from the shelves. "We're in all the same classes. Mr. Reese helped me find the right books Saturday, so I know exactly what you need."

Callie and Raven went to the checkout counter with their loot: five casebooks, half a dozen spiral tablets, green and yellow highlighters, pencils and an assortment of other things. The man behind the counter was handsome—the kind whose looks fit him best later in life. Callie guessed that he was probably in his mid-sixties. His slightly wavy hair was almost pure gray, except for the bits of black at his temples and in his mustache. He had two deep laugh lines that gave him a serious look and a slight midriff paunch that reminded

Callie of her own father. The memory sent a sharp pain through her heart, so she quickly put it away.

"What did you do with the books you bought Saturday, burn them?" John Reese smiled broadly as Raven approached.

"These books are not for me; they're for my friend, Callie," Raven said. As she spoke, Raven placed her hand over Callie's, which was resting on the counter. "But," Raven leaned on the counter and lowered her voice, "if I have to burn every book in this city in order to visit you, then that's just what I'll do."

Reese let out a booming laugh.

"No honey, just keep making this old man's day and you're always welcome."

When Reese got to *Cases and Materials on Property*, Reese asked Callie why she didn't buy canned briefs, which are outlines that summarizing the cases that a student is called on to explain, or 'brief.'

"My dad was a court bailiff for over thirty years, and he told me that he could always spot the lawyers who never took the time to read their cases when they were in law school because they sometimes tried to get by without reading all their cases for court. He said it backfires on them and hurts their clients. I promised him that for the first year, I wouldn't take shortcuts."

"Sounds like your father is a smart man," a voice from behind them said. Callie and Raven turned to find a man approaching them with the bold stride and deep, cultivated voice usually associated with a physically imposing figure. But he wasn't a big man. He was of average height and weight, yet looking at him, the word *average* didn't come to mind.

"Michael Joseph," he said as he extended his hand to Callie. His hands were smooth and his smile was a bright, white specimen of expensive dentistry.

She pretended not to notice that as they shook hands, his eyes were locked onto Raven.

"Senator, it's good to meet you," Raven said. "I've followed your career since day one. I know you hear it all the time, but I'm one of your biggest supporters. Raven Holloway."

Callie smiled at Raven's flattering lie. She'd just moved to Texas. How much of a Joseph watcher could she be?

Senator Joseph then turned to Callie. "You're Sonny Stephens's daughter, right?"

"Yes, I am."

"I knew your father well. I'm sorry for your loss." He stepped backward and took a good look at Callie. "I should've recognized you the minute I walked in. You look just like him! Prettier, though." The senator turned serious again. "We met at his memorial service. Sorry that I didn't remember at first."

"That's okay. My family was surprised that so many people took the time to attend."

"Sonny was a wonderful man, always looking out for the other guy. If you're anything like him, you're already ahead in the game," said the Senator.

Mr. Reese, changing the subject asked, "Mike, guess who they have for property?"

Senator Joseph's sharp eyes twinkled. He had nice eyes. "Adel?"

Mr. Reese laughed and nodded yes.

"If you can make it through Professor Lenton's property class, then you've got it made," Senator Joseph said.

"That's right," Mr. Reese agreed. As he handed Callie her book bag, he added, "Y'all stick together. You'll need friends to help you make it through."

Senator Joseph snapped his fingers and said, "As a matter of fact, Professor Lenton's invited me to address the Student Bar Association this Friday. I hope to see you both there."

It was clear that he was speaking to Raven. Callie glanced at the Senator's left hand. He wore a wedding ring.

Raven smiled at the Senator and threw in something extra with her eyes that gave her smile a provocative edge. Callie made a mental check mark beside her initial assessment of Raven. This woman had *that thang* all over the place.

❧   ❧   ❧

On the drive back to campus Raven told Callie why she decided to become a lawyer.

"I decided to go to law school when I found out that the folks making the real money weren't the scientists, but the patent attorneys," Raven told Callie.

As she pulled into the law school parking lot and maneuvered her car into a space marked reserved for faculty, Raven explained, "Last year I developed a system that was guaranteed to generate at least thirty-two million dollars in revenue over the next three years. The lawyers who made sure that our company had exclusive rights to the new process made three to four times more than I did." She swallowed the last chunk of a super-sized Milky Way and added, "All I got was a year-end bonus."

Raven finished her story as they entered their case analysis class. "I figured, screw that. It's time for me to start getting paid."

❧   ❧   ❧

As soon as he left the bookstore, Senator Joseph placed a call to Adel Lenton. "Adel, it's been a while since I've done anything for the school," he told her. "I'd be more than happy to give a speech to the SBA, if you can set it up for this Friday."

O MAR FAXTON HIT the replay button on his CD remote control and leaned back into the smooth coolness of his leather sofa. He'd been unsure about making such a major purchase just before starting law school. Not that money was hard to come by, but who knew when the golden goose would stop laying eggs? Just three weeks into the semester and he knew that getting it was a good idea. Nothing soothed away the tension of a long day like his sofa, except, of course, his music.

"Somebody's sleeping in my bed," Dru Hill's lead singer crooned. Omar added his own velvety bass, "sleeping in my bed, messing with my head." He knew all about that, having spent time in many beds not his own.

Omar took a sip of wine and picked up his civil procedure book. He felt sorry for Professor Wizen, the hunch shouldered little man who taught the course. Omar couldn't imagine repeating the same boring stuff over and over again for twenty years. Every case came down to who to sue, when to sue or where. How exciting was that?

Still, Omar planned to master civil procedure, put in enough effort to get the American Jurisprudence award, called Am Jur for short, given annually to the student who made the highest grade in the class. So what if getting an enema was more thrilling than plowing through *Pennoyer versus Neff* for the umpteenth time? The real deal, no matter how much substantive law one knew, was to know the rules. Cases with merit were thrown out of court every day because the attorney failed to file his case on time or to notify the right people in the correct manner. An opponent who was a master of the rules could beat even star litigators.

Omar knew that law was like life—manipulate the rules or be manipulated.

"Rule number one," Omar said aloud as he rubbed the sofa, "never buy something for a man thinking you gonna share it with him." Shelly, who wrote the check for Omar's leather sofa, his bedroom furnishings and even his tuition, should've been able to recite that one in her sleep. Omar had given her plenty of opportunities to apply the rule, but like most women, she relied more on his smile and his touch than on her own experiences. Shelly, a beautiful blonde, was Omar's golden goose of the moment.

Shelly had clear blue eyes, bleached and straightened teeth, a perfect nose and great legs. Her derriere was a tad flat, but hey, nobody's perfect. She worked out with a personal trainer four days a week, and never ate anything that tasted good. Shelly was Jennifer Lopez fine. Matter of fact, J Lo didn't have a damned thing on Shelly.

Omar remembered the day he met Shelly, not that it was special to him—he simply made a point of remembering everything about his affairs. Winslow Huffmeyer, president of the computer company where Omar was employed as an account executive, had rushed into Omar's office with such energy that Omar figured the company must have closed on a lucrative government contract.

"I'm getting married," Winslow blurted out.

"That's wonderful," Omar said sincerely. Winslow, lacking his own interesting persona, always came up with excuses for going out with Omar, with the intent of salvaging the surplus from Omar's exciting lifestyle and claiming it as his own. Omar detested spending time with Winslow—he was a fat, humorless pain in the ass. It bugged Omar that Winslow's main reason for hiring him was because Winslow got off on having an ex-pro football player around. Omar reduced their leisure time together by introducing Winslow to a few other middle-aged football groupies, but he hadn't been able to completely shake the guy. Marriage, he thought, would take care of that.

"You and Marie, right?" Omar asked, referring to Winslow's date (business functions only) for the past five years.

Winslow sighed and his smile vanished. "Marie's a great gal, but no, it isn't her. I just met this young lady two weeks ago," he said, excited again. "She's a goddess. You've got to meet her, Omar."

"Okay, maybe next week–."

"We'll be married by next week. You've got to meet her now," Winslow insisted. "She's right outside."

Thirty seconds later Omar laid eyes on Shelly for the first time. He immediately knew that she was too much woman for Winslow Huffmeyer.

Omar started out being nice to Shelly simply because she was the boss's wife. He could tell from the casual way that Winslow treated her that Shelly quickly went from "goddess" to latest acquisition. Whatever passion Winslow had was saved for Winslow Computers.

A couple of months into the marriage, Omar asked Winslow, "How are things with you and Shelly?" He didn't care one way or the other about the newlyweds, but Winslow had wandered into Omar's office for the third time that morning, and each time he'd stare out the window or finger Omar's jazz figurines, and Omar had work to do. Winslow obviously wanted to talk about something, and Omar guessed that it must be personal.

"Fine, but it's funny. Now that I have her, I realize that there's nothing wrong with being a bachelor." Winslow looked at Omar's expression and added, "Don't misunderstand, Shelly's a great gal. I guess that I'm a guy who needs a woman, but I don't have time for her to need me. I think she's getting restless."

"Take her to Argentina with you next week," Omar suggested.

Winslow shook his head, "She'd be in the way. Shelly went with me to Mexico City, and boy, what a disaster! I missed a dinner meeting because she insisted that I take her out."

Omar knew that Winslow's Mexico City trip lasted six days, which meant that he had plenty of time to devote one evening to his wife. If Omar had gone with him, Winslow would've insisted that they hit the hot spots every night.

"Hey pal, do me a favor, take Shelly out while I'm in Argentina. She's young, maybe she misses being with people her own age." Winslow's look was so apologetic; one would think he was asking Omar to look after an untrained pet.

Omar let Winslow awkwardly stand there for a moment while he pondered whether the request presented a burden or an opportunity, then he said, "I'm over thirty, and how old is Shelly, twenty-four? I doubt that she'll enjoy my company, but I'll do what I can."

Winslow stayed in Argentina for three weeks, and about two weeks after his return he called Omar into his office. "Please, let's sit here," Winslow said as he ushered Omar away from his desk and toward the sitting area, which was off limits to employees, even Omar. Generally only clients signing multi-million dollar contracts got to tread on the Oriental rug and sit in the custom leather chairs. Omar figured that Winslow was about to close a deal with him. But what the hell, he was prepared.

"Thank you for saving my marriage." said Winslow, who took Omar's silence for modesty. In reality Omar was too shocked to speak. "Truth be told, I was starting to think I'd made a mistake, I just knew Shelly'd ask me for a divorce. I don't know what you did, but son," Winslow grabbed Omar's shoulder, coach style, "you worked a miracle. Shelly's happy; she finds things to do on her own now, and she's okay with me spending time with the business." Winslow pressed an envelope into Omar's palm. "I know that looking after Shelly probably cut into your personal life, but it did wonders for mine and I want to say thanks."

Omar waited until he was alone to open the envelope. Winslow's handwritten note said, "On behalf of Winslow Computers, thank you for thinking outside the box and going beyond the nine to five routine. Sincerely, Winslow Huffmeyer, President." Omar tossed the note aside and looked at the check. Five thousand dollars for sleeping with Shelly. Omar knew that his services were worth more, but given the circumstances, he was pleased.

While Winslow trotted the globe, Omar showered Shelly with attention and listened for hours as she agonized about her passionless marriage. At first the dinner and hotel tabs were on Omar, or, more precisely, on Winslow Computers, since Omar charged everything to his expense account. As Omar and Shelly's trysts became more meaningful (Omar's words), he insisted that their temporary love nests be lavishly appointed. He and Shelly couldn't express their true feelings in a run-of-the-mill-hotel, after all. He convinced Shelly that she deserved the best, and that Winslow, the insensitive bastard, ought to pay the bill. It never crossed her mind that Winslow was already footing the bill, so Shelly paid cash for everything and Omar continued to be reimbursed via his expense account. Their arrangement was perfect because Omar had already decided to go to law school, and he didn't want to work or to raid his investments in order to support himself. The expense account money, which totaled two grand or more each month, went directly to his education fund and allowed him to dump another lady friend whose usefulness was about done.

Omar got to the point where he really liked Shelly, would've been her lover for free, but to maintain his edge, he told himself that if he had to caress Shelly's meager butt for an entire afternoon his consolation prizes ought to include four-star accommodations and a panoramic view of downtown Dallas.

Next came money spent not on them as a couple, but on Omar exclusively. Shelly gave him emergency loans that were never repaid and bought all his clothing. On the day that Shelly plunked down four thousand dollars for a beautiful mahogany bed that took six months to hand carve, Omar celebrated by borrowing a thousand dollars from Shelly and partying with two topless dancers who knew how to break in a mattress.

Shelly didn't do all this because she was stupid. On the contrary, she was well-educated, traveled extensively and had an abundance of common sense for a twenty-four-year-old. Shelly did it because she loved Omar and she was ready to give up Winslow, her family, her church and her standing as a Dallas socialite to be with him. Omar was fine with that, just so Shelly's standard of living didn't decline. He told her that she deserved to live in the manner that she'd become accustomed to during her one year with Winslow. Shelly agreed and began funneling even more cash to Omar so that their life together would be financially secure. She had also prepaid the rent on Omar's condominium for an entire year. Three months more and Shelly planned to leave Winslow and move in with Omar. Her lover had other plans. Whoever heard of taking in a goose that had stopped laying golden eggs?

Shelly's time with Omar was almost up. He was thinking of cutting it short, especially if things worked out with a classmate who'd caught his eye. What a stallion: exquisite skin, long legs, seductive lips and (unlike Shelly) a perfect rear. Her looks and her aloof attitude had gotten underneath Omar's skin; he had to have her. Omar sensed that she wasn't the sort of woman who he could easily play. When they made eye contact, which was happening with increasing frequency, her look was always direct, sexy and cold. Still, she drove a nice car and wore expensive clothes, so it was worth a try. Even if she wasn't meant to be his next provider, Omar would have a grand time finding that out.

$\mathcal{B}$RETT MILSTEAD STOOD on the steps of the Monroe Law Auditorium and studied a campus map. The University Books Superstore was only three blocks outside the western edge of the campus. But Monroe Law Auditorium was on the east side of the two hundred fifty acre campus.

Brett made his way toward the Superstore. The enormous oaks lining Monroe U's sidewalks blocked the Dallas late-September sun, but Brett still felt like he was in a sauna. He ran his fingers through his wavy chestnut hair three times and made a mental note not to do it a fourth time. Brett's dad, Andrew Sr., and his older brother, Drew, were both bald. No need to help the process along in his own case.

When Brett finally made it to the western edge of the campus, he peered down the street and into a different world. The Superstore's giant neon sign beckoned, but between the store and Brett lay three blocks of pure 'hood. Brett thought; it probably isn't a good idea to walk to the bookstore. Not safe. Probably couldn't catch a cab in this part of town either, and even if he could, what cabby would agree to take him only three blocks? Brett consulted the campus map again and found the on-campus bookstore operated by the university. It was, due east—less than one hundred yards from the law school.

Although mid-term exams were only a few weeks away, Brett had yet to buy his first book. He'd had to make due with library books until his financial aid came through. After watching Brett return the books at midnight each night, only to check them out again early the next morning, the librarian finally said, "Keep them until you get your own. You're the only one using them anyway."

Brett estimated his average cost per casebook, even if he chose used ones, would be forty dollars at the Superstore. He'd overheard other students say that the prices at Monroe U's bookstore were at least ten percent higher than those of off campus bookstores.

Brett couldn't afford to spend a penny more than he had to. He couldn't even afford the Chicken Shack Snackie Pack of fried chicken and french fries that most of the other law students survived on. Calf's liver was cheaper. During the past week Brett had eaten liver and onions with rice for four days in a row. No vegetables. By the fifth day Brett felt so stuffed and uncomfortable that he splurged and bought broccoli and yellow squash. Vegetables, bought in sparse quantities, were less expensive than laxatives. More satisfying too. A few vegetables were one thing, but he couldn't justify overspending on books when making the short walk to the Superstore would save him at least sixty dollars.

But, as Brett's father would say, "Being poor is no excuse for being dumb."

Brett wasn't really poor. His father's personal injury practice generated enough money for Drew and Brett to attend the best schools and for their mother to keep a flat stomach, rock hard breasts and a face stretched so tautly that her lips never quite touched. Brett didn't have money because Andrew Sr. wasn't altogether behind his decision to attend Monroe.

Indeed, being poor was no excuse for being dumb. Spending extra money on books because he was land locked within the university's boundaries was just a price he'd have to pay for choosing Monroe.

In reality Monroe chose him, a fact that Brett had already given a revisionist twist. He preferred to link his Monroe experience to Texas tuition, which even for out-of-state students, was much lower than that of other states.

"Choosing" Monroe cost Brett more than safety and access to his father's bank account. "No friends, no culture, no decent study partners," Drew had reminded Brett on the drive to the Milwaukee Airport.

The list became longer and more depressing, "No tennis, no Chi Nu fraternity brothers, no visits from Cyndi," Drew emphasized the last drawback. "And, no cheating on Cyndi."

Brett ran his fingers through his hair as if to punctuate each prohibition. Drew noticed and eased up a bit. "It's still a good deal, buddy," He'd given Brett a pat on the shoulder. "Once you get your degree, no one will know where you went to school and when you go into private practice with Dad, no one will care."

Brett, deciding that his well-being was worth at least sixty dollars, folded the map, shoved it into his back pocket and headed east. *This isn't so bad* he told himself. The students in his property class, even the women, reminded him of Bryant Gumbel; well-groomed and well behaved. They all spoke pretty good English, too.

This could be a good experience. He figured that the Asian students would finish at the very top of the class but he and the other two dozen or so white students had a good chance of finishing in the top ten percentile, no sweat. Brett believed that he would fare well because no matter how high in the class the Asian students finished, they wouldn't get the top job offers. Personally, Brett thought that the Asians should get the jobs, but they didn't fit the law firm culture. Although the ones he got to know in undergraduate school were friendly enough, they still didn't have American-style congeniality. Asians didn't look the part, either—especially the men. Blacks at least knew how to look acceptable. He believed that with this being Texas, the Hispanics might stand a chance. As for the Africans and the Middle-Eastern types, Brett figured that they wouldn't even sign up for interviews.

With the Asians out of the way, Brett just knew he'd be a prime prospect for major law firms that recruited at Monroe. He still couldn't get over the fact that major firms even bothered to come to Monroe, because (Brett believed) the best black students attended predominantly white law schools. Whatever the firms' reasons, Brett was glad that top-shelf firms such as Eaglewhite and Thorpe had a few Monroe graduates on their hiring committees. So what if he didn't get into Georgetown, or Stanford or any other good law school? Brett still had a shot at landing an associate spot at a reputable firm. No way was he going into private practice with his dad. For the first time since getting off the plane at the Dallas/Fort Worth International Airport, Brett felt good about choosing Monroe Law.

In rating his chances of garnering a top-notch job, Brett didn't take into account his grades thus far—he had yet to make higher than a C minus on a pop quiz. But he was sure that once he had books of his own, ones that he could make notes in, he'd have no problem catapulting into the top tenth percentile of the class.

As soon as he neared the student center, Brett's optimism crashed. He stopped and stared at the sea of people congregated on the steps of the building. Where the hell did they all come from? Why were there so many of them crowded onto the steps? Didn't they have classes to attend? These folks didn't remind him of Bryant Gumbel at all. They seemed so *black*! Far too black, in both color and attitude. Every single student looked, to Brett, like a rapper, or the kind of girl rappers rhyme about. Brett started to panic enough that his ears turned pink.

He ran his fingers through his hair five times before he took another step. To regain his composure, Brett whispered softly to himself, "Walk with confidence, eyes straight ahead, but keep the peripheral areas in sight."

To his left a group of girls dressed in orange and gold appeared to tap dance while emitting high-pitched shrieks. A crowd gathered around and urged them on. *It's a black thang*. Brett thought about the slogan that sprang up on T-shirts and television years before. The slogan ended with the assertion, *you wouldn't understand*.

Brett ran his fingers through his hair one last time, squared his shoulders and pushed through the throng of spectators and toward the student center's entrance. He wasn't at Monroe to understand. Getting a law degree was his only goal.

THEY ROUNDED THE same corner, from opposite directions, with such force that the basketball tucked underneath the arm of the shorter man bounced away in one direction while the other man's papers scattered in another.

"Whoa," the taller man stepped back. "I need to slow down."

"Same here man, sorry about that," the shorter man said as he stooped to gather the wayward papers. He kept one eye on his basketball, which had rolled near the steps leading from Monroe's graduate dormitory to MLK Boulevard.

"I've got this covered," the taller man said as he also reached for the papers. "You'd better grab your ball before it's too late."

After gathering papers and basketball, the two men introduced themselves.

"Omar Faxton," said the shorter man. Though Omar wasn't as tall the other man, he was at least six feet. He wore a sleeveless T-shirt that revealed his muscular arms and chest. Omar had the physique of a natural, all-around athlete.

"Keith Dawson," said the taller man, extending his hand. He too, was handsome; his ebony skin, deep-set eyes and prominent cheekbones gave him an imperial air.

"I know who you are," Omar said. He then raised his deep voice and spoke in a southern falsetto, "Leave the room, Mr. Dawson."

Keith shook his head and said, "Professor Lenton got me, didn't she?"

"You were the sacrificial lamb for the day, man."

Omar glanced at Keith's papers. "I didn't mean to hold you up."

"No hold up. I'm here to return some borrowed notes." He nodded toward Omar's basketball. "Surprised to see you holding anything but the pigskin, you any good with that?" Keith asked.

"So you think you know me?" replied Omar.

"Without a doubt, Chicago Bears, tight end, couple years back?"

Omar enjoyed being recognized, and he liked the way Keith played it cool—like it was no big deal. So he did the same.

"I should've gone to the NBA. That's how good I am with *this* ball. Care to find out for yourself?"

"I hoop enough to take you on. I just need to drop this stuff off and get my gym shorts out of my car. Where do you play?" Keith asked.

"At the high school across the street. Some of the kids over there are pretty good." Omar said.

"I'll meet you there in five minutes."

⁂

Keith put four quarters into the dormitory lounge soda machine.

"What do you want?" he asked Omar.

"Anything cold."

Keith pulled the two sodas from the slot and passed one to Omar, who had already stretched out on the sofa, one leg dangling over its arm.

"Man! That was just what I needed," Keith said as he took the seat across from Omar. Keith stretched his neck, leaning his head first to his left shoulder and then to the right. "All the tension in my neck and back is gone. There's nothing like playing ball to relieve stress."

"I'll tell you what I need to relieve stress—some of these chocolate honeys running 'round here!" said Omar, who was ready to talk on one of his favorite subjects.

"There are some fine sisters here," Omar continued. "Sitting next to them all day, smelling their perfume, checking out the little feminine things they do. It's getting next to me."

Keith smiled and leaned forward, grasping his empty soda can with both hands. "I'm from Atlanta, and we're known for having fine women, but I've never seen so much beauty in one spot. All persuasions, from light to dark, naturals to hair hanging down their backs."

Omar picked up the description. "Lean, athletic ones, sisters with hips, and they all go hard!"

Keith summed it up: "I feel like a kid in a candy store. But 'cause there are so many men here, it's like the candy gets to choose the kid."

"Yeah, it's wild. In the pros I kicked it with all types and I didn't have to do a thing to get them, but I'll bet the women here have expectations."

"That's because they're bringing a lot to the table."

"Sounds like you've been checking things out, made any moves yet?" Omar asked.

"Nah. And I'm not looking to get into anything. I've got six lovers for the time being. They're all leather bound and hard as hell to read."

Omar laughed. "Sounds like some women I've known."

"What about you?" Keith asked.

"I can tell you who's at the top of my list, Raven Holloway, know who I'm talking about? The long-legged sister with the wild hair who sits on the third row, left side, in Lenton's class? Omar grabbed the basketball with both hands. "You see this? Raven's ass is like this. Perfectly round. She's a damned blue-chipper, and she knows it. I like a woman like that."

Keith had certainly noticed Raven, she wasn't the kind of woman that a man could miss. He considered Omar's evaluation of Raven. "Yes, she is fine, no doubt." He stroked the beginning of a beard that always appeared in the late evening hours. "But there's something about Raven that strikes me the wrong way. I can't put my finger on it, but she doesn't do it for me."

"You ever meet a woman who didn't have something wrong with her?" Omar asked, but he didn't wait for Keith's answer. "They're always scheming on a brother. That's why I don't get caught up emotionally. I don't care what Raven's game is. I just want to be her man for a night or two. That's it."

Keith didn't feel the same way. "Most women I've come across are sweet as can be, like the one who's always with Raven, Callie Stephens. She's as pretty as Raven, but in a different way. And the woman's got style, but she doesn't flaunt it, you know?" Keith looked to see if Omar agreed with him.

"I know Callie. Her locker is right above mine. Man, every morning before Lenton's class, I'm here, opening my locker." Omar dropped the basketball and squatted, his hands in mid-air. "Raven and Callie walk up to get into Callie's locker. Next thing you know, I've got ass all in my face!"

Keith laughed, "I can think of worse ways to start the day. No wonder Raven's on your mind."

"When Raven's around she's all I see, but the more I think about it, Callie's tight too. Of the seventy or so women in the class, she's got to be in the top five. But me? I have to have number one," Omar said.

"So," said Omar, abruptly switching to teasing Keith, "you don't only lie about your game, you lie about women too. My guess is that you've got your eye on Callie."

Keith held up both hands in a gesture of surrender. "You're right. I'm checking her out every chance I get. Lots of the girls here are young, twenty-one, twenty-two. I prefer a woman with a little background and perspective. I'll tell you something else. After midterm exams are over, I'm asking Callie out."

"Go for it." Omar said as he stood up. "I'm hooking up with Raven, so we'll probably hang out together."

"You talk like it's a done deal. Women like that, you know they've both gotta have a man somewhere." Keith said as he stood and gave Omar a friendly slap on the back.

"Yeah, but somewhere ain't here. Once I get some time with Raven, any other man can forget about it." Omar stretched and picked up his basketball. "Time to hit the books," he said.

"Have you joined a study group yet?" Keith asked.

"No, I've been doing my own thing, but I wouldn't mind hooking up with someone. What did you make on Lenton's first quiz?" Omar asked.

"An eighty-eight."

"I did about the same. Want to get together tomorrow, after contracts?"

"Sounds good to me." Keith said, giving Omar another pat on the back. "Look man. Good game. Good conversation and good advice."

"What's that?"

"If you hadn't pointed out that I've already zeroed in on Callie Stephens, I don't know when I would've noticed it myself; probably not until I saw her with someone else."

PROFESSOR LENTON'S LANGUID southern drawl provided the perfect background acoustics for Omar's thoughts. The class had just turned in its midterm examinations and Professor Lenton, rather than releasing them into the mid-October sunshine, insisted on taking a few moments to preview the assignment for the coming Monday. While his classmates took notes, Omar sketched Raven Holloway's profile. He was a talented artist who found that sketching was the best way to get to know a woman, often better than she knew herself. Every woman he'd ever known possessed unappreciated beauty. Beyond the obvious assets or liabilities of face and figure, every woman had something all her own, a particularly graceful gesture or expression that made her shine, if only fleetingly. Omar's trained eye could spot a good heart, trustworthiness (to the limited extent that any woman could be trusted), untapped sensuality and dozens of other sterling character traits. Omar lost count of the times that he'd gotten in good with a woman by complementing her on a quality that no other man had noticed.

Sketching also helped Omar to detect the flaws. A woman needed to be told at just the right time that, yes, her ears were noticeably large—no hairstyle could hide that. Or that she was too yellow or too dark to be considered pretty. The physical flaws were good, but Omar got the most mileage out of the emotional impairments that his sketches captured. He was always on the lookout for a chin that showed occasional weakness, shoulders that stooped under certain conditions or a perpetual smile that turned downward for half a beat at the mention of a particular topic. Knowing what hurt a woman deep inside was Omar's specialty.

His sketch of Raven was about half done. She was more beautiful, more physically perfect, than he'd realized. But Omar wasn't satisfied. Although he captured the outward Raven, he couldn't pick up anything, good or bad, on the emotional level.

As Professor Lenton dismissed the class, Omar put away his sketchbook and decided not to wait any longer. Whatever there was to find out about Raven Holloway, he would find out the old-fashioned way. Although the two of them had done little more than swap greetings and exchange a few glances, Omar's gut told him that he could be with Raven during the four-day midterm break. Time to make his move. He picked up his books and made his way toward Raven.

"Excuse me," Omar said as he gently touched Raven's hand. "I've seen you around, Raven Holloway, right?"

"Yes, I am, and you've done more than see me around Omar. Seems like every time I turn around you're staring at me. When I'm at Callie's locker with her, I'm half afraid that I'm about to give you a heart attack."

Attitude. Omar knew it was coming and came back at her full force. "So we're skipping the small talk? Fine with me." He stepped closer to Raven and lowered his voice. "I've been staring, and you like it. Let me take you out to dinner tonight."

"I already have plans."

"That's cool, but I'm getting with you before this semester is finished. That's a fact, Raven. I figure it might as well be right now, while we have some down time. When do you want to see me?"

Raven looked dismissive and bored. "What makes you think I want to see you?"

Omar didn't say anything, he wasn't one to blink first. Raven wasn't the type either, but there was no need for him to know that, and she was ready to find out if Omar could fit with her program.

"What about Friday night?" Raven asked.

If she went out with Omar on Friday night and things clicked between them, her Saturday and Sunday would be on.

"Friday's good," Omar said, as though he read Raven's thoughts, "That way we will have the rest of the weekend to get to know each other. I want you to dress up. Be ready at seven."

Omar kissed Raven on the corner of her mouth, turned and walked away. He hadn't asked for a telephone number or address, but Raven knew that Omar would find her.

CALLIE TOOK HER first sip of a giant margarita and finally began to relax. This time it had been her turn to show Raven a Dallas treasure. Raven suggested that they go to Juan's, an upscale North Dallas eatery, but Callie said no.

"We haven't eaten at a decent restaurant in six weeks, let's go somewhere special," Callie said as she directed Raven to Dallas' east side, the heart of the city's Hispanic population. The place, Cantina de Carlos, was as plain as Reese's Bookends on the outside. But once inside, diners felt like they had stepped into the Mexican Yucatan.

"How are you going to spend your weekend?" Raven asked as she sipped her drink.

"Studying."

"You can't study all weekend. That'll make you crazy."

"Until I get some studying done," Callie told Raven, "I can't think about what else I might do."

"I'm going to read the cases assigned for next Monday, but aside from that, I say it's time to have some fun," Raven said.

"You deserve it, Raven. You've given one hundred percent all the way around, but what drives me crazy is that you make it all look so easy," Callie told her friend.

"Easy, like what?" Raven asked.

Callie ticked off a list: "You've made great grades on every pop quiz, and when we study together, you usually grasp the concepts way before I do. And you're always looking out for me. Remember when I caught the flu and missed two days? You showed up at my place with copies of your notes and homemade vegetable soup. Or what about the time I ran out of gas on the interstate?"

Rave gave herself a pat on the back. "I'm a superwoman."

Callie laughed and said, "You're my hero. I admire you."

"Thanks." Raven tossed her thick mane, "You've got some good qualities too, and I think you're going to make it through school. You just need to be more confident."

Callie laughed because the thought of merely making it through never crossed her mind. "Raven, don't take me seriously, I'm gonna do fine. You're looking at a natural worrier, that's all."

"You think that's all it is? Oh well," Raven said shrugging her shoulders.

"So what's up for the weekend?" Callie asked.

Raven narrowed her eyes into tiny slits as she visualized her weekend. "I'm heading over to The Clipper and have my girl Francine give me the works—manicure, pedicure, facial. I might even get a bikini wax." Raven pushed the pause button on her fantasy so that she could order another top-shelf margarita, her third, and the queso dip as an appetizer.

"A bikini wax!" Callie laughed. "You must think you're at UCLA or somewhere else that has a decent beach and weather that won't turn from hot to cold in a split second. This is Dallas!"

Raven turned up her nose and said, "This is a big, backwards cow town, for sure, but the good thing is I don't have to go to the beach to have my bikini wax admired. That can be done in the privacy of my own home."

Callie smiled and shook her head. It had taken her about a week to pick up on Raven's haughty side. Callie chided her friend: "You mean there's a man in dinky little Dallas good enough to see your bare skin? Who is he, anyone I know?"

Before Raven could answer the waiter brought Raven's drink and appetizer and asked to take their orders. Callie halfheartedly ordered the taco salad, without the sour cream and the guacamole. She promised herself that she would order the enchiladas on her next visit. Raven ordered the Mexican platter: two beef enchiladas smothered in ranchero sauce and cheese, a taco, a chalupa, rice, beans and flan for dessert.

Once the waiter left, Raven told Callie that she had a picture of a man in her mind's eye that would be an excellent private companion. "He is tall, on the good side of six feet and he's good to look at—not a pretty boy, though I've had more than a few do me right—but a man with a strong jaw line and pearly white teeth. And he's a man's man, you know?"

"No wimps allowed," Callie added. "He's athletic–"

"–and golf doesn't count, unless he's got serious bank," Raven offered.

Callie listened while Raven described her version of the perfect man. When Raven finished, Callie said, "You gave a pretty good description of your bikini wax man; he sounds like more than just a fantasy. Is there something you're not telling me?"

"With me there always is," said Raven as she drained her glass and let out a long sigh of satisfaction.

O MAR WATCHED RAVEN finish her pecan brownie a la mode. He'd never seen a woman with an appetite quite like Raven's. As he looked at her smooth brown shoulders and toned arms, revealed by the strapless dress that she wore, Omar wondered where the calories went. Raven's dress clung to her like plastic wrap, and Omar could tell that her body was curvy and tight. He'd dated some fine women, but not one could compare to Raven.

The evening was going well. Omar had no problem finding Raven's apartment, an expansive flat on the third floor of a nondescript warehouse on the outskirts of downtown. Omar sank into Raven's royal blue sofa and admired her place while she did whatever women do as they keep a man waiting. Her taste was different from Omar's, more Spartan. The blonde hardwood floors gleamed so brightly that during the day they reflected Raven's wrought-iron coffee table and dining room set almost as clearly as a mirror would. The walls were gray and completely bare. A large stained glass rendering of an African Madonna and Child secured by a heavy crimson cord hung from the rafters directly above the dining room table. Omar knew quality art when he saw it, and this was most certainly an original by a very talented artist. The only other furniture in the room was a stereo that bathed the apartment with the soothing sounds of an alto saxophone. Raven wasn't a member of what Omar called the "potpourri set," women who filled every corner of their surroundings with flowery, feminine things. Her taste was extremely understated and very expensive. This, for Omar, was a good sign.

Before they left her apartment, Raven scribbled a quick note and left it on the dining room table. "My housekeeper is dropping by while we are out," she'd explained. Omar shrugged and smiled. The place was already immaculate as far as he could see.

Omar took Raven to DeLongchamp, an intimate European restaurant atop an office building in chic North Dallas. The restaurant was a favorite of power brokers who liked to wheel and deal and be waited on hand and foot at the same time.

The temporarily spurned mistress of a Congressman who wanted to embarrass her lover in front of his colleagues first brought Omar to DeLongchamp. As Omar and Raven entered the restaurant, Omar nodded a silent greeting toward a table where four men sat, including Senator Michael Joseph.

"Mr. Faxton, good evening, your table is ready," said the maitre d', who greeted him and sat the couple at an out of the way candlelit table that provided a romantic view of the North Dallas skyline. A light rain had begun to fall, adding to the ambiance. Without a word from Omar, the maitre d' left and reappeared with a bottle of wine. He presented it to Omar and said, "I think this will be to your satisfaction, sir."

Omar wanted Raven to be impressed, and she was.

Their conversation was lively and far ranging. Unlike his usual dates, Raven didn't seem interested in Omar's past, but his resume was one of his strongest points. He had to put it out there. First he asked about her.

"Where's home, Raven?"

"Wherever I am for the moment."

"No, you know what I mean. Where did you grow up?"

"Like I said, wherever. My dad's in the military; we've lived all over."

Raven didn't ask him the same question, but Omar launched into his own story as though she had.

"I'm from Chicago, spent my whole life there. I played football for Northwestern and then I played for the Bears, but an injury ended all that. So three years ago I moved here, took a job at Winslow Computers, got bored with that and decided on law school. My life now isn't as exciting as it was when I played ball, but considering where I started out, it's a minor miracle that I've made it as far as I have."

He sat back, waiting for Raven to ask questions so that he could fill in the blanks. But she didn't say a word, so Omar let it go. He could tell his story later. He primed her for information once more.

"Do you have brothers or sisters?" Omar asked.

"No, I'm an only child."

"So after your folks had you they decided one was enough?" he said lightly, jokingly.

"They tried, but things didn't work out." Raven said. Omar detected the first signs of boredom, but he couldn't get next to Raven if he couldn't see inside her, so he took his chances and delved into a subject that was none of his business.

"Too bad that fertility drugs weren't widely used back then."

Raven smiled, but her voice was flat, "I come from perfect stock, Omar, fertility wasn't the problem. It died."

"It what?" a confused Omar asked.

"The other one. The baby. It died."

"Oh, that's too bad." Omar was moderately sympathetic, but most of all he was curious, perhaps there was something here he could use. "What happened, premature birth, crib death?"

"You're being rude, you know?" Raven said as she folded her arms and leaned forward. "First of all, I told you that my family is perfect, defect free, so no, there was no premature birth or crib death. There was an accident, and it died."

"I'm sorry if I seem rude, but I asked because I'm interested in you," he truthfully told her. He wouldn't ask about the accident, but he wondered whether the baby lived long enough for Raven to have memories of her little sister or brother. "How old was the baby when it happened?"

"Three. My parents were upset at first, but things worked out," said Raven smiling at Omar. "Like you said, one of me is enough, I specialize in being a handful."

"So how's it you're a handful?" asked Omar, seeing an opportunity to change the subject.

"I'm spoiled. I enjoy decadent indulgence."

"I can see that from the way you eat."

"What way?" Raven replied as she slowly ate her ice cream.

"You know what I mean," said Omar, who had eaten grilled chicken and steamed vegetables. "Stuffed mushrooms, lobster with pasta in a cream sauce, two cognacs and now chocolate and ice cream. I'd be rolling on the floor by now if I'd eaten all that."

"I have a huge appetite, Omar. If there's something that I like, I indulge myself until I'm satisfied. Sometimes that takes awhile."

"Does that apply to food only?"

"Not just food," she said. "Whatever I want, I get, and I savor." Raven liked where the conversation was headed. She decided while dressing for dinner that she would let Omar service her that night. Since moving to Dallas, Raven had chosen to rely on her own devices to meet her sexual needs, and given her skill and fully equipped toy chest, she achieved more than adequate satisfaction. But to become utterly sated, Raven needed another person—someone to marvel over being chosen by her. Raven glanced at her watch. Her housekeeper would be leaving her apartment in just a few moments, time to move things along.

Raven leaned into Omar and said, "There are all sorts of things that I can't get enough of. For example…" She whispered something into Omar's ear.

"I can do that," he replied.

Omar motioned for their waiter to bring the check. He hoped that Raven wanted to go back to her place rather than to his. Friday was

Shelly's regular night to come over; Winslow thought it was the girls' night out. He imagined Shelly parked outside his condo, wondering where he was and why her key no longer worked. No need for a scene, at least not yet.

"So what now?" he asked.

"Take me home," Raven replied.

Omar was so ready to be alone with Raven that he was tempted to pull two one hundred dollar bills from his wallet and not even wait for change. But business was business. Even though Raven set him on fire, Omar wasn't in the market for a high-maintenance woman. He had to know if Raven could afford for him to be her man.

"You're not going to believe this," said Omar, opening the eel skin wallet that Shelly had given him earlier in the week. He impatiently snapped it shut.

"What's wrong?"

"I'm carrying a new wallet, and I forgot to put cash in it."

"They take credit cards, I'm sure."

"Raven, I don't have anything. No cash. No cards. Nothing. I'm such an idiot!"

Raven folded her arms and gave Omar a wary look.

"I'm so embarrassed Raven, especially with this being our first date." Omar's tone changed from agitated to subdued. "I guess I was moving too fast, my mind was on seeing you."

"Really," Raven replied. Omar thought he detected a bit of sista attitude in her tone. If things were to work out with them, she'd have to get rid of that.

"It's the truth," Omar said as he used his index finger to etch tiny, invisible circles on Raven's bare shoulder. "Why don't we do this," he continued in a confidential tone. "You take care of the bill and I'll hook you up later. It's time for us to get out of here." He leaned over and kissed her. "I promise to pay more attention to details for the rest of the night."

Raven studied Omar for a long moment, then smiled and said, "I don't have much cash, but I saw an ATM in the lobby." She picked up her purse and kissed Omar full on the lips. "I'll be back in a minute."

Raven went straight to the maitre d', slipped him a twenty and asked that he call her a cab. She gave him her best smile and said, "This is just between us, okay?" He gave her a brief nod and immediately picked up the telephone.

As soon as the elevator doors closed, Raven laughed aloud and shook her head in disbelief, "That simple-minded tightwad tried to play me." Too bad, Raven thought—he'd put her in the mood. "Oh well," she said, talking aloud again, "his loss."

At first Raven thought that the lobby was deserted, and then she spotted Senator Michael Joseph, who stood alone, gazing out at the nearly deserted rain-slicked street. She studied his profile. Based on the things that he said during his speech to the Student Bar Association, Senator Joseph had to be over forty-five, but you couldn't tell from looking at him. He was well-dressed; he'd worn an expensive suit when he visited the law school, and tonight he wore a tuxedo that accentuated his broad shoulders. Every time that Raven had seen the senator, his curly hair looked as though he'd just had it clipped. His face was lean, like the rest of his body, and his eyes and smile conveyed a slightly superior attitude. Senator Joseph tried to hide that side of his personality, unless he had to let it out, but Raven was almost as good as Omar when it came to reading other people. She saw his confidence, his smugness. Senator Joseph wasn't too much taller than Raven, only about five-foot ten, but his commanding demeanor showed that he'd go up against any man, any day. He wasn't quite a little Napoleon, but almost.

Raven walked up and extended her hand. "Senator Joseph, good to see you again. I'm Raven Holloway, a student at Monroe. We met at Reese's Bookends and again at the Student Bar Association reception."

"Ms. Holloway, I remember you. You asked lots of questions about the legislative internships." As he held her hand, Senator Joseph flashed Raven an arrogant smile that suggested how important he was and how fortunate she was to be in his presence.

"I'm glad that I made such a lasting impression. Although I'm only a first-year student I want an internship this summer."

"Well, it's like I told the SBA, the internships normally go to second-year students, but I'd be glad to talk to you about it some more, anytime. Just call me." Senator Joseph scanned the lobby then asked, "Where's your date?"

"He's still in the restaurant. I'm taking a cab home."

"Oh." Senator Joseph gave Raven a concerned look. "That brother must be crazy, letting you go home alone. Dallas can be dangerous."

Oh yeah, Raven thought, ritzy North Dallas must be the crime capital of the whole world, but the expression on her face spelled out vulnerable with a capital V.

"There's no way I'm letting you take a cab home Ms. Holloway," Senator Joseph said. "Let me give you a ride."

Raven glanced at the black Mercedes roadster parked at the curb. The parking attendant was walking toward them with keys in hand. The rain had stopped and the air was sweet—a little warm, but not very humid. An excellent night to ride with the top down.

"Thank you, Senator Joseph. You're a lifesaver."

"Please, call me Michael."

Omar handed his American Express platinum card to the waiter at DeLongchamp just as Raven opened the door to her apartment.

By the time Omar pulled into the garage of his condominium, Senator Joseph was nude, lying on an antique rug and oversized pillows in the middle of Raven's living room and sipping champagne. He was bathed in the glow of more than fifty candles that were already lit when he and Raven entered her apartment. Senator Joseph kissed Raven softly and didn't think twice about his good fortune. For men like him, getting some on the fly was *de rigueur.*

THE MIDTERM WEEKEND was a special time. According to Monroe lore, the weather was always sunny and brisk during the three and one-half day break. Football weather. From the third-floor windows of Monroe's law library, one could see that the promise exceeded itself this year. The sky was pure pale blue, sprinkled with just enough clouds to make it picture perfect. Autumn leaves stirred in the wake of freshly washed cars as the Monroe student body went about making the most of the beautiful Saturday afternoon.

A slight glance out the window and Callie could have seen all this. But she sat, as she had all day Friday and all Saturday morning, with her back almost completely to the window. Just one glance to take in the beauty of the day might have saved Callie a world of trouble down the road.

"That's Callie Stephens, isn't it?" asked Omar. He used his T-shirt to wipe the perspiration from his face as he looked up into the library windows.

"Yeah. I can't believe that she's not taking a break like everyone else. I'll bet the library is almost deserted," replied Keith. He took in Callie's profile, her long brown legs extended, heels resting on the table in front of her. A golden sunbeam lit her frame, making her all the more stunning. Keith felt an involuntary tightening in his chest.

"Not on your job, huh?" Omar asked.

"What do you mean?"

"You told me that you were going to ask Callie out after midterms. Thursday night and Friday night are gone, and I can tell that this is the first that you've seen of her. Tonight's the night, Keith. Everyone's going to Janna's party, cutting loose. If you'd asked Callie out, she'd be at the beauty shop or manicurist. How's a brother like me supposed to keep hope alive when you're such a sorry role model?"

"Good question," said Keith. He shoved the basketball into Omar's hands. "I'm going to get cleaned up, hustle back over here and do some fast talking. I'm taking Callie out. The day isn't over yet." Keith turned and sprinted toward his car.

During their conversation, Omar never took his eyes off Callie. Lately he'd begun to pay more attention to her, and he agreed with Keith; Callie was as much a woman as Raven, but in a different way. Omar made it a point to engage in friendly banter with Callie whenever they ran into one another at their lockers. She wasn't a high-end fashion horse, like Raven, but her clothes, shoes and jewelry bespoke old-line class, which made sense to Omar, since he'd heard that Callie's father had been a lawyer. Omar waited until Keith was out of sight before he started up the library steps, two at a time. Now that Omar knew where he stood with Raven, he could move on to plan B. True enough, the day wasn't over, but it was a lot later than Keith thought.

❧   ❧   ❧

"Hey, I've been all over the place looking for you."

Callie smiled at her attractive interloper. Omar Faxton was one of the few men in her class with whom she did more than just exchange daily greetings. She looked forward to seeing him each day because his witty, warped observations about law school life always made her laugh. Callie liked to tease Omar that he was gifted, not with a sixth sense, but a sick sense.

Omar made Callie feel like blushing as often as he made her laugh. He complimented her daily and seemed especially taken with her eyes. She made a swift head to toe appraisal of Omar. His muscular, honey-colored arms gleamed with perspiration and his sleeveless T-shirt stuck to his skin, etching every detail of his well-built chest.

Callie had never seen Omar in shorts before. His legs looked so good that they seemed to beg to be touched, just as his smooth face and strong torso did.

Callie dismissed her thoughts and retreated to the familiar territory of light-hearted joking. "One of the places that you probably won't find me is on a basketball court," she said.

"Okay, so I'm exaggerating. But I'm just telling you girl, I've been looking for you. Thinking about you, too. Why else would I come in here, all funky and sweaty?"

"You smell like a man to me," Callie said and then quickly looked away.

She didn't shift her gaze before Omar read what was in her eyes. Shy women wore their lust awkwardly. Omar liked that. To him it meant that a woman would do for love, things that she would ordinarily never, ever do.

"Why aren't you somewhere stirring up that magic potion sisters use to mesmerize men?" he asked. "Aren't you going to Janna's party tonight?"

"Well, if I were going I would be there to have a good time, not to mesmerize men. But I can't go. This *Pennoyer* case has me all tied up. I've read the thing at least a half dozen times, and I still don't get it."

Cha-ching. Omar hit triple seven. "Civil procedure is my best subject."

"I've noticed. You seem to have it all figured out."

"Look here, Ms. Stephens," Omar said, squatting so that he was eye level to Callie, "I'll help you with *Pennoyer.* I'll spend all day Sunday with you going over *Pennoyer* and the other civil procedure cases too. Just, please, come to Janna's party with me tonight?"

Callie could hardly concentrate on Omar's words. His masculinity, accentuated by the sticky sweet aroma of his sweat, struck her hard. The man smelled like well-worn leather. She remembered reading somewhere that a man's scent was a primal mating attraction. She believed it. Callie tried to focus on Omar's words but that only made her notice how kissable his lips were. She masked her attraction with a flippant comment.

"What's wrong, your date cancel at the last minute?"

"No. I waited until the last minute to ask the only woman who I want to be my date. I had to build up my nerve. Brothers don't like to be turned down either, you know." Omar moved closer to Callie, caught her glance and held it.

"Come on, Callie. Like I said, I've been looking for you, and I don't mean just today, or just this weekend." Omar may not have had much allegiance to anyone or anything, but when he had a strong rap, he stuck with it. "I'm getting to know you before this semester is over, I promise you that. It might as well be right now, tonight, while we have some down time."

Callie cleared her throat. "What time shall I be ready?"

❀   ❀   ❀

Callie used one toe to gingerly test the steaming, scented bath and felt a delicious shiver run down her spine. Before stepping into her bath, she made sure that everything was perfect: candles lit, lights low, jazz on the stereo and wine near by. Omar's invitation took Callie back to her time at Radnel, days of hard work and relaxing, solitary nights, when she would take the time to regroup, turn her back on AIDS' unrelenting demand for attention and get back to Callie. As she thought about what her date with Omar would be like, Callie resolved to stop being so uptight. Like Raven always said, if a little fun caused them to flunk out, they were not meant to be lawyers anyway. She was submerged in bubbles up to her chin when the telephone rang.

"Hello."

"Hey Callie, this is Keith Dawson."

"Hi, Keith. What's up?"

This was certainly a surprise. Callie knew Keith through Omar, but not well. She couldn't imagine why he would call her at home.

"Not much. Did I call at a bad time?"

"No, not at all," Callie said, making swirling motions with her legs as she spoke. "I'm not sure that I've ever talked to you over the telephone, that's all."

"I've been trying to catch up with you all day. First, I went to the library, but the desk clerk told me that you left about a half-hour before I got there. That was around noon. Since then, I've been trying to find your phone number."

Callie giggled and Keith asked, "What's so funny?"

"I've got to stop spending so much time in the library. Folks think that I live there."

"Well, I'm sorry that I missed you. I want to ask you something and face to face would've been better."

"Over the telephone is fine, I hope. What is it, Keith?"

"First, let me apologize for my timing. Believe me, it in no way reflects my level of interest." *Where did that stiff line come from*, Keith wondered as he stumbled ahead. "I want to take you to Janna's party tonight. Dinner before hand would be nice."

"Keith, what a thoughtful invitation. Someone else has already asked me to the party. I'm sorry."

"So am I." Keith didn't realize how badly he wanted to get to know Callie until that moment. "Some other time?"

"I hope so. I'd like that," she replied. Callie didn't want Keith to think that she was giving him a polite brush-off, so she added, "I was just invited a few hours ago. If you had asked me sooner, I would've said yes."

Callie hummed along with the jazz music as she let the bubbles envelop her once again. *Why is it always feast or famine with men?*

❧   ❧   ❧

That said complaint, summons, afficavit of Mitchaell and of the "editor" of the "Advocate" aforesaid, and entry of judgment, were in the judgment roll, made up by the clerk in the case, but the order for publi-

cation of the summons aforesaid wasn't placed in said roll by said clerk, but remains on the files of said court; and that when said court made said order for publication....

If *Pennoyer* had Callie all tied up then it was most certainly had Brett in a death grip that he couldn't break. He reached for another Ritz cracker, shoved it into his mouth and tried the sentence again. Still, no light came on for him.

"I hate this crap!" Brett exclaimed aloud and slammed his civil procedure book shut. For weeks now he'd been wading, all alone, through the incomprehensible muck called case law. Life at Monroe hadn't become the easy walk that Brett predicted it would once he got books of his own. Reading a dozen or so cases every night and trying to figure them out without anyone to discuss them with was bad enough, but so far his classroom experiences had been even worse. He expected to be among the small number of students who were nonplussed by having to field questions from professors while standing before the entire class. Instead he stumbled and fumbled his way through the living hell of oral presentations just as the average student did.

Once, in Professor Lenton's class, caught between saying "went" and "had gone," Brett heard himself saying, in a thin, trembling voice, "had went." The guy seated behind him, whom Brett suspected was offended by Brett's presence at Monroe, said in a mocking tone, "My man must'a taken Ebonics 'fore he stepped off in here."

Brett's grades on the few written exercises that the 1-L class had taken prior to midterm exams were on par with his oral performances. He hoped that he'd done well enough on the midterms to give him solid Bs in most of his courses. The trouble with midterms was the same as the trouble with everything else; it seemed that everyone belonged to a study group except him. Brett had no one to talk to.

Lack of scholastic companionship wasn't the only thing bothering Brett. Naturally outgoing, even with strangers, Brett was lonely at Monroe. He missed the company of his buddies and of his girl, Cyndi. He'd shared a few lunches with some of the whites in his class and even a few of the Asians, but couldn't connect. There were a couple of black guys in his class who Brett found witty and interesting from a distance. He'd overheard them talking about playing basketball after class and had been tempted to ask if he could join them. Brett played high school basketball and was good enough to be selected All District. He also played on his college team. As much as he wanted to ask the guys, Omar and Keith, if he could join them some evening after class, Brett never did. He didn't know why.

The only person he did talk to was Janna, who sat next to him in most of their classes. Janna was a petite, talkative young woman who reminded Brett of Renee, his childhood friend and next door neighbor. Brett lost his virginity to Renee, so the comparison was, for him, a good one. Janna even looked like Renee, especially when she tossed her braids over her shoulder and laughed. In his mind's eye Brett saw Renee, red hair swinging, her smile lighting up the room. He never considered, before meeting Janna, that people of different races could be alike beneath the skin.

During the two weeks before mid-terms Janna talked to Brett almost everyday about coming to her party during the mid-term break.

"Come on Brett, you'll have fun," Janna told him.

"Janna, I'd like to, but I can't. Besides, I won't know anyone there."

Janna tossed her braids and punched Brett playfully in his chest with her index finger. "You'll know me. The other people there will be our classmates and a few of my other friends, that's all. Come on Brett," she continued to cajole him. "I'll even teach you how to dance."

He laughed and shot back, "What makes you think I don't know how?"

Brett declined the invitation and on Saturday night was all alone, with the exception of his friend *Pennoyer*. Janna did get him to agree to have lunch with her on Sunday, the day after the party. He was looking forward to it, but worried about how much lunch would cost and where they could go so that they wouldn't be seen by lots of people. People, for Brett, meant whites.

He ate a few more crackers, ran his fingers through his hair a half dozen times and reopened his book. Something had to change for the better, and soon.

$\mathcal{J}$ANNA'S PARTY WAS casual and Callie wore a clingy sweater and short skirt. She looked sexy and her bearing was so naturally feminine that Omar almost felt as though he was escorting her to a black-tie affair. She wore her hair in a loosely pinned upsweep. Wisps haphazardly escaped, gently framing her face. They partied hard, dancing on most songs and laughing a lot in between.

"Okay, that's it!" panted Callie, thinking that their fourth consecutive dance groove had finally ended as she headed off the floor.

"No way, girl. This is the extended remix," Omar grabbed Callie's hand and pulled her back into the crowd.

But the next one was a slow song. Omar boldly pulled Callie to him.

"I thought you said—"

"I lied," Omar whispered into her ear. "I knew that if I kept you dancing long enough they'd kick in a slow jam."

Callie felt awkward, stiff in his arms. Omar's hand brushed the nape of her neck. "Relax," he said and held her a little closer. By the end of the second song, Callie gave in to the rhythm and Omar's tender pull.

"Cal, you feel so good," he told her, and he knew that it wasn't just because Callie was the only woman, besides Shelly, who he'd been that close to in months.

When the DJ picked up the pace, Callie and Omar exited the dancing throng and found a quiet place to sit. "Where's your girl?" Omar asked.

"Raven hooked up with some wonder boy last night, I guess they decided to make a weekend of it."

Omar frowned. "Wonder boy! Is that how she described the guy?"

"No, those are my words," Callie said. She couldn't believe that she'd told Raven's business so easily, but she felt comfortable with Omar, better than she'd felt in months. "She told me about him Thursday night, and the way she described him, he sounds perfect."

Omar leaned back in his chair and sipped his drink. He'd half hoped that Raven would see him with Callie, but knowing that she gave him high marks was satisfaction enough, so what if she skipped out on him? She was too bitchy anyway. He hadn't expected Keith to show, but if he had Omar wouldn't have felt bad about it. To Omar getting a woman was just like everything else, the superior competitor prevailed.

Janna came through doing the host thing. "Are you two okay, need anything? Callie I love that skirt!"

While Janna and Callie talked clothes, Omar checked Callie out and decided that he didn't need an audience to make the evening worthwhile.

After the party, as he and Callie walked to his car, Omar stopped suddenly, stepped directly in front of Callie and gently unpinned her hair. "I've wanted to do that all night," he told her, and as he used his fingers to fluff her hair he kissed her lightly on her forehead. Callie didn't respond, but Omar thought he saw her eyes glisten with tears. What was that all about, he wondered? Omar's instinct, the one that guides a man toward a particular woman, told him to take it slow, Callie was definitely not Raven. He didn't want to blow it, and his reasons were not all calculated. Omar needed time to sit back and figure out what he wanted to do with her. When he got her home, Omar gave Callie a big hug, another kiss on the forehead and that was all.

The next day Omar made good on his end of their bargain. "You think you've got it?" he asked Callie.

"I've got it. Absolutely."

"Then explain it to me."

Callie took a sip of her soda, leaned across the table and gave Omar a look of mock consternation. The two of them had been sitting at Callie's coffee table, legs akimbo, for hours, while Omar tutored Callie in civil procedure. Now he wanted to know if she understood it.

"This guy Pennoyer was a deadbeat client, the kind we never want to have, who ran up a bunch of legal fees and skipped the state. He still had property in the state so the lawyer sued Pennoyer, got the land and sold it to pay Pennoyer's debt. Now here comes Pennoyer saying, 'Hey, you can't sue me, I don't live here anymore. Haven't you guys ever heard of personal jurisdiction?'"

"So what did the court say?" Omar asked.

"The court said, 'Yes, Mr. Pennoyer, we have heard of personal jurisdiction, and you're right, you can't be sued if you didn't have at least minimal activities going on in this state. Give this man back his land!'" Callie said, banging her fist on the coffee table as though it were a gavel. She continued, "*Pennoyer* is a dusty old case that's difficult to get through, but it's meaning is simple."

"All right then!" Omar shook his head in approval.

"Thank you so much Omar, you really broke this stuff down for me. Now I have a whole new attitude about how to analyze these cases. I can't believe all the time I wasted, just because my approach was wrong. I owe you big time," Callie said.

"You don't owe me a thing, we had a deal, remember? You went to Janna's party with me, and I unlocked the mysteries of the law for you."

"Last night my mind was on all this," she replied, gesturing at the books and papers scattered on the table. "I don't know if I told you, but I had a good time."

Tell me something I don't know, thought Omar. In truth, being with Callie had been a breath of fresh air.

"Omar, did you hear me? I said I had a good time last night," Callie repeated.

"Sorry, my mind wandered. I told you that getting together would be fun." Omar took a tablet and pencil from the table, leaned back against the sofa and continued talking to Callie. "It won't be the last time, will it?"

"Not if you don't want it to be," she replied, her eyes half shaded by long, beautiful lashes.

Ah, there it was, the sudden shyness that made Callie seem so innocent. Omar put pencil to paper and began sketching.

"I don't want it to be the last time. To me, you've always been pretty and friendly, fine, too. I look forward to seeing you every day." Omar continued flattering Callie, but his words were true. "So far you've missed two days of class, right?"

"Yeah, I did. Why do you remember that?"

"Because I didn't know what to do with myself! Not seeing you threw me off, I felt like something was missing. That's when I knew for sure that I wanted to try and spend some time with you."

Omar studied Callie and thought: *If she were a white girl she would be as red as a rose right now.* Could he capture her blushing in his sketch?

"Sometimes when a brother admires a woman from afar for so long, the way I've been doing with you, he builds her up in his mind, imagines that she's all that," said Omar. "When he finally gets to spend time with her, she may be just the opposite. A stone bitch, 'hood rat, airhead, or whatever."

"The same thing happens to us," said Callie. "So which one of those things am I?"

"You're a bitch," Omar said with a straight face. He laughed at the surprised look on Callie's face. "Teasing you is so easy it ain't fair. My point is, you're exactly what I imagined you to be: intelligent, down to earth, kind-hearted and lots of fun. To top it all off, you've got a smooth, feminine style that sets you apart."

"You can't tell all that from just one date, Omar."

"True, but this helps," he nodded toward his sketchpad and kept drawing as he talked. "I see something else—a vulnerability that I can't put my finger on, a sort of sadness. Want to tell me what that is?" he gently inquired.

Callie hadn't talked about it. She refused. Her mother and her brother, Trent, began counseling just after her father died, but Callie wouldn't join them. She couldn't imagine talking about it, especially to some psychologist who had heard it all before. With Omar she felt relaxed, totally at ease. Callie looked into his brown eyes, saw that his concern was genuine and decided to release a little of what weighed heavily on her heart.

"You see me missing my dad, he died this past summer." Callie said hesitantly. "It hits me hard sometimes. Times when I least expect it."

"Times like last night, on the sidewalk in front of Janna's house?" Omar ventured.

"Yes." Again, the tears flowed. Callie allowed a few to fall. "And when you call me Cal—he called me that."

"I'm sorry, I didn't know. Should I stop?"

"No, hearing you call me that gives me a bittersweet feeling, mostly sweet. It makes me think of the good times." She laughed, wiped her tears away. "He only called me Cal when I had done good. I could always tell when I was in trouble because then I'd be 'Callie Yvette Stephens.'" She continued between sniffles, "That's about all I can tell you right now, Omar. It's too difficult for me to talk about, even to my family."

Omar reached across the table for Callie's hand and held it tightly.

"I understand, because I've been there myself. I was surrounded by other people, by *family*," said Omar, giving a derisive laugh that Callie didn't understand. "But," he continued, "there was no one for me to turn to, no one who could comprehend what was going on inside me. When you feel like talking or crying or you just don't want to be alone, I'm here." He paused, giving his words time to sink in. "Look at me Cal," Omar commanded. Callie raised her bowed head and met his eyes again. "I'm here," he said urgently, "Okay?"

"Okay," Callie agreed. She began to smile. "Why such kindness?"

Omar smiled too, and said, "When I needed someone, I'll bet that if I'd known you, you would've been there, although you would've been just a cute little pony tailed girl at the time."

"What happened?" she asked.

Before beginning his story, Omar clutched Callie's free hand, holding both was more dramatic. He intended to give her his standard 'poor boy beats the odds and makes good' story, the one he tried to tell Raven. The words that came from his lips surprised him as much as they did Callie.

"When I was growing up," Omar began, "I had an aunt, my mom's baby sister. Her name was Rita, and I was just crazy about her. Rita was only 13 years older than me and she loved me too—at least that's what I want to believe. To me, Rita was the greatest person on earth, always laughing, teasing and having fun. She was real cute as I remember it, kind of honey-colored with these beautiful brown eyes."

"Like yours," Callie threw in.

"Yeah, I guess. Well, like I said, I thought that Rita was the best. My folks didn't though. They were real Holy Rollers who always said that Rita was fast and irresponsible, you know, a first-class sinner. Rita didn't come to our house much, but when she did, oh man!" said Omar, his eyes lighting up at the memory. "She'd walk through the door; I'd hear her calling for me. 'Where's my boy?' I'd run and jump into her arms, and she'd twirl me around and ask, 'Are you my boy? 'Cause my boy is special!' I'd scream over and over, 'Yes, Aunt Rita, yes, I'm your boy.'" Omar frowned and said, "My folks hated that."

Omar stopped talking for what seemed to Callie like a very long time. He squeezed her hands again before continuing.

"When I was six, Rita was killed, stabbed by a dealer called Billy C. It happened right in front of our house. She owed him fifteen dollars."

Now it was Omar's turn to look away. Shame or sorrow, Callie couldn't tell which, clouded his handsome face.

"Oh, Omar," was all that Callie could say.

"After the funeral we had a huge dinner at our house," he continued, speaking just above a whisper. "You know how adults say things around children, thinking that children aren't smart enough to catch on? That's what happened to me. That's how I found out."

"Found out what?"

"All that stuff about me being her boy wasn't just fun and games." Omar's lips twitched oddly. It seemed to Callie that he looked through her as he spoke. "Rita was my mother."

By now Omar was squeezing Callie's hands so tightly that it hurt, but she didn't care. "So the people who you thought were your mom and dad were really your aunt and uncle," concluded Callie.

"Not quite. My mom was really my aunt. But my dad was truly my dad. Rita was my grandmother's youngest child, and my folks raised her. From what I can gather, my dad, Reverend Omar Faxton, Sr., began molesting Rita as soon as she hit puberty," Omar's expression was ugly and bitter.

"Where are your folks now?" Callie asked.

"Either in Chicago where I left their black asses, or dead. Who cares?"

Omar released Callie's hands and resumed his sketching.

They sat in silence for the rest of the afternoon.

That night Omar stayed awake for as long as he could. He studied his sketch of Callie and tried to discern her weaknesses, but his mind refused to cooperate, all that he could see was he and Callie sitting across from each other, holding hands and sharing intimacies. Why had he told her the whole truth? That was something he never did. At three a.m., Omar finally gave in to sleep and was immediately overcome by dreams of Rita, switchblade protruding from the middle of her chest, chasing him through the halls of Monroe law school.

Callie tossed and turned in her own bed, her mind replaying Omar's story. Why is it, she wondered, that families have to be torn apart by one person's dirty secret?

O MAR DROVE TO the basket. He could feel the shot going in. The kid appeared out of nowhere. He slapped the ball down hard; it ricocheted off Omar's shoulder and bounced out of bounds.

"Omar, I don't hear you talking all that trash now," Keith said as he took the ball out. He chided Omar about what would surely be the last play of the game. "What you wanna bet, my boys and me get off on this play? What's left, man? Let's see," said Keith, counting the bets that Omar had already lost. "You owe me ten dollars. You have to pay for my car detailing and what else, what else?" Keith snapped his fingers in mock forgetfulness. "Oh yeah," he continued, as the other young players laughed, "you have to pick up the tab for me to take a honey on a date, and I'm not talking about the Chicken Shack."

"Screw you Keith; ten dollars ain't shit, your car's so raggedy that detailing won't help and you don't even have a woman," Omar responded. "Just play ball."

Keith put the ball in play. For the next several seconds, the court was a collage of flailing black arms and legs, and colliding bodies. Little Cory passed the ball to Keith who was immediately double-teamed by Omar and two other players. Just as he thought he would have to eat crow, Keith glanced to his left and saw the light. Set Shot was planted in his favorite spot, completely unguarded. Set wasn't strong enough to drive to the basket like some of the others, but once that little dude planted himself in a particular spot, watch out. Keith faked a pass to Little Cory, did a three-quarter spin and passed off to Set.

Set put the ball up. Nothing but net.

"Game over," Keith said, as he slapped Omar on the shoulder, "We win, *again*."

"So, are you talking shit for the rest of the evening or do you want to get in one more game before it gets too dark?" Omar asked. He was a consummate competitor who didn't joke around when he was on the bottom.

Keith had the good luck to pick Little Cory and that damned Set for his team. All Omar had was a goofy fat-assed kid who couldn't catch a ball, even if he'd had sixteen arms, along with three other boys who thought they were too cool to hustle.

"I can't play another one. My mama's fixin' meatloaf tonight," the fat one said.

"If you guys need another player, I'm in."

Everyone on the court looked to the sidelines, where Brett stood waiting for their answer. He looked as uncomfortable as hell and eager to play at the same time.

"Milstead, right?" Omar asked. Damned if his luck was about to change today. Still, even a white boy couldn't be worse than Fat Ass.

"Right," Brett answered.

"Sure you're in—my team," Omar said to Brett. He turned and swatted Fat Ass on the butt. "See you later man," he told the smiling, rotund teenager, "don't do like you did last night, save some food for the rest of the family."

"Forget you," the boy laughed, and off he went.

The pace of the game was leisurely, almost boring, until the score reached ten all. Omar knew that this was the time when Set Shot became lethal. If that little marksman got hot, Keith's whole team would catch the fever and blow Omar and his boys out for the third straight game. Omar's team needed to keep the pace fast, keep Set running. And, of course, they needed to score.

Omar spied Brett, who was wide open and motioning for the ball. Omar hesitated and then passed the ball to a gangly kid named Robert. The boy caught the pass, licked his lips and proceeded to do some funny sort of dribbling that was supposed to be cool.

"Get your slow ass to the basket!" Omar yelled, but he was too late. Robert was so caught up in his style that he didn't even see Keith, who came in from his left and easily snatched the ball away. Keith passed off to Set and, swish, the score was suddenly eleven to ten.

"I was wide open!" Brett shouted at Omar.

Omar held up both hands, conceding his error.

On the next play Keith's team gained control of the ball almost immediately. Little Cory, who was a decent player for his size, was angling for the basket, but Robert, motivated by having ruined the prior play, was all over him. Finally Little Cory took his shot. The ball bounced off the rim and Keith went up for the rebound. Quicker than lightening, Brett snatched the ball from Keith's grasp and sped down court for an easy lay-up.

"Son of a bitch," Omar said softly. The game stopped as all the players looked at Brett through new eyes.

"What are you guys staring at?" Brett wanted to know. Loose and at ease, he forgot that he was the new kid on the block. With a basketball in his hands, Brett was in his element. He threw the ball to Omar, winked, and said, "Let's put this puppy to bed." Brett ended up scoring the final shot, giving Omar's team a much-needed win.

After the game Keith, Omar and Brett walked back to Monroe together. Omar talked his share of trash; it was his team's most impressive win, and he wasn't about to let Keith get away unscathed. As soon as their feet hit Monroe pavement, however, the talk turned to law.

"Meet you in the library at eight?" Keith asked Omar, who nodded yes.

"Starting this late, I guess you guys will only get a couple of hours of sleep, like me," Brett said.

"No, you'll be up all night by yourself," Omar said. "We've already prepared for property and civil procedure, so tonight all we have to cover is case analysis."

"Tell me something," Brett said. He hadn't talked to anyone about law school, and his need to do so outweighed his urge, innate in every law school student, to never let your colleagues see you sweat. "Do you find this stuff as difficult as I do? When I received my midterm grades, I was blown away, man! Take property—Lenton gave only three A's, and there are at least sixty people in her class. Wizen's civil procedure grades were just as bad. I made a D in Wizen's class," Brett confessed before he could stop himself. "I know that you guys gotta be hurting."

"Lenton's exam was difficult," Keith said sympathetically.

"What did you get?" Brett brashly asked a taboo question. Asking a person about his grades was as uncouth as asking about his salary or how much he paid for something. The question invited a lie or a rebuff.

"I made a B+," Keith said.

"I made the highest grade on Wizen's exam," Omar threw in.

"You're kidding!" Brett said sounding as though he thought that they were. "I assumed that Philip Tang made the highest grade in just about all our classes. I mean, the top students are pretty easy to spot."

Omar and Keith exchanged a glance that Brett saw but didn't comprehend, until Omar spoke.

"And exactly who are the top students?" Omar asked.

"Well, you know…," Brett stumbled and stroked his thinning pate. "I guess…I don't know," he admitted with a shrug.

"I guess you don't," Keith said. He and Omar walked away, leaving Brett in his usual state—alone and confused.

"**W**ANT BUTTER ON your popcorn?" Omar shouted from the kitchen. "Callie!" he called again.

"What?" Callie shouted back. She'd heard Omar's question, but was too distracted to answer, her eyes glued to Omar's big screen television.

Omar, bearing popcorn, sat down on the sofa next to Callie. She scooped up a handful, her eyes never leaving the screen.

"Yuck! It's all wet!" she said, staring accusingly at Omar. "I hate butter on popcorn, why'd you go and do that?"

"You're so cute when you're angry," Omar teased. As far as he was concerned, Callie was cute just about all the time and when she wasn't cute, she was sexy. He pulled Callie closer to him. "I thought I'd seen my last football freak, then I run into you." He leaned toward her, "If you weren't so–"

But Callie wasn't hearing Omar; she leaped from his arms and screamed at the television set. "Catch the ball! Oh, man!" Callie moaned and sat back down.

Fascinated by her enthusiasm and overt oversight of him, Omar watched her. He'd had plenty of women put on the 'I love sports' act, and he knew the difference between that and the real thing.

Omar settled in and observed Callie. She wore a little tank top, shorts and flat sandals; her hair was pulled back in a ponytail. Callie was most alluring when she was unadorned, and her natural beauty pulled Omar in. He always stuck to a strategic plan with women, and he'd already decided that he should take Callie slowly. They'd kissed and fooled around a little, but they'd never had sex. He wanted to keep it that way until Callie wanted him so much that she couldn't stand it.

But as Omar watched Callie, the tables turned and he forgot about his plan. Omar walked over to the television and turned it off. Callie looked at him, and because his eyes said it all, she said nothing, simply went to him.

As they kissed, Omar undid Callie's ponytail and ran his fingers through her hair. She pressed closer to him, then moved slightly away and began untucking his T-shirt.

"Wait," he whispered. "I want to do this right." Omar lifted Callie and carried her into his bedroom. Although he set aside his technique to get Callie into bed, Omar went back to it once he got her there. He tried a few fancy tricks and was so into doing his thing that it took him a few minutes to notice that Callie wasn't into it.

"What's wrong?"

Callie gave Omar a deep, slow kiss, then said, "I know that you know lots of...*things*," she touched his face, and continued, "but with me, I just want you to do what comes naturally."

Omar was taken aback; he'd run his game for so long, he wasn't sure what came naturally. He uttered words foreign to his tongue, "Why don't I follow your lead?"

Within minutes Omar and Callie were flowing together, naturally, and it was the best love he'd ever had.

For a law school student, where you study is as important as how you study. Some find that the quiet, scholarly atmosphere of the law library helps them to focus. Within that group are students who need the open space and unobtrusive presence of other students, so they claim squatters rights to tables, chairs, or even the floor of a particular aisle. Students who enjoy the accessibility of the library resources, but ruminate best in complete privacy, choose study carrels. Other students can't study anywhere but home, either because

family obligations make it necessary or because the familiar surroundings and comfort at their fingertips make the task easier.

Callie and Raven chose a place to study that combined the con-
templative mood of the library with the comforts of home. A fairer
statement is that the two women were chosen for the honor of using
what was probably the best study facility in town, the backroom of
Reese's Bookends. Every year John Reese chose a couple of 1-L students who showed promise and allowed them to study in the spacious, comfortable area alongside his office. The backroom, as it was
called, had overstuffed chairs, a sound system, and a refrigerator that
John Reese kept stocked with all sorts of drinks (no alcohol) and
microwavable food. The walls of the backroom were lined with
shelves holding reference books that 1-L students normally needed.
On one of his frequent visits to Reese's Bookends, Michael Joseph,
who was himself a graduate of the backroom, suggested to John that
the privilege of studying there should be extended to Raven and Callie. John agreed and gave each woman a key to the backroom, which
had a separate entrance, so that they could come and go as they
pleased.

On this blustery autumn evening in November, which actually felt
more like winter, Raven and Callie reviewed each other's case analysis term papers.

Raven read for a moment, then scribbled something on the paper
that she was reading, "This is good, Callie, but why don't you consider phrasing it this way?" She thrust the paper toward Callie.

"Sure," Callie replied without so much as glancing at the change
that Raven made. Raven noticed that within the past half hour, Callie
hadn't made one comment about Raven's paper. Plus, Callie was
humming again. For days she'd been going from one love song to
another. At the moment she concentrated on a Babyface tune.

Raven put down the paper and affectionately shoved Callie on her
knee to get her attention. "So who's got you tripping?" Raven asked.

"What are you talking about?" Callie tried to sound baffled, but she couldn't hide the smile that played on her lips.

"*What if we were wrong about each other, what if you were really made for me?*" Raven sang in a translucent soprano that was, like everything else about her, flawless. She then asked, "Is it Omar Faxton?"

"How'd you guess?"

"It wasn't hard, Callie. When you and Omar's paths cross, it's like you both want to linger, but don't want anyone to notice. Since when has it taken a whole five minutes for you to throw things into your locker? Then there's this idiot grin that the both of you can't manage to wipe off your faces. See there it is now," said Raven, pointing at Callie. "The brother must go hard, considering the way you've been humming—morning, noon and night." It was more of a question than a statement.

"Actually we're taking it slow, or at least we were until last night." Callie said, putting aside Raven's paper as she spoke. She'd been anxious to share her feelings about Omar with Raven, but she also treasured the fact that only she and Omar knew how right their flow was. Callie began to explain, "Omar's fine, one hundred percent he-man, agreed?"

"Agreed," Raven said, nodding. Since their fiasco of a date (which Callie knew nothing of) Raven and Omar had maintained superficial pleasantries, but nothing more. Each held a healthy respect for and wariness toward the other. No matter what she thought of Omar, Raven couldn't deny that physically, he was tight.

"But, that's not the best thing about him. Aside from all that he's…," Callie gazed toward the ceiling and searched for the right words, "…he's tender, just a tender, sweet, beautiful man." Callie stopped, amazed at how good saying the words made her feel. "Besides you, Omar is the best friend that I have here at Monroe," Callie said, and continued, "That's where it all starts, you know?"

"Whatever. But I want to know *when* did it start? Come on, give up some details!"

"It started during the midterm break. We went to Janna's party together, then we started spending time together, just talking about our lives, school, our ambitions, world peace, you name it. For two whole weeks, Omar never did more than give me a goodnight peck, but never on the lips."

Raven frowned at this, which prompted Callie to say, "I know. I was dying inside for something more! A real kiss—anything to let me know that it wasn't a buddy situation. I'm not like you Raven, I can talk a blue streak to you or in class, or on a job, but with a man I'm attracted to, I can be very hesitant and self-conscious."

"All right, all right!" Raven waved her hands impatiently. She sensed that Callie was leading up to the good part, and she wanted her to get there already.

"So after a couple of weeks, we started fooling around a little bit, you know, but the clothes stayed on, body parts stayed put. It was like he wanted to take it slow."

"So, anyway," continued Callie, deliberately lowering her voice and slowing her pace, "last night we were at his place watching the Dallas Cowboys and San Francisco 49ers go at it. We're loud and unruly, or at least I was. Arguing about a play, popcorn's flying everywhere..." She stopped mid-sentence and addressed Raven's look of exasperation, "All of this is essential to the story, trust me." Raven rolled her eyes, but she said nothing.

"Then, late in the fourth quarter, with the score tied..." Callie interrupted herself again. She asked Raven, "Did you see the game?"

"Forget the damn game, and I'm going to have to kill you in a minute if you don't hurry up and get to the point," Raven ordered.

"Remember when Dallas' defensive back intercepted the ball and ran it back 85 yards?" Callie asked, but didn't wait for an answer, "Well I'm screaming and yelling, and out of nowhere, Omar up and turns off the TV!" said Callie as she sprang from her chair to demonstrate. "I turn toward Omar to ask if he's lost his mind, and he's got this funny look on his face. Next thing I know, we're in his bed." Callie collapsed into her chair, sporting a satisfied look. "By the way…who won the game? We never got back to it."

Raven smirked and said, "Either he's refined his approach, or you're very easy to please."

Callie's eyes flashed, "What's that supposed—"

Raven shoved her knee playfully, "I'm just teasing, girl, I'm happy for you." Callie still looked annoyed, so Raven picked up the big bag of peanut M&Ms that was on the table and held it out to Callie. "Candy?"

Callie looked warily at Raven and then reached into the bag. "Sometimes you tease too much" she said as she crunched the candy. Callie dropped the subject and turned her attention to Raven's term paper.

That night the two women called it quits at midnight. They moved silently and hurriedly around the backroom gathering their things and straightening up, both anxious to get home to their warm beds. The ringing of a telephone disturbed the silence.

"That's mine," Raven said, as she rushed toward her Coach satchel and removed a slim cellular telephone.

Raven turned her back to Callie as she answered her call, but privacy within its walls was one thing that the backroom didn't provide. Callie couldn't help but overhear Raven's part of the conversation, especially once her voice took on an annoyed edge.

"It's already midnight," Raven glanced at her watch and said to the caller, "and I'm exhausted. What about tomorrow?"

She stood, frowning, and listened to her caller, who, Callie guessed from Raven's end of the conversation, had launched into a scolding monologue.

"Okay," Raven finally said as she let out a small breath, "I understand. I'm sorry. See you in a few." She pressed the 'end' button on her telephone and stood silently for a few seconds before turning to face Callie.

"Look," Raven ran her fingers through her hair as she spoke. "I'm gonna stay here a little longer, so you go ahead, I'll finish up."

"Are you sure?" Callie asked. To her, Raven looked more than end-of-a-long-day tired, she looked drawn. She hadn't looked that way before the telephone call. "Do you need me to stay with you?" Callie asked, although she didn't want to stay. Callie was still irritated by the snide remark that Raven made about Omar, but she would stay if Raven needed her.

Raven laughed, picked up Callie's purse and books and said, "That's just what I don't need." Raven handed Callie her belongings and walked her toward the door.

"Goodnight," Callie said as she unlocked the door and peered around the deserted parking lot.

"Goodnight," Raven replied. She grabbed Callie's hand just as Callie was about to shut the door behind her. "I appreciate what you said tonight," said Raven.

"About what?"

"About me being your best friend at Monroe. Growing up in the military I didn't have a chance to make many friends at all, let alone best friends. I know I'm bitchy sometimes, and you always put up with me."

"Anyone who had an opportunity to get to know you the way I have over these past months would want to be your friend, Raven," Callie said. She could see that her words meant a lot to her normally cool, unflappable friend, so she forgave Raven and generously added more. "You're kind. I've lost count of all the nice things you've done for me. You're everything that a person would want in a friend, except…" Callie frowned.

"What?"

"You're so good looking, you constantly upstage a sister. That ain't right," Callie teased. They both laughed.

"Well, thanks Callie. You're my best friend, too, and not just at Monroe." Raven looked at her watch again and said, "You'd better go." Callie gave Raven a quick hug and then sprinted to her car.

Once Callie had driven away, Raven turned her attention to a car parked at the curb, which Callie hadn't noticed. The car, still without headlights, drove onto the parking lot. The driver, duffel bag in hand, walked hurriedly toward Raven.

"Couldn't you have gotten rid of her sooner than that?" he greeted her.

"I'm sorry honey," Raven tousled her hair once more, adding a sensuous flair that was absent when she did the same thing while talking to Callie. "I'm so tired, baby. Can't we go to my place?"

"I *told* you over the phone that I have a six-thirty flight to Austin, and I don't want to be late!" *Sometimes*, the man thought, *no matter their age, position or perceived intelligence, women have to be talked to like small children.* "This place is only ten minutes from the airport. Your apartment has got to be twenty-five minutes away." Michael Joseph softened his tone as he placed an arm possessively around Raven's waist, led her inside and closed the door behind them. "Besides," he said, "this is where I spent some of my most memorable nights when I was a student. It turns me on."

$\mathcal{B}$RETT THOUGHT THAT the change of atmosphere would do him good, keep the panic that regularly clutched at his chest from completely consuming him. At first it seemed to work—the library study carrel made him feel scholarly. He made it through the torts review materials at record speed, but then torts was his best subject. Case Analysis and contracts were challenging, yet manageable. But when he got to property and civil procedure, Brett shut down. Damn it, why couldn't he understand this stuff?

Brett tilted his chair back and rubbed his eyes with his fists. It's Friday afternoon, he thought, although he'd vowed not to count the days. After a full week of study time, final examinations would begin Monday. Brett reasoned that Friday night and the weekend would be more than enough time for him to master the two problem courses, but in his heart he knew that was a lie. If he didn't get manna from heaven, in the form of huge clues on what property and civil procedure were all about, Brett was in danger of flunking both courses. Flunking out of a black school. *Wouldn't that be some shit?*

"Time to take a break," Brett said aloud as he hopped from his seat and opened the door to his study carrel. Another thought, even more forbidden than thinking about how few days were left before exams began, crossed Brett's mind. Maybe Janna was at the library. *Maybe I'll run into her. Maybe this time I'll*—. Brett forced his mind to go blank as he headed toward the library stairs.

Brett took the stairs to the basement level. He stood in the doorway checking for signs of life. Most of the students studied on the upper floors, because the basement level was always five or six degrees too hot or too cold. At the moment the basement was a human meat locker. As he cruised the aisles, Brett saw that most of the tables were empty—basement study was for those who craved quiet and didn't mind the discomfort. Brett rounded a corner and walked upon Keith and Omar. Course books and hornbooks for every first-year class were neatly stacked at one corner of their table.

"Hey fellas, what's up?" Brett greeted them.

"Nothing but the law, my man, nothing but the law," Omar responded in a friendly tone. He liked Brett, and so did Keith. Undaunted by their awkward parting the first time that they played basketball, Brett came back the next afternoon and every one after that. Although he lacked Omar's athletic versatility, Brett knew the game and was an aggressive player—scrappy like Allen Iverson. Pretty soon their pickup games began to attract a small crowd. They even caught the eye of the high school's basketball coach, who, on his way to his car late one afternoon, looked their way just in time to see Set do his thing. The coach stayed through that game and the following one. Omar and Keith hadn't spent much time with Brett off court, but they always walked back to Monroe together after the games and shared easy conversation between classes. They always discussed basketball, never school or grades.

"How's it's going?" Brett asked, gesturing toward the books.

"Pretty good. We've finished going over everything, for the first time at least, except for property," Omar said.

"Oh," Brett replied, and asked, "When are you reviewing property?"

"We're getting started in a few minutes, but now is a good time for a break," Keith answered Brett. He took his jacket out of the seat next to him and placed it on the floor. "Sit for a minute," he told Brett.

Brett sat. When he ran his fingers through his hair a few times without saying anything, the other men could predict what was coming. They had talked about it beforehand and agreed that it was only a matter of time before Brett broached the subject.

"I want to ask you guys something," Brett began. He glanced briefly at both of them, trying to decide which one would best receive his plea. Although Omar was his teammate, Brett felt that his best bet was to direct most of his attention toward Keith. Omar could be a little hard sometimes.

"Would it be okay for me to join you, for the property review, I mean?" Brett asked and steeled himself for their answer. He knew that they had more reasons to say no than to say yes.

A study group is a close-knit thing. The mix has to be just right for it to work. Omar and Keith spent the entire semester studying together; their styles complemented each other. If Brett's style was different from theirs, his presence could throw them out of sync. At this stage, a few days before final exams, there was no logical reason for them to take that chance. Being a part of a study group, especially one consisting of just two people, was a lot of work. Brett glanced at the table again and saw that the men had taken the time to type out-lines for each subject. All that Brett had was an assortment of hand-written notes, which, typically, he forgot to date and organize. Why should he be allowed, at the last minute, to reap the benefits of Omar and Keith's semester-long efforts?

The best reason for them to turn down Brett's request was that he'd already confided to them that his grades were poor. He had nothing to offer. In essence, Brett was asking to partake in a gourmet meal that he didn't help to prepare and might not have the stomach to digest.

Keith tactfully addressed that point. "Maybe what you need, Brett, is to see if one of the 2-L tutors can help you out," he looked toward Omar, who sat there twirling a pencil between his fingers. Omar looked bored and a little agitated. "Omar and I—well—we're moving pretty fast here," Keith finished.

Brett frowned at Keith. That was a terrible idea, and they both knew it. This close to final exams all students, even the second and third-year tutors, were looking out for themselves. Not one of them would have time to spend going over another student's class work. Brett's only chance along those lines would be if he could pay and pay well, so a tutor was definitely out of the question.

He tried to make his response sound casual, "A tutor? That's a thought, but I'm pretty sure that they're all tied up with their own work."

"Well–" Keith didn't know what else to say. He didn't particularly care if Brett joined them as long as he didn't slow them down. The question was, where was Omar on this?

Any doubt about Omar's position swiftly vanished when he asked Brett, "How come you're asking us Brett? Why aren't you hanging with the other white folks or with Philip Tang and his crew?" He got in Brett's face. "They're the ones gonna make the grades, right?"

But Brett was in no mood to be intimidated. He came right back at Omar, "Yeah, I thought they were going to be the top grade get-ters, and you know what, I wasn't the only one. Some of you *brothers* thought so, too . Don't think that I didn't hear the talk."

This bit of information took Omar aback, because he knew that it was true. During the first weeks of the semester Omar paid closer attention when the Asian and white students spoke in class. His rea-son, which he would never admit to anyone, including himself, was that he assumed, even while fighting against the idea, that the non-blacks always had something important to say. Omar considered himself to be an enlightened black man, but he waged an eternal, internal battle to beat down the notion that he was inherently infe-rior. He suspected that Keith fought the same fight; many blacks did.

Brett seized upon Omar's momentary flash of doubt and pushed the same button again, "So I was wrong. So I stereotyped. Big deal. You guys did the same thing when you assumed that I couldn't play ball."

An upper-class student walked toward their table and told them, in that superior tone that everyone used with 1-Ls, to either lower their voices or take it outside. Brett calmed down and went on,

"Look, I already apologized for what I said before. If you don't want me to study with you, just say so, but don't tell me it's because of something I said weeks ago."

Besides asserting himself, Brett knew that he needed to make a sales pitch—convince the men that including him would be to their advantage, or at least not to their disadvantage.

"Why did you choose Monroe?" Brett asked, looking first to Omar.

"Connections," said Omar. "A man, a *black* man, who does well here is going to do well on the outside. Monroe graduates are everywhere, always willing to help a fellow alumnus."

When Omar finished, Keith said, "Full scholarship."

"I barely got in because my LSAT scores weren't all that great," Brett admitted. "I'm a smart guy, did well in undergraduate school, graduated with honors even. Monroe considered my entire record when other schools wouldn't give me the time of day. I've done okay here, in some of the classes. I'm pulling an A in torts, maybe in contracts."

Keith seemed impressed and Omar appeared, for the first time, to actually listen. "My problem is," Brett continued, "that sometimes I don't test well. I don't know why that is, and I've stopped trying to figure it out. I do know that I do better when I have someone to discuss things with. Hell, anyone would do better." Brett then gestured toward Omar. "If you've missed the issue in a case, Keith can set you straight. If both of you are off course you can discuss the issue until you figure it out. Me? *I've got no one to talk to.* When I'm wrong, I stay that way. That's my problem with property and civil procedure. Somehow I've gotten on the wrong track and because I study alone, I can't right myself. It's not that I'm dumb or slow on the uptake. I'm alone. That's all."

Brett sat back in his chair, feeling better than he had all week. He'd laid his cards on the table. Keith and Omar had a decision to make and whatever the outcome, Brett decided, it was cool with him.

Keith, Brett was sure, had been convinced. Omar would resolve things and when he fixed Brett with a cool stare, Brett had an idea of what to expect.

"We're doing this, not because of what you said," Omar told him. "This is because if you're not around next semester, this fool here," Omar nodded his head toward Keith, who wore a slight smile, "might start kicking my ass on the basketball court. I can't go back to that." Omar made a fist and extended it to Brett who met it with his own.

"It's time to study," Keith said.

CALLIE CLOSED HER eyes and savored the moment. The first semester of law school was behind her and although grades wouldn't be posted until after the first of the new year, she knew that she'd done well. Being in school brought Callie the comfort that she needed, especially after her Radnel experience and her father's death. She pulled the quilt up around her neck and snuggled deeper into Omar's arms. The fact that the first semester was a success wasn't the only thing that pleased Callie. She and Omar became closer each day; he was wearing away at her vow that she would date casually during law school, nothing too deep.

Earlier that evening they had gone out to dinner (Callie's treat) and then rented four old movies. The couple got cozy on Callie's sofa, popcorn within arms reach and started with *Cotton Comes to Harlem*. Omar made it through that one and halfway through *Imitation of Life* before Callie realized from the soft steadiness of his breathing that he'd fallen asleep. She made a few feeble attempts to extricate herself from his arms and move to her rocking chair in order to give Omar more room to stretch out. Every time she moved, however, he stirred slightly and held her closer.

Callie watched *Imitation of Life* to the end, where Sarah Jane chase her mother's funeral procession down the street. She decided to watch another movie, even though it wouldn't be as much fun without Omar's wisecracking color commentary. She glanced across the room at her desk. Three numbers, 1:30, illuminated the darkened room. Callie decided to close her eyes, just for a minute. When she opened them, it was three a.m.

When she and Omar spent the night together, Callie always fell asleep the instant their bodies parted and she never woke until after Omar touched her again, so she'd never seen him in repose. Callie studied her lover's face. Gone was Omar the confident, sexy man. In his place slept the sweet young boy that he'd described to Callie.

"Shh…," Callie whispered to Omar as she gently push back the quilt and stood. "Shh," to the sleeping man-boy who reached out for her. Callie unzipped her jeans, stepped out of them and removed her bra without taking off her oversized Monroe T-shirt. Then she slid quietly beneath the quilt and back into her man's arms.

❧   ❧   ❧

"So, how does it feel?" Omar asked as he sipped his coffee and smiled mischievously across the dining room table at Callie. Before them lay an old-fashioned country breakfast—steak, scrambled eggs, grits and biscuits. Omar laughingly called the feast that Callie threw together 'heart attack on a plate.' He devoured two steaks and at least six biscuits that were heavily buttered and crammed with peach preserves.

"How does what feel?" she asked, a big, silly grin covering her face.

"The morning after. Was it as good for you as it was for me?" Omar teased.

Callie threw her napkin at Omar. "We didn't do anything."

"Yes we did girl, you did some things to me—amazing!" Omar shook his head. "You just don't remember."

Callie, still sporting a huge grin, leaned back in her seat and gave Omar a bit of his own medicine, "No matter what I did, if I don't remember, then it wasn't as good for me as it was for you."

Although nothing sexual had taken place between them the night before, both Callie and Omar were aware that something happened, something between them changed. They shared a deeper intimacy that neither had known two people could experience without making physical love.

Callie toyed with her grits and thought *having him in my life makes the holidays bearable.* She'd called Omar the week before Thanksgiving and invited him to spend the holiday with her family because she felt it was the hospitable thing to do. He'd declined, and Callie was relieved, justifiably as it turned out. Thanksgiving without her father had been so melancholy and her mother's false cheeriness only made matters worse. The woman acted as though her life hadn't been irrevocably altered. The atmosphere was so intolerable that Callie, Trent, and her mother, Cordelia, abandoned the house to the ghost of the late Mr. Stephens and took in a movie. Their mood wasn't happy, exactly, but at least they had two hours of peace. All day long Callie relived the night before Thanksgiving, which she and Omar spent together; that's what got her through the holiday.

Omar had told Callie that he already had Thanksgiving plans, and she hadn't inquired further. He never would've told her the truth—that her invitation was shock therapy for him. Omar began questioning whether he'd become too wrapped up in Callie. Something deep within him craved Callie's companionship, sought her out whenever possible. But Omar was nobody's fool; he still had to pay his rent. The time that Omar spent with Callie was carved from Shelly's allotted time. Sooner or later Shelly would get a clue and then where would he be? Callie was definitely comfortable financially, but from what Omar could tell, she wasn't in a position to take care of a man with his tastes.

As soon as he'd hung up from talking to Callie, Omar called Shelly.

"Thanksgiving in Cozumel—doesn't that sound good?" he said when Shelly answered.

"Thanksgiving with my husband sounds better," Shelly retorted.

"Bullshit."

Shelly hung up, leaving Omar momentarily stunned, he *was* losing it! He called Shelly again.

"Honey, what's wrong?"

"It's been two weeks since I've seen you, Omar, you tell me what's wrong!"

"Studying takes all my time, Shel, I told you it would be this way."

"Omar, the only thing you can give me is time. If you're too busy for a girlfriend, just say so!" Shelly snapped. Her pique excited Omar, and he made up his mind to bring her back into his fold.

"I'm sorry, let me make it up to you. Let's go to Cozumel, my treat."

After more begging on Omar's part, Shelly relented and they left for Cozumel on Thanksgiving evening. The trip had gone so well that they decided to go to Aruba during the days between Christmas and New Year's Day. Omar loved Callie down before he left for Cozumel and again when he returned on the Sunday after Thanksgiving, so Callie was cool, he was cool and Shelly was, too.

Callie poured Omar another glass of orange juice and thought about inviting him over for Christmas. Meeting family for the first time usually marked a milestone in a relationship. That the meeting would take place on *the* holiday, Christmas, added to its significance. She had a fleeting thought that Omar might be put off by the invitation; maybe he'd think she was moving too fast. Callie decided that after last night and this morning, she had no need to feel insecure.

"Omar," she spoke softly, her eyes questioning, "would you like to spend Christmas with my family and me?"

Omar's smile faltered. He expected another playful missive from Callie, not realizing that she'd moved from banter to a serious topic. The idea of spending Christmas with Callie's family, or any family for that matter, was unsettling. Omar hadn't done that since he left home at sixteen. Every holiday between Rita's death and the day he shut the door on his life with the Faxtons had been a time of loneliness and hurt. Omar's idea of celebrating was to do what he planned with Shelly—travel to a far away place and leave tradition behind.

Callie took Omar's obvious discomfort as a sign that he was about to give her a tactful excuse. "Oh, it's okay—" she stammered. Callie rose from her seat, reaching for both their empty plates, "It was just in case—it's no big deal." By now Callie was halfway to the kitchen, her back to Omar as she talked.

Omar joined Callie in the kitchen. She didn't look up as he walked toward her, concentrating instead on rinsing the dishes and placing them in the dishwasher as though it was the most important thing that she would ever do. Omar placed one hand gently on her shoulder and said, "Callie Yvette Stephens, you're acting like I hurt your feelings, don't be so sensitive. I haven't even given you an answer yet. Before I do, I have one question."

"What's that?" she asked, still not looking his way.

"Are y'all having turkey?" he asked, "'cause you know I don't eat swine."

$\mathcal{K}$EITH LOOKED AT his watch. It was time to make the call. He took a deep breath before dialing the Atlanta telephone number. "Hey buddy, Merry Christmas," Keith said cheerfully into the phone. The depression that held him in its grip since Christmas Eve night somehow lifted and deepened at the same time. "Was Santa good to you?"

Keith listened, shaking his head in agreement and sometimes laughing at what he was hearing on the phone. Keith asked a few more questions. Which toy was his favorite? Had he and his mother been to grandma's house yet? With every answer Keith's heart grew heavier. Why couldn't things have turned out differently?

"Let me speak to mommy. Oh and K.J.," Keith paused, then asked, his voice raspy, "Daddy loves you K.J. You know that, right?" Keith cleared his throat and added, "I'm sorry that I'm not there with you."

"Yes daddy, I know. I love you too, but I gotta go. I left my PlayStation on."

K.J. dropped the telephone receiver and raced away. Keith could hear him shouting "mommy, telephone," and imagined his eight-year-old son barreling down the hallway like a tiny hurricane.

"Hello?" the sweet voice touched Keith's heart as it had for the past 15 years, even during the bad times.

"Merry Christmas, Vicki."

"Keith," the woman's voice tinkled like tiny bells, "K.J. didn't say it was you. Merry Christmas yourself."

"How's everything?"

"Fine, everything's fine. K.J. loves the toys that you sent him. And the sweater that you sent me is beautiful. You always knew how to dress me."

"Yeah, well–" Keith couldn't think of what to say. Of all the changes that had taken place during the past two years, not knowing what to say to Vicki was what surprised him most. It was also the thing he most regretted. Perhaps if they hadn't run out of things to say he would be there, in Atlanta, instead of Dallas, miles away from the people who meant more to him than his own life.

"Keith, I wish you'd come home for Christmas. We're having dinner at your mother's house. It won't be the same without you. We miss you."

"Vicki, it would've been a mistake. You know that."

"It wasn't a mistake at Thanksgiving, was it?" Vicki heard the plea in her voice and loathed herself for it. Keith was the only man she'd ever loved, and her feelings were slow to fade, making her afraid that she'd never get over him.

Keith winced and hung his head. "No," he lied, "Thanksgiving wasn't a mistake. I'm saying that we both need to move on with our lives, that's all."

Since the beginning of school, Keith had managed to get to Atlanta every three weeks, thanks to a sympathetic cousin who worked for Delta. Even though the flight was only two hours, there was never enough time for him to do anything but scoop up K.J., hang out for a day and a half and then return him to Vicki.

The Thanksgiving weekend was a long, lazy vacation, by comparison. His mother, who loved Vicki like a daughter, insisted that with Keith's sister and her family driving in from Virginia, there wasn't anywhere for Keith to sleep in the house where he grew up.

"You go on over to your own house, with K.J.," she'd said. "You need to spend every minute that you can with that boy."

During the day that's exactly what Keith had done, but nights were an altogether different matter. He slept in the spare room on

Wednesday night. Thanksgiving Day was surreal, they behaved like a happy family, for KJ.'s sake, Keith kept telling himself. On Thanksgiving night he found himself in the bedroom that he shared with Vicki during their tumultuous marriage. Her familiar caress soothed his soul, wiping out his loneliness and anxiety. Keith took full advantage of Vicki's love. He was ashamed.

He ended the conversation. "Merry Christmas, Vicki. Give K.J. a kiss for me."

Vicki didn't put down the receiver until a recording came on telling her to hang up. She pretended to be on the phone because salty tears, her new best friends of late, rolled down her face. She knew how to make herself stop crying; Vicki had a trick, a painful one, that worked every time. She replayed in her mind the day that she told Keith about the baby. A few hours after they talked, she walked into their bedroom and overheard Keith, who was in the bathroom, talking on his cell phone. She heard say Keith, "I think she planned it to keep me here." More was said, and every word cut Vicki like a knife. When Keith's conversation ended, he'd sat there and cried.

Reliving the memory wounded Vicki, but it also dried her eyes. K.J. had seen enough tears, and Vicki, for her part, was tired of crying.

       ❧   ❧   ❧

Raven sat in her parents' sunny Southern California living room and tried to decide which gift to open first. She chose Callie's. "Ahh, an anthology of black fiction. This," Raven said as she scanned the table of contents, "is from my best friend, Callie."

Jacqueline Holloway, who at sixty was an older, lighter complexioned version of Raven made all the more stunning by her crown of salt-and-pepper hair—searched her daughter's face. "A best friend?" A curious smile played on the older woman's lips. "I'm impressed," she said and took another sip of her coffee, which was bolstered with three shots of cognac. Jacqueline knew that she was drinking too much, too soon, but with Raven in the house, what choice did she have? Once the girl left, Jacqueline would return to her normal drinking routine, one scotch for lunch and another for dinner would be sufficient.

Raven tossed the book aside and reached for the tiny box that Senator Michael Joseph slipped into her coat pocket just before she boarded her flight to San Diego. "You think you're impressed," Raven addressed her mother, but didn't look at her. "Wait until you see this." Raven removed the necklace, a pear-shaped emerald surrounded by diamonds. She held the necklace aloft so as to catch the morning light that streamed in through open blinds.

Raven's dad let out a soft whistle and said, "Somebody thinks you're real special, baby girl. Why you didn't bring him home to meet us? All these years, as beautiful as you are, you've never brought a man home for me to check out."

"This one, Daddy, you'll definitely get a chance to meet. But right now he's not in a position to do that," Raven blithely said as she placed the necklace on the floor and grabbed another box.

Jacqueline looked at her husband and shook her head. *He's so stupid, even for a man*, she thought. "You had me worried, talking about having a best friend," Raven's mother leaned forward, picked up the discarded necklace and placed it on the coffee table. "But I see," she added, making eye contact with her daughter as she did so, "that you're still the same old Raven."

॰ॐ॰   ॰ॐ॰   ॰ॐ॰

On Christmas day, Brett ate so much that he almost got sick. *Say what you will about mom*, Brett thought, *but she definitely knows how to choose a catering service.*

That night he and Cyndi went to a movie and then checked into a hotel. It was their third rendezvous in five days, but you couldn't tell by Brett.

"Slow down, Brett." Cyndi gave her boyfriend a slight shove and began unbuttoning her blouse. "I know you missed me, but you're about to rip my buttons off. I don't know what's going on with you," Cyndi said, leaning back and closing her eyes. "But whatever it is, I like it."

Brett kept his eyes wide open, staring at Cyndi's rapt face. If he closed them, there was no telling whose face he would see.

❧   ❧   ❧

"Baby, are you sure that you don't want some of this ham? It's honey-glazed," Callie's mother said to the handsome young man.

"Haa–!" Callie burst out laughing, but Omar kept a straight face and said, "No, thank you ma'am. This turkey is so good that I don't have room for anything else."

❧   ❧   ❧

Shelly Winthrop took her cellular telephone from her purse and pressed the redial button. She covered one ear with her hand to block out the clamor of hundreds of post-Christmas travelers.

"Hello this is Omar Faxton. At the beep, you know what to do."

Shelly decided to leave a verbal message. Punching in her cellular telephone number, even with *911 added, hadn't done any good so far.

"Omar, you're cutting it close, babe. It's already three, our flight leaves in two hours. I hope that you're on your way. Please call and let me know that everything's okay." Shelly sighed and absently shoved the telephone into her bag. She tried to read a magazine but couldn't keep her eyes on the page for more than a few seconds without looking up, hoping to see Omar walk her way. He'd stood her up before, especially lately, but never anything like this.

Shelly waited five minutes and then reached for her cellular phone again. She pressed the redial button, abruptly canceled the call and dialed a different number.

"Hi, Dana, it's me," Shelly said when her best friend answered. She tried to sound cheery, but Dana, who knew the whole sorry story of Omar and Shelly, wouldn't be fooled. "Throw a swimsuit and some other stuff into a suitcase and come to the airport, pronto. You're going to Aruba."

❦   ❦   ❦

Callie's mother was responsible for Omar's decision to be a no-show for the Aruba trip. After Christmas dinner they sat around talking about all sorts of things. Omar mentioned that he liked gumbo. Cordelia Stephens said, "Baby, I make the best gumbo this side of Louisiana. I'ma make some tomorrow, just for you." After that, nothing could have lured Omar to Aruba, not because of the gumbo, but because of the offer. While his lovers did things for him all the time, never had a woman with strictly maternal intentions gone out of her way to please Omar.

The morning after Christmas, Omar called Callie as soon as he thought that she was awake.

"Are you going to your mother's house today?" he asked. She said yes, but not until later in the afternoon. Omar suggested that they visit Cordelia that morning; he wanted to take her to breakfast. "After all," he explained, "Miss Cordelia's cooking for me. I need to show my appreciation."

Omar wasn't able to coax Cordelia out of the house. "Honey, I put my gumbo on an hour ago, and I cook it real slow. I can't leave right now," Cordelia said as Omar and Callie followed her into the kitchen. "But, how about pancakes?" she asked Omar. "Or would you rather have homemade biscuits?" They ended up spending the whole day with Callie's mother.

Omar loved watching Cordelia move, listening to her talk. She was straight southern, and called Omar "baby" or "sugar" twice for every time that she called him by his given name. She didn't have on any makeup, not even lipstick, and her hair was short and curly. Cordelia was short, and in Omar's opinion, she looked exceedingly fine to be the mother of two grown children.

"I can't believe you two are mother and daughter," Omar said as he served after-dinner dessert. "You don't look or act anything alike."

"No," Cordelia agreed. "Callie is her daddy up and down." But Omar could see that Cordelia was the source of Callie's goodness, and that pleased him.

The next day Omar's excuse was that Cordelia was probably lonely; the first Christmas without her husband had to be hard. When Callie left her mother's house that afternoon, Omar opted to stay. The next morning he hadn't even bothered to call Callie, just made a beeline to Cordelia's.

At one point during the week, Callie's mother told her, "That poor boy clings to me like an attention-starved puppy. He needs a lot of love Callie."

"I know." Callie answered. Cordelia read in her sensitive daughter's eyes that Callie looked forward to being the source of that love. She could be so naive sometimes.

"No, I don't think that you do. It might sound romantic, might make you feel needed. But having a man soak up all you have to give and then want more—it can be hard." Cordelia replied.

Callie listened to her mother but didn't respond. As far as she was concerned, Cordelia assumed that her own past foretold Callie's future. But Callie wasn't Cordelia and Omar wasn't like Sonny Stephens. Not at all.

"*R*INGGG…ringgg…!" Callie glanced at the clock on her nightstand. Only seven a.m. That damned Omar was such a morning person. Callie tried to sound annoyed when she said hello, but Omar's attentiveness pleased her.

"Yes, Omar," she said in greeting.

"How did you know it was me?"

"You're the only person who would dare call me this early."

"I'm the only one who thinks of you the moment my eyes open," Omar cooed.

"Omar, your rap is so weak sometimes. Those high school boys you play ball with must have given you that line," she teased.

"Woman, I called you to say Happy New Year, and look how you're treating me."

"Happy New Year? That's two days away!"

"Well, you know what they say, baby. A New Year, a new you? Because I've got you in my life, I'm already a new man. As far as I'm concerned the New Year is already here." Omar meant every word. He could feel himself changing and didn't know if he wanted to fight the feeling or give in. Omar decided that until Shelly returned from Aruba, he could afford to give his emotions free rein.

"I want you to pack a bag. You'll need clothes for three days, including a couple of sexy, dress-up outfits. I'll be at your door in forty-five minutes," Omar instructed Callie.

"What are you talking about? Where are we going?" Callie asked. They hadn't talked about taking a trip. Omar hadn't even mentioned

New Year's Eve, although Callie assumed that they would spend it together.

"Do you trust me?"

"Of course."

"Then don't ask questions. Just be ready when I get there," he said and hung up the telephone.

An hour later Omar and Callie were on Interstate 20, headed southeast. When they crossed the state line into Louisiana, Callie looked at Omar, excitement shining in her eyes.

"You're taking me to New Orleans," she declared.

❧   ❧   ❧

Omar exited the expressway and turned onto Canal Street. They drove along Canal toward the Mississippi River. Downtown, throngs of black children milled about the fronts of seedy shops that stood next to grand hotels. The once showy strip had fallen on hard times in recent years, but like all of New Orleans it revived itself and lived on.

"I haven't been here in years," Callie said as she took in the dilapidated stores and swank hotels. "It's like driving down Hollywood Boulevard in Los Angeles, just doesn't live up to expectations."

"Maybe not now, but during Mardi Gras, Canal Street is the place to be. The Mardi Gras parade takes the route we're taking now. It's wild," Omar said as he pointed straight ahead. "Wait until we get closer to the French Quarter, it's nicer there. My favorite hotel is down that way."

"Is that where we're staying?" Callie asked. On the way down, she bugged Omar for more details about the trip. Was this a spur of the moment thing or had he planned it? How long would they stay? Did he know people in New Orleans, or were they on their own? How did he know that she would agree to come?

Omar made a right turn onto St. Charles before answering, "Let's get a bite to eat," he said, "and we'll talk about it."

They ended up in the city's Garden District at a wood-framed house that had been converted into a restaurant. As the maitre d' approached them, Callie cast a doubtful look at her slacks and sweater, which looked nice, but were more comfortable than elegant.

"You look fine," Omar said as he place his hand at the small of her back and urged her forward. He took a deep breath and followed her.

Although it was only mid-afternoon, Omar ordered a bottle of champagne.

"Champagne," commented Callie, arching one brow. "That's certainly special."

"I'm hoping this will be a special time," Omar answered.

Omar's fine dining experiences were far more extensive than Callie's. She puzzled over the menu and the pronunciation of certain dishes, and asked the waiter so many questions, until Omar finally suggested that he order for them both.

"You're an expert at this, Omar. I'll bet you wine and dine women all the time," Callie said, only partly in jest.

"I've done my share of good living with women," said Omar, his expression earnest, "but you're messing with my game."

"How so?"

"Callie, I'll be honest with you. I've known a lot of women. *A lot.* I've had trouble in my life, but for whatever reason, having a woman has never been a problem." He took a sip of champagne and continued, "Having any woman you want, well, after a while, it can make a brother have a real cavalier attitude."

"What do you mean?"

He answered frankly, with no sense of embarrassment, "Usually I only want to know one of two things about a woman—is the money right or is the sex good. And I want to know upfront. Beyond that I'm never too interested, don't get involved emotionally."

"What about me?"

"Well, you're certainly not handing out major cash," Omar laughed, relieved at an opportunity to break the tension. "As for the other," he added with a smile, "good, oh yes, but that's not the only thing that's got me going."

Callie didn't know what to say, so she waited for Omar to continue.

"I'm telling you this because I want you to understand where I'm coming from," said Omar, as he gave a nervous dry cough and reached for Callie's hand. "There's something about you, Cal…something that touches me here," Omar gestured to his heart. "Other than Rita," he continued, "I've never trusted or loved anyone. Until now."

Omar felt a hot, unfamiliar sensation rush from his chest to his head, settling just behind his eyes. He realized that he wanted to cry. Omar leaned close to Callie and whispered words he'd uttered often but never meant until that moment, "I love you."

Callie dropped her fork and held him tightly.

The next day was New Year's Eve and Callie was the early riser. She shook Omar, "It's time to get up."

"I can do that," he said, reaching for her.

"No." Callie scooted out of bed. "I mean up, and *out*."

Omar raised his head far enough to check the time. "It's only eight thirty, come back to bed, girl."

But Callie was already headed for the shower. "I want to see everything!" she shouted from the bathroom. Omar didn't move.

Callie peeked out of the bathroom and said, "I could use some help."

With that, Omar was up, and within the hour, they did go out.

They made the obligatory stop at Café du Monde, where they planned their day over beignets and chicory coffee.

"Let's go to St. Louis Cathedral first, then check out the Riverwalk," Callie suggested. "But the Riverwalk might be more romantic at night, maybe we should go to the cathedral now, then the cemetery, but back to back, I don't know, maybe–"

"We'll take a carriage tour first," said Omar, helping Callie from her seat, "and play it by ear from there." Omar had been to New Orleans twice that year already, both times with Shelly, so it didn't matter to him what they did, as long as Callie had a good time.

Their driver was a convivial native of the city who introduced himself, as Jet, short for Jet Black, he told them.

"Git on out da fella," Jet urged his horse, Napoleon, forward. "Since y'all the only ones I'ma give you my special tour." He took them up and down the streets of the Quarter, describing sites along the way in equal doses of humor and New Orleans speak.

"Across der be the voodoo shop. Gitcha somthin' outta der, this gal never leave you 'lone," Jet said and winked at Omar. "Course, way she sittin up under you, I guess that ain't no problem."

Jet pointed out famous jazz clubs, hotels and homes. On passing a strip club he told Callie, "Dat's where dem pretty gals be, pretty boys too, don't know where you goin.' Don't let dis here fella out your sight, he git switched up on you."

After the ride they took in the sites near Jackson Square and had a late lunch of seafood po-boys.

"Want to take a siesta?" Callie asked after they finished their sandwiches. They been out for over three hours and given their lack of sleep the night before, Callie was tired.

Omar didn't answer, just looked at her.

"What?"

He grabbed her around the waist as they ambled toward their hotel. "Never thought I'd have a friend like you," he said.

That evening they enjoyed a sumptuous six-course meal and then went to a jazz club. At eleven their waitress brought them party hats and noisemakers.

"You know what," Omar said as he twirled his hat on one finger, "this isn't where I want to be."

Callie and Omar brought the New Year in from their hotel balcony, where they sipped champagne and watch fireworks explode over the Mississippi river. Their night, spent alone in a quiet little hotel on Chartres Street, was sweet and slow. Omar Faxton, in his lifetime, would never again know such peace.

"Brett!" Keith shoved his way through the crowd of students jockeying for position in front of the grade postings. He finally reached Brett, who was too intent on studying the grades to hear his friend's greeting. Keith couldn't read Brett's face, so he stood stock still until Brett said, "Yes!" and made a corny slot machine gesture.

"Brett," Keith said, punching Brett's shoulder, "good to see you buddy."

"Hey, Keith! Merry Christmas, Happy Kwanzaa, Happy New Year and all that. I made out pretty good in property. I owe you and Omar big time." As he spoke Brett tugged at the soul patch that he impulsively grew during the winter break, and scanned the maze of students scurrying about the hallway.

Suddenly, Brett's eyes lit up and he smiled. Keith followed Brett's gaze and found himself looking at cute little Janna, with the braids.

"Hi," Janna said to them both, but her attention focused on Brett. Keith didn't know Janna well, but he liked her because she was always carefree. Her braids did her justice like no other woman he'd ever seen. Janna, like Brett, was young, 22 at the most, and at first glance she looked more like a high-school senior than a law student. Always fresh, the rigors of law school never showed in her face or disposition. A lot of guys were interested in Janna, she carried herself with the grace of a dancer and always smiled. As far as Keith could tell, she saw only Brett.

Janna gestured to her earrings; earth-toned metal set off by small jewel-colored beads with an African motif that suited her style. "Brett," she said, "thanks for the Christmas gift. I love them."

Keith had seen Brett turn red before, but never like this. To his credit, Brett didn't move one finger toward his head, just fingered his soul patch a bit.

"Just my way of saying thanks for all the help you gave me last semester." Brett tried not to sound as pleased as he felt.

Janna checked her watch, "I've gotta run. You know how Lenton is about starting class on time." She chided Keith, "*You* know, if no one else does." Then Janna turned to Brett again, and asked, "Dinner this week? I'll cook."

"Sure, see ya," Brett said as Janna tossed one last quick smile their way and headed down the hallway.

Keith ribbed Brett. "Why does Janna get a gift, and all I get is a thank you? I never would'a pegged you for a dark meat man! You had us fooled."

"Janna and I are friends, that's it. I've got a girlfriend back home."

"Well I sure could use a friend like that—all cute and sexy, ready to cook for me."

Brett saw his opportunity to turn the tables on Keith, and he wasn't about to pass it up. "I've got a friend like that, Omar's got a friend, and what have you got? I think you've been spending too much time with those little high school boys. Is that your thing?"

Keith laughed. "Screw you, Brett," he said and then asked, "Who's Omar got? I thought he was still solo."

"Nah, he and Callie Stephens are an item."

The two men had been walking toward the library, but this last piece of information stopped Keith in his tracks.

"Callie Stephens! Are you sure?"

"Yes. I saw them last night, at a little coffee shop in Highland Park. Janna told me that they went to her party together, so I guess that's when it started. For whatever reason, they've been keeping it on the down low."

"Down low?" Keith smiled at Brett as they entered the library. "Pushing up on sisters, hanging with brothers, talking the talk. Next thing, you're gonna be asking for a wave cap."

That night Keith and Omar met at their usual spot in the library basement. Keith mulled over whether to ask Omar about Callie. He understood, on an intellectual level, that Callie hadn't gone out with him simply because she had other plans. She didn't reject him. Emotionally, however, Keith's feelings were still tender, close to the surface. The scars from his split with Vicki were so slow to heal. Keith hadn't asked Callie out again. He didn't want to hear her say the dreaded word: no. He didn't ask her out, but she was never far from his thoughts. Keith had it bad for Callie, and he'd decided over the winter break to take another chance. But before Keith could do that, he needed to know if what Brett said was true.

"Look here, Omar, Brett told me that he saw you and Callie hanging out. Mind if I ask what's up with that?" Keith said, getting right to the point.

"No problem, it's no big deal," said Omar, and looked Keith in the eye. "You acted like you were scared to step to her, so hey, I figure she's available. Besides, she's the one who approached me. She's a nice girl. We kick it sometimes. That's about it."

"Brett told me that you took her to Janna's party."

"I didn't exactly take her," Omar lied to support his prior lie that Callie made the first move. "We sort of ran into each other there and ended up together."

Omar knew without a doubt that Keith knew he was lying, and he enjoyed Keith's knowing. Omar noticed for the first time that Keith, when he chose to, could be a hard core brother; he liked that, too.

"Why so secretive, man?" Keith wanted to know.

"Just because you didn't know doesn't make it a secret," said Omar. He did with Callie what he habitually did with all his women;

he neither denied her nor showed her off. He hadn't completely trained Shelly not to pop up when she felt like it, and until he'd done that, Omar couldn't afford to show Callie much public affection.

"Yeah. That's fucked up, Omar," Keith responded. He stared stonily at Omar before saying, "But you know what? It's done, no problem. Let's get back to work."

Keith remembered his conversation with Callie as though it had just happened. How could he forget it, when he replayed it, word for word, at least every other day? Callie told him that she'd been asked to Janna's just hours before Keith caught up with her. Omar undercut him, Keith was sure of that.

Driving home that night, Keith thought about his conversation with Omar. He couldn't blame Omar for beating him to Callie, after all the playing field was level and wide open. It was Omar's chickenshit lying that pissed him off. Keith looked at himself in the rearview mirror. *Like you can talk.*

*T*HE SECOND SEMESTER of law school is a moment of truth for 1-L students. Grades from the first semester, posted behind glass on Monroe Law's main hallway, tell the tale with certainty. Although the grades are posted by student identification number, the truth leaks out. Students who do well don't try to hide it. First semester braggarts who fall short become withdrawn and start living in the library. Some, like Arlena Colten, the daughter of a federal judge, take one look at the boards, as the posting area is known, walk away and never come back.

Callie, Raven, Keith and Omar all did well. Raven, who never worried, never studied past midnight and never went out of her way to impress anyone (unless she had an ulterior motive), did best.

"All A's, and the highest grade in every class," Raven told Callie as they studied the boards.

Raven's perpetual smugness irritated Callie, who quipped, "Not in every class."

Raven squinted at the board and smacked her palm against the wall, "Who the hell beat me in civil procedure? Damn cheat!"

Callie wasn't looking at just her own grades, she knew Omar's student I.D. number and realized that he Am Jured civil procedure, as he set out to do. Raven made the highest grade in every other course.

"You Am Jured five out of six classes, Raven; what's wrong with giving someone else credit once in a while?" Callie asked. She didn't tell Raven that the grade was Omar's. Let her find out on her own, she thought.

Raven paid no attention to Callie. "Probably cheated with the professor's help," she fumed. "I knew I should've gone to a white school!"

Callie watched Raven shove her way down the hallway toward the library. She gave a heavy sigh and looked at the boards again.

"Three A's and three B's," she whispered, as she studied her own grades. Even though she began the winter break with confidence, Callie suffered a panic attack just before classes resumed. Her grades placed her within the top 15 percent of her class. *I guess I can hang*, she thought, and set out to find Omar.

"Where's Raven? I hear that she's the one who aced everything," Omar said after accepting a lingering congratulatory kiss from Callie.

"Don't know, don't care. Raven's in one of her moods; she's upset because she didn't Am Jur Civil Pro. I didn't tell her that it was you."

"Good, I'm looking forward to doing that myself."

But within the hour Raven, her mood completely changed, cornered Callie. "I can barely make it down the hallway without professors and students stopping me, asking if I'm the one. Do you realize that it's been six years since anyone Am Jured all the first-year classes?"

"Didn't know that," Callie said. She wasn't surprised that Raven had conveniently forgotten about Civil Pro.

"Even Dean Burthood made it his business to seek me out, and the rest of the men, well, you know they've already been checking me. But now!" Raven let out a huge breath, "It's almost too much to take in at once. And of course Michael called, sounding awestruck."

Although Michael demanded discretion, Raven told Callie about their relationship when she called Callie over the holiday break. Callie didn't approve, but she didn't criticize Raven either. She only hoped that Raven didn't get hurt.

"How did he find out so soon, isn't he in Austin?" Callie asked, but she already knew the answer. Michael hadn't called; Raven called him. But to Raven stories sounded better if she was the one on the attention-getting end.

Just then Professor Lenton walked up, "Congratulations Ms. Holloway, spectacular performance."

Callie suddenly felt small for being jealous of her friend. For the rest of the week, Callie was happy to watch Raven accept her sudden celebrity status with the same gracious aplomb that she did everything else that went her way.

JOHN REESE WATCHED his two protégées and the rest of the 1-L class very closely. Years back he'd discovered that a person's true nature shone through during the first year of law school.Callie was the person Reese would want on his side when things got tough. She seemed cautious about who she let into her inner circle, but once there, the person had a loyal friend for life. Late one evening Reese received a shipment of manuals. The shipment was four days late, and Reese expected an onslaught of computer science students the next morning. He had to get the manuals processed and on the shelves before he left that night. Fit older gentleman that he was, Reese gave it a good shot, but when he opened the fifth box his lower back wouldn't cooperate. When she emerged from the back room to take a short break from her studies, Callie found him sitting dejectedly among the seven boxes still to be opened.

"What's going on Mr. Reese," Callie asked as she stretched from side to side, "need some help?"

"No, baby girl, just taking a break," Reese said as he tried to downplay his predicament, but Callie could see the disappointment in his eyes.

"I'm done with my studying, so why don't I put on some coffee and keep you company?"

After their second cup, Reese reluctantly walked over to the unopened boxes.

"Tell you what," Callie said, "why don't you add these manuals to inventory records while I shelve them?" Callie shushed his protests. "I need the exercise," she said.

While Reese worked on the computer, Callie turned up the stereo and at two in the morning, placed the last manual on the shelf. Reese found out later, from Michael, who'd heard it from Raven, that after Callie left Reese's Bookends, she went home to finish writing a paper that she handed in just as Reese rang up the first computer manual sale. That marked the only time in her life that Callie pulled an all-nighter.

Raven was another matter. Reese knew that she and Michael were lovers. At first it didn't bother him. Michael was your garden-variety powerful-man-whore who'd sexed enough ingénue law students to form a nice-sized sorority. Michael, his wife Grace, and their two boys were like family to Reese, so he counseled Michael from time to time on his bed-hopping ways. The first time Michael and Raven met, Reese knew that she would be Michael's pick, at least for the first semester. When the young women left the bookstore, Reese had opened his mouth to say something, but Michael said it first. "I know, I know," he'd said, "don't get anything on the outside that I can't take home."

But this time, Michael's was a goner—Reese saw too much of him. Time spent in Dallas meant that he wasn't in Austin taking care of business. He also heard that Michael was spied several times in Dallas, and even once in Austin, with a beautiful young woman who wasn't Mrs. Joseph. Reese was afraid that Michael's marriage and his career were both at risk. He broached the subject one afternoon.

"I received a call from Jimmy Davis this morning," Reese said. "He wanted to know what happened to you yesterday. Thought I'd have an idea."

"That white boy thinks I'm his field hand," Michael said, his eyes darting around the room, never resting on Reese.

"That *white boy* is Speaker of the House, Mike," Reese spoke firmly. "He was depending on you to line up three more votes for the Grimes Highway Bill. Three votes, plus yours, that's all he needed to get the thing passed." Reese didn't hide his disappointment, "Hell, you weren't even there to cast your own vote, let alone round up the rest. Four years of work down the tubes. A new piece means that much to you?"

Michael eyed his friend. "You want to talk about her, Reese, show some respect."

"Okay, then," Reese said and eased up on the sarcasm. "What's with you and Raven Holloway?"

"I don't know," confessed Michael. He spread his hands as if he hoped to pull the right words from thin air. "Reese you know me better than anyone. You know that political power, public recognition, money, I live for all that stuff. But the rush I get from being with Raven," Michael let out a low whistle. His mouth, hard before, softened. "I don't know what it is, but when I'm with her I know I'm the man."

"Mike, you've had beautiful women before, blue-chippers every time. What's different about Raven?" Reese asked.

"Raven is the only woman I've ever known who is everything in one package, and it's all strong, you know what I mean? That girl can cook, from down home to gourmet, then turn around and help me decipher complex regulations. Remember that speech I gave in January that all the newspapers hailed as the best address given from the Senate floor in the past two years? Raven wrote that! Sat down at her computer and popped it out in less than an hour."

Reese wasn't impressed. So the gal was a born speechwriter. So what?

"I meant what I said before about you showing Raven some respect, but I have to tell you, in bed, Raven is…I can't even describe it. She's got me whipped, man."

Reese looked skeptical, so Michael asked, "Remember how crazy I was about Adel?"

Reese remembered. Adel Lenton could have been Mrs. Michael Joseph if she'd wanted to. Michael must have asked her to marry him a half dozen times, but she chose academia over being a politician's wife. A trim fellow to begin with, Michael lost over fifteen pounds when Adel let him go. Grace, bless her heart, was merely an outstanding second-round pick.

Michael spoke again, "Adel can't hold a candle to Raven."

Only then did Reese start to comprehend the depth of Michael's feelings for Raven. This was dangerous. He tried to get the younger man to take a different view.

"I understand where you're coming from," Reese began, "but you gotta put this thing in perspective. Your outside woman might be all that you say, but still she's an *outside* woman. You've got a family, Mike! And a career that you worked hell of hard to establish." Reese hoped that his earnest words would make a difference. "You can't be gallivanting all over the place with the girl! Grace loves you, and she puts up with a lot, too much. You've always given her the courtesy of never publicly embarrassing her, but you're cutting it close this time."

As Reese spoke, Michael nodded in agreement. He loved Grace, though he'd never given much thought to fidelity. Grace wasn't the type who could keep him out of other women's beds. Even so, she was an excellent wife and mother who didn't deserve to be hurt. Most importantly, if Grace ever decided to divorce him, under Texas community property laws, she'd get half of the modest fortune that Michael had amassed.

"I know that I'm a damn fool to be seen with Raven in public," Michael admitted. He fell silent, remembering how Raven used Valentine's Day to train him. For weeks Michael had brushed off Raven's demand that he spend Valentine's night with her. He told Raven that she had to be crazy; everyone would know what was going on. On

February tenth, Raven turned off her cell phone and left it off. Over the next three days Michael didn't get any work done, and missed a meeting that it had taken him months to arrange. On Valentine's Day he took the first flight from Austin to Dallas and surprised Grace by taking her to a long, romantic breakfast and giving her an expensive bracelet.

He spent the afternoon searching for just the right gift for Raven. As the art dealer prepared Michael's acquisition for delivery to the hotel suite that Michael reserved for the night, Michael called his broker. "I need an extra thirty-five hundred in my checking account by morning," he'd said. "Sell something."

At seven in the evening Michael and Raven stepped through the doors of DeLongchamp. Michael and Grace celebrated their anniversary at DeLongchamp every year. For Michael, it was a special place, a place for politics and for his wife. He'd never spoiled its sanctity until Valentine's night. Even the normally unflappable maitre d' looked disturbed.

Michael agreed with Reese that he was taking a gamble, "You're right, Reese. It's just that Raven's the kind of woman who gets what she wants. Considering what she's done for me, I want to be the one to give it to her."

Reese lost his patience. "What she's done for you? All I hear is that she fuc–," Reese stopped himself, lowered his voice, and said, "Michael you'd better straighten up, or your gonna be known as Michael Joseph, *formerly* of the Texas Senate!" Reese turned his back on Michael and went into the back room.

Michael sat for a moment, half hoping that Reese would return. "Old bastard," Michael said. He picked up the telephone and dialed Raven's number.

R EESE WANTED TO rush back out to Michael and let him know the truth. Let him know about the flat sexual way that Raven stared at Reese whenever she, Reese and Michael happened to be in the same room. Reese wasn't deluded into thinking that Raven wanted him, but he did know that if bedding him would serve some purpose for her, she would do it in a heartbeat. Reese wanted Michael to see that Raven gave herself for profit or sport, never for love—let him know something a friend back in D.C. told Reese about Raven.

When Reese became wary of Raven, he'd known just who to call.

"Reese, you old hound, good to hear from you," said Gary Fellow, greeting his friend. Reese and Fellow went back a long way, to their days at Fort Hood. Over the past forty odd years, their relationship had been constant, though it wasn't an everyday or even every year thing. Once they lost contact for three years, but as true friends will, they found each other.

After inquiring about family, health and so forth, Reese got to the point.

"Gary are you still with the Department of Defense?"

"Yep, but this is my last year, I retire in June. Will you and your wife come out for my party?"

"Sure thing," Reese replied. They were past due a trip to the East Coast. "Look here, you ever hear tell of a young woman named Raven Holloway? She was some kind of scientist or something...."

"Ha! *The Raven*...who at Defense doesn't know her?" Gary interrupted Reese with a dry laugh that held no humor. Then he asked, "What's your connection to Raven?"

"She's a student at Monroe, a friend of a friend. Something about her strikes me the wrong way, Gary," Reese said. He trusted Gary and felt comfortable giving full vent to his doubts about Raven. Reese would tell all, except for his friend's name.

"Trust your instincts, that gal's poison," Gary admonished. He then told the story of Raven Holloway. She was, by all accounts, brilliant, a rising star at a research firm that did eighty percent of its business with the Department of Defense. The company used Defense grants to fund one major research initiative per year. Having one's pet project chosen for funding was the pinnacle of professional achievement. The firm's scientists and engineers fiercely competed for the honor.

"Raven and a Dr. Vakar presented separate projects that vied for the top pick. Vakar's intelligence was off the charts—pure genius," Gary said.

"Sounds like Raven didn't have much of a chance," Reese interjected.

"Sure she did, because while Dr. Vakar's project was out there, real vanguard technology, Vakar's self-confidence was zero. Personality, I'd rate a negative six."

"Insecure," Reese commented.

"Yep, exploited to the hilt by Raven. She got next to Vakar, initiated an affair, pretty hot from what I understand. Screwing on lab tables, in environmentally secure rooms, stuff like that. Doc was deep in love, never had anything like Raven."

"Humm," Reese said. He felt like he'd hit a replay button on a recorder, only now the voice was Gary's instead of Michael's.

"Raven convinced Dr. Vakar that Vakar's project contained a flaw that would be embarrassing and career-ending when discovered," Gary continued.

"Then everyone would know that Vakar was a lightweight. Vakar's big fear come to life," Reese said.

"Right. Vakar's only hope, according to Raven, was to destroy the data containing the error," said Gary.

"I'll be damn."

Gary couldn't tell Reese the specifics of Dr. Vakar's project but he did say that Defense wanted it more than it had wanted any civilian design within the last few years. When it came out that Vakar destroyed everything: notes, the prototype, even the proposals submitted to the screening committee. Defense took its money elsewhere.

When questioned Dr. Vakar admitted everything, but refused to believe that Raven acted out of malice and defended her until the evidence against Raven became pretty overwhelming.

"Raven's gotten next to my friend the same way. Gary, I'm scared for this guy; he's going to destroy his family and his career for her. What about Dr. Vakar, did he lose his family?"

"Did he...?" Gary sputtered. He emitted another brief, dry laugh. "Dr. Vakar had a family. And I shouldn't be laughing, because Vakar lost more than just family. There was her husband Dr. James Vakar, and their three children. Vakar's first name was Vanessa."

"You kiddin' me! So what happened, Vakar's husband leave her?"

"Yes, but that wasn't the worst of it. Once Vakar faced reality, she decided to cooperate in an investigation that could've ended with criminal charges being brought against Raven. Although the feds had plenty, Vakar's testimony was crucial. A week before her final meeting with the investigators, Vakar died. Anaphylactic shock, which was crazy, since she knew that she was allergic to shellfish. Even carried injectable epinephrine with her at all times."

"Say again?"

Gary explained in layman's terms. "Vakar was allergic to shrimp; she didn't go near the stuff and carried medication with her at all times. Even though she knew it could kill her, she apparently ate some shrimp, couldn't get to her medication in time, and died."

"NEXT UP," THE barber snapped his crisp white towel and looked toward the threesome. Omar pointed a thumb toward Keith, who said, "Special guests first." Keith, Omar, both barbers and every customer in the shop focused their attention on man number three. Brett.

"Are you sure that you can do me?" Brett spoke to the barber but didn't move from his seat.

The barber replied, "Son, get in this chair. Here I am, cutting hair for over thirty years and you got the nerve to ask me that. I got plenty black customers with hair finer than yours." The barber took one look at the top of Brett's head and fired another salvo. "If I didn't have no more hair than what you got, I'd be a little over protective myself."

Keith and Omar settled back into their chairs. They shared the morning paper, sipped their coffee and enjoyed Saturday morning in the 'hood. It had been Brett's idea to come to the barbershop with them. When he walked into the door, Brett seemed taken aback that the barbers were black. He was still learning that an entirely different America existed right beneath his nose. Hanging with Keith and Omar, Brett could do everything that he wanted to and never cross paths with another white person.

"What's up Mr. Carlton, Jess," the man said to the barbers as he entered the shop.

"Ain't nothing, Post," Mr. Carlton responded. Mr. Carlton, his clippers precariously close to Brett's nose, looked toward the man as he spoke.

The man turned to take a seat. He spotted Keith and Omar, who were engrossed in the paper, and didn't look up as he entered.

"How are you gentlemen doing today?" the man asked.

"Hey coach," Omar said. He moved the newspaper from the seat next to him to make room.

"Omar Faxton," Omar said as he clenched the man's hand.

"Don Post," said the man, who both Omar and Keith recognized as being the high school basketball coach.

The Saturday morning barbershop crowd, in syncopation with their brothers in barbershops everywhere, launched into a conversation. They covered professional sports, politics and neighborhood gossip. Brett garnered instant respect when Don Post complimented him on his game.

Keith replaced Brett in Mr. Carlton's chair. He leaned back for a close shave. He said to Don, "Coach you gotta admit, little Set is the joint. He runs rings around those other boys."

"Shut up before I cut your throat," the barber said.

"He's tough," Don agreed. "Where does he go to school?"

"Doesn't he go to Franklin?" Omar asked.

"No. He's not one of ours. I talked to the coach over at Dupree. Set Shot doesn't go there either."

Keith realized that he didn't know much about the young men he spent at least five hours a week with. He made a mental note to get closer to his hoop partners.

Keith wasted no time. On Monday evening after the last game, he motioned for Omar and Brett to go ahead without him. Keith slung one sweaty arm around Set's shoulder, and said, "I think I owe you a soda. Want to go to the Chicken Shack with me?"

Keith and Set settled into their tiny booth at Freddie's. They didn't talk much, but instead concentrated on devouring greasy fried chicken and french fries. Set ate all three of his own pieces of chicken and one of Keith's. Keith waited until Set dug into his sweet potato pie before he began the conversation.

"Set, you're pretty good, you know. You're playing varsity, right?" Keith asked.

Set nodded no.

"They've got you on JV?" Couldn't be, with his talent.

"I don't play for no school," Set said. He stared out the window. For all his confidence on the court, Set spoke in a small voice and stole glances at Keith. When he spoke, Set either looked at his food, or out the window.

"Oh." Keith said. He let a moment pass before asking, "Do you go to Franklin?"

Set nodded no again. He hunched into his seat.

"Where then?"

Set sucked his teeth and said, "I'm s'pose to go to Dupree. But they be trippin' over there, so most of the time I just be hangin' out."

"Mmm," Keith nodded that he understood. He took two more bites of pie before asking another question. "When's the last time you went to school?"

"I don't know, before Christmas." Set said. "They be acting all fraud, know what I'm sayin'? I ain't got time for that."

"Who? Gangsters giving you trouble?"

"Nah, it's the teachers. They always picking on somebody for no reason, trying to embarrass you and stuff."

"What do your parents think about you not being in school?" Keith asked. He didn't know whether Set even had parents. A surprising number of children were completely on their own. Most had one parent, but precious few knew what it meant to have a mother and a father.

"My mama don't know yet," Set admitted, and gave Keith a look that said he would like to keep it that way. "Jimmy, that's my stepdad, he been trying to get me to go back."

"Jimmy's got the right idea," Keith said as he leaned forward and forced Set to look at him. "Set, you're a good kid, so I'm going to tell you like I would tell my own son. A black man without an education is null and void." Keith pointed out the window to the corner across the street. Young men, their forty ounce bottles concealed by brown paper bags, hung on the corner, silently sipping their potion and watching the world pass them by. "See that? There's always room for another black man. Is that what you want?"

"No. I want to be a pro basketball player, then I want to be an accountant. They good with numbers, right?"

"Yes."

"So am I. I make good grades in math. My math teacher wanted to put me in the advanced class, until them other fools butted in."

"Who?"

"My other teachers, the ones I took English and history and social studies from."

"Your grades in those classes not so hot?"

Set returned to his shell. He cast his eyes downward as he nodded yes.

Keith picked up the greasy foil and napkins that littered their table. He tossed them into the nearest basket. "Let me give you a ride home, Set."

INTERLUDE

*T*HE NEXT NIGHT Keith, Brett and Omar took a rare break from their rigorous study schedule. After their pickup game, the trio headed to Omar's condo to watch the first game of the NCAA Final Four playoffs. During half time Keith told them about his conversation with Set Shot.

"Sounds like maybe he can't read," Brett speculated.

"That's what I think. I met his folks—nice people, but I doubt that Set can depend on them for help," Keith said. He turned to Omar, who was channel surfing, switching from one sporting event to the next. "Omar," he said, "you're the idea man. What can I do to get Set back into school?"

"Teach him to read, I guess," Omar replied absently.

"Yeah, I..." Keith stopped midsentence. Someone was at Omar's door.

Omar looked at his watch, muttered something and stared at his front door. He didn't move.

"You want me to get that for you?" Brett asked after the buzzer rang for a third time.

"No. This won't take but a minute." Omar dragged himself to his feet and headed toward the door. He opened it and stepped outside, only half-closing the door behind him. Keith and Brett craned to get a glimpse of the visitor, but Omar's frame blocked their view. All they could tell was that the person was much shorter than Omar. From Omar's side of the conversation, they guessed it was a woman.

Keith felt a little nervous. Maybe it was Callie. He and Callie enjoyed a casual, friendly relationship; she seemed oblivious to his feelings for her. So far Keith had avoided being with Callie and Omar at the same time, and he would just as soon keep it that way. While Callie didn't notice the way he felt, Keith wasn't so sure that he could front Omar as easily and he didn't want to find out. Keith's heart sank to his feet when Omar stepped aside to allow his visitor to enter.

"Brett, Keith, I'd like you to meet Shelly," Omar guided the woman toward the sofa. "Shelly, this is Keith." Omar waited for Shelly and Keith to exchange hellos before turning to Brett. "And this is Brett." Brett looked dumbly at Shelly without acknowledging Omar's introduction or Shelly's friendly hello. "Brett!" Omar snapped curtly, whereupon Brett came to himself and gave Shelly a short wave.

Shelly began working her magic to put the men at ease, "It's so good to finally meet y'all. Omar talks about you all the time." She gave a small laugh and added, "I was beginning to think that you guys didn't exist. You probably thought I was a figment of Omar's imagination."

Omar shot Keith and Brett a glance. *Don't say a word.* Keith ignored him. "You know Omar," Keith said to Shelly, "he can be so private. He hasn't told us nearly as much about you as he should've."

"We both keep pretty quiet about things," said Shelly, giving Omar a look that spoke love and conspiracy simultaneously. Omar tossed her an inscrutable smile and then riveted his attention to the television. "Dana—she's my best friend, knows everything." Shelly turned to Keith again as she spoke. "I don't discuss it with anyone else."

"We're Omar's best friends, right Brett?" Keith said.

"Huh?" said Brett. His shock at seeing Omar with a beautiful, well-heeled white woman cloaked Brett like a thorny cape. Brett looked from Shelly to Keith. "Did you say something?" he asked.

"I said we're Omar's best friends."

"If you say so."

Shelly felt like slapping Brett. Omar and Keith didn't seem to read his mood, feel the vibes that he emitted, but Shelly sure did. Omar might be one of Brett's best friends, but Brett didn't like him dating a white woman. Omar wasn't the only one living beyond the pale; in Brett's eyes Shelly was a whore. A spectacular specimen of American beauty, but a reject nonetheless. She hated herself for letting the Bretts of the world get to her. Shelly redoubled her efforts to display the strength of her bond with Omar.

"I know something that he didn't tell you, because I haven't broken the news to him yet," Shelly said and smiled directly at Brett.

She's pregnant they thought in unison.

"Although we decided against it at first," Shelly spoke matter of factly, unaware that the trio hung on her every word, "we're definitely going to have a wedding. Nothing elaborate. Just a little something that best friends will be required to attend." The effervescent Shelly beamed.

Omar let out a huge sigh that the other men took as one of relief. They were only half right. Gratified that Shelly wasn't pregnant, Omar was also pissed that she spilled the beans on their relationship. While Shelly chatted on, Omar's mind raced, trying to decide the quickest way to get rid of her, other than straight up tossing her out the door. He didn't want the guys to know about Shelly's marital status or his financial arrangement with her. Omar followed Brett's gaze to the fat diamond wedding set that adorned Shelly's left hand. Only one secret left to save.

As if cued by a malevolent spirit, Shelly said to Omar, "Honey I found the Charles Johnson figurine that you want. You didn't tell me that his work was so expensive. We need to talk…"

"We sure do babe." Omar snapped to his feet and grabbed Shelly's hand. He smiled at her just the way she liked as he pulled her to her feet. "Come with me."

Safely behind his bedroom door Omar grabbed Shelly by her hair and gave her the most passionate kiss that he could muster. "It's so good to see you," he whispered. Omar shoved Shelly against the door and lifted her so that she could wrap her legs around his waist. Unlike the kiss, this part was real for him. Right now Omar hated Shelly, could rip her head right off. That turned him on. Omar and Shelly made lightening quick, furtive love and it was good for them both.

Omar zipped his pants and checked himself in the mirror. He looked at Shelly, who, even though he'd given it to her standing on her feet, had a hazy aftersex glow on her face. She made no attempt to get herself together, just leaned against the door, eyes still closed. *She's too stupid*, he thought.

"I'm going back out there. Once you get all fixed up, you'd better go." Omar tempered his words with a kiss and a smile, "Otherwise I'd want to stay in here with you all afternoon." He paused before opening the bedroom door. "Oh, leave me a little something on the dresser? I'm sorta light right now."

"So," Keith broached the subject as soon as Omar returned from walking Shelly to her car, "what's up with that, Omar?"

Omar waved his arms dismissively, "Oh, Shelly? She's cool."

"Must be more than cool; you guys getting married."

Omar was suddenly glad that Brett noticed Shelly's wedding band. He took the easy out that it provided, "What am I gonna do, participate in bigamy? Shelly's already married, didn't you check out her rock?"

"Why are you dating someone's wife?" Brett wanted to know. His words were sharp and accusing.

"I didn't plan it," Omar lied. "That's how things went down." Omar was tired of being on the receiving end of probing questions. He decided to flip the script. "Haven't you ever wanted a woman you shouldn't have?"

"No," Brett replied, but his bright-red color and soul-patch tugging gave him dead away.

"Then why are you so red, man? What are you hiding?" Omar pressed his point.

"Janna," Keith explained. He still wanted to know where Callie fit into all of this, but there was no way that he would ask, flat out. Better to let the conversation flow and see what happened. Besides, it was time to call Brett on his race fixation.

"Janna?" Omar feigned ignorance. "What's forbidden about Janna?"

"Janna and I are just friends," Brett responded defensively. "I've got a fiancée back home. Her name's Cyndi, and she's great. I mean Cyndi's good looking, she's sweet and fun—I—there's no way—what would I want with–," Brett sputtered.

"If you don't stop tugging at that jacked-up thing, you're gonna jerk it right off your chin," Keith offered.

"What would you want with Janna?" Omar jumped in again. "Hell, what's not to want? She's tight, and she wants to be down with you. You ain't getting it nowhere else, so what's the problem?"

"She's black!" Brett spat.

"No shit." Keith said. "The blacker the berry."

"True my brother," Omar said and walked over to get some dap from Keith, who ignored him.

"What does that mean?" Brett wanted to know.

"The blacker the berry, the sweeter the juice," Keith spelled out what was a truism for many men of all colors. "Black women, they're the best."

"That's racist," Brett said.

"No it isn't," Omar was less combative now. He was out of the spotlight, at least temporarily. Plus women were his favorite topic. "It's just a compliment, you know, like saying blondes have more fun."

Keith seized upon Omar's statement, "Tell us which is true Omar. You've got both."

"The truth is, variety is the spice of life," Omar quipped. He stood up and faced his guests. "Look here guys, Shelly's my girl and so is Callie. You've seen them both, which one would you cut?"

When neither Brett nor Keith answered his question, Omar said, "What? You expect me to believe that neither of you has ever been involved with more than one woman at once?"

Vicki's stricken face flashed before Keith's eyes. While earning his college degree at night school, Keith became close to a classmate, Adrienne Wools. He found that he could talk to Adrienne about things that Vicki wasn't interested in. Adrienne's looks were understated at best; she couldn't touch Vicki in that category. Still, Keith found himself intimately involved with Adrienne. He loved things about her that were completely different from the things that he loved about Vicki, who was a woman who knew how to attract a man—Adrienne was a woman who knew what to do to keep one. Keith often wondered whether he would've gone on having them both forever if Vicki hadn't found out.

"Yes," Keith answered Omar truthfully, painfully. "I've had two women at the same time, two good women. We all ended up hurt."

"Who were they?" Omar asked.

"One was my wife," Keith sighed, "The other, maybe the love of my life."

Keith told his story. A private man, he'd never shared the long version of what went wrong in his marriage with any man. For Keith's twenty-fifth birthday, Vicki wanted to do something special, but Keith told her that he needed to stay at the library until midnight. Rather than having Keith forego a celebration, Vicki decided to surprise Keith at school by bringing him a birthday cake and a bottle of wine. She arrived at the library at about ten-thirty, but couldn't find Keith anywhere. His car was on the parking lot. At a quarter until midnight, Vicki watched with unbelieving eyes, as Keith drove up to the library in a car that she didn't recognize. He got out of the car, walked to the passenger side and opened the door for a tall, busty woman. Vicki's disbelief turned to shock and hurt as she watched her husband, the man she'd loved since she was fifteen, kiss the woman and hold her close with such passion that Vicki could feel their intensity through the glass doors of the library.

"What happened after Vicki found out?" Brett asked.

"I promised to stop seeing Adrienne."

"But you didn't," Omar filled in.

Keith leaned back and stared at the ceiling. "I tried. But I swear to God, I loved Adrienne."

"What was it, was she the best looking woman you ever had?" Brett asked.

"Not really, Vicki's the beautiful one. She still has her cheerleader figure to this day. Adrienne's lusher. She's got hips, a sexy little pooch. Adrienne's pretty, but with her it was more than her looks. It was her way."

"What way?" Brett asked.

"I was going through changes, trying to work, take care of my family and go to school at the same time. Some days, seeing Adrienne, or just hearing her voice, were the only things that kept me going."

"How long did it last?" Omar wanted to know.

Keith was embarrassed by the answer, but he'd gone this far, might as well keep it real. "Another three years. Vicki knew how I felt about Adrienne, but she didn't know what to do about it."

"Why not get a divorce? Sounds like you and Vicki were finished," Brett asked.

"Man, I thought about it all the time. All the time. But,…this might sound crazy…I still loved Vicki. It wasn't a passion thing, but it was real. We were a family—Vicki, my son and me. A man just can't walk out on that, and it wasn't just that I couldn't. I didn't want to. My dad died when I was eight, and my mom never remarried so there wasn't a man around. I didn't want my son to grow up lonely for a dad, the way I did, and I didn't want another man spending time with him, or my wife."

"I'm with that," said Omar. He wasn't into all that guilt stuff that Keith poured out, but this he understood. "I could live like that, respectable husband and father, with a hottie on the side. Why'd you opt out?"

"I didn't. Vicki got pregnant. The first person she told wasn't me, it was Adrienne."

"Damn," Omar and Brett said at almost the same time.

"Yeah. Adrienne put up with a lot. They both did. But since Vicki and I already had one child, Adrienne knew that with another one, I'd never leave, so she ended it."

"That should've fixed things between you and Vicki," said Brett.

"Nah," Keith's tone was harsh, bitter. "Vicki miscarried. After that we tried to make it work for another year, but neither of us could get over losing the baby, or my affair with Adrienne."

Omar was amazed that Keith, who seemed so much in control, had such a drama-filled past. He couldn't believe that Keith had the best of both worlds and ruined it by deciding to get a divorce. What a wimp. It seemed to Omar that despite being heartbroken, Vicki was so dependent on Keith that she would've grudgingly endured his continuing affair with Adrienne. Based on Keith's description, Adrienne was alluring, but just plump enough to be grateful that she'd landed a man as attractive as Keith. Sure she was angry when she found out about the baby, but she would've gotten over it if Keith had done some proper lying, begging and pipe laying. Omar feigned sympathy for Keith, but from that moment on he deemed Keith a fool. Omar loved Callie, and Shelly loved him. He had them both and would keep it that way for as long as he wanted.

THE FOLLOWING SATURDAY morning Omar called Keith at seven-thirty. "Ready for the barbershop?" he asked.

"Count me out, I've got something else to do. I'll get a haircut this afternoon."

Omar put on a pot of coffee and fixed himself a bagel. He opened his blinds to see if the weatherman's promise of a clear, kite-flying March day had come true. Frost covered Omar's windowpane and when he touched it the chill caused him to draw his hand quickly away. The temperature couldn't have been higher than thirty degrees. A gray shroud enveloped cars, trees, everything that should've been within easy eyesight. On Friday the high had been seventy-two degrees. Unpredictable late-winter temperature swings were the only thing about Dallas that Omar didn't like. Be that as it may, a morning like this one was very good for some things. Omar decided to go back to bed. He wanted Callie with him.

"Hello." Callie's crisp, wide-awake greeting was Omar's second surprise of the morning. His early morning telephone calls always came before Callie or Keith woke up. This morning they both sounded more alert than Omar did.

"Hey, girl," Omar deliberately enhanced the throaty sleepiness that was fast fading from his voice. He yawned deeply and then said, "Why don't you come over and keep me company." It wasn't a question.

"I'd love to babe, but I can't. As a matter of fact, I'm headed out the door. Running late." Callie sounded rushed. She didn't tease and flirt the way she normally did.

"Where are you going?"

"To Reese's. I'll be finished around ten, I can come over then," Callie said.

Omar wanted to chat, but he got the impression that Callie was in a hurry. "Call me," he said and hung up the telephone. Omar plopped back into his bed, trying to ignore the heat that talking to Callie fired in his groin. He was taken aback that Callie put him off; Omar was accustomed to women adjusting their schedules to fit his, not vice versa. Omar thought about finding a willing substitute to satisfy his needs. Shelly couldn't do Saturday mornings; he'd have to go into his inventory. A bulky, well-worn organizer lay on Omar's nightstand. He stared at his trusty friend, feebly willing it to help him recall visions of a hot body doing him just the way he liked. Nothing. No vivid flashback, no name. Omar's mental exercise only served to make him go limp. He would wait for Callie.

SET COULD BARELY look at the woman. She was so pretty! He thrust his hand forward and connected with the rich softness of her grasp. "Nice to meet you Miss Stephens."

Callie told the boy, "Don't you dare call me Miss! I'm not that old. Call me Callie."

"Okay, Callie," Set flashed a self-conscious smile and reluctantly let go of Callie's hand.

"Let's go inside. It's freezing out here," Callie said as she unlocked the door to Reese's Bookends' backroom and led Keith and Set inside.

After they were seated, Keith took charge. Callie watched the way that Set followed Keith's every move. It was obvious that the young man idolized Keith, and Callie understood why; Keith was so reassuring. Set seemed sweet, but as withdrawn as he was, Callie doubted that he shared his inner-self with very many people. Keith talked to the young man with immense respect and kindness. He made it sound as though the three of them were embarking on an important project and that each of their contributions to the effort was unique and important. *He's got it right*, Callie thought of Keith. Few things were more important than knowing how to read.

Keith's role was to help Set get up to speed on the substantive content of the subjects he needed help in. Callie's job was to evaluate Set's reading ability and help him improve his skills. Beforehand Callie and Keith discussed whether Callie should teach Set to read under the guise of helping him with one of his subjects. Being unable to read was embarrassing, and Callie was concerned that he would reject help rather than allow her to witness him faltering over simple words.

Keith insisted that they be completely upfront with Set. "He's a black man, Callie, the brother has to learn to deal with the good and the bad."

Callie and Keith immediately discovered two things about Set. First, he was of average intelligence and should have no trouble keeping up with his schoolwork. Secondly, his reading deficiencies weren't as severe as they'd feared. Callie unnerved Set in the beginning, but by the end of their session he could look at Callie and simultaneously comprehend what she was saying. His desire to read overcame his bewitchment, at least while they were in the thick of unlocking the mysteries of phonics. Once they finished, Set took to studying his feet, the walls—anything that would help him keep from gaping at the beautiful angel who was teaching him to read.

"Set, what's the plan?" Keith asked as the boy packed his books to leave.

"I'm s'posed to go back to school Monday. On Wednesdays, after we play, and on Saturday mornings, I'ma meet y'all here," Set said, repeating the actions that he, his parents and Keith decided upon. "And," he emphasized the part of their pact that was most important to him, "this is between us, our secret."

"That's it. You hang, my brother, you hear?" Keith patted Set supportively as he led him to the door.

"I hear you," Set answered Keith before turning to say goodbye to Callie.

"You'll be here Wednesday, right?" he asked, venturing a final, bashful look at Callie.

"Wouldn't miss it."

After he locked the door behind Set, Keith turned to find Callie wearing an odd smile. "What's so funny"? he asked.

"Set's such a cute kid. He reminds me of my little brother, Trent, when he was a teenager, all sugar and shyness around the opposite sex."

"Probably not around all females. You have that effect on men, Callie."

"Yeah, right." Callie busied herself organizing the materials that she used to assess Set, so she didn't notice that Keith's expression was much like the younger man's had been. Keith's eyes roamed Callie's body from head to toe, his mind vainly willing him to stop, every sensuous inch of the way. He imagined himself taking advantage of their time alone to let her know how he felt. Damn, the woman was everything he wanted! Looking at her now, he wondered how Omar could even think about another woman. But of course, Keith knew how. He reminded himself for the thousandth time that Callie was Omar's woman, or at least one of them.

"I'm grateful for your help," he said, moving the conversation onto safer ground. "So is Set Shot."

Callie turned and smiled at Keith. She had no idea what that simple gesture did to him. "Glad to help. It's a good thing that you knew about my volunteer work with the reading counsel. Teaching a person to read isn't difficult, but it does take some special training." Callie asked Keith a question that she hadn't thought of before. "How'd you know about that anyway?"

"You mentioned it one day in the Student Bar Association office."

"I chatter on and on when I talk to you; I don't even remember telling you."

"Does that mean you find me easy to talk to?"

Callie faced Keith and looked at him squarely. "Yes," she admitted, "easier than almost anyone I know."

"Callie–" Keith began, his feelings on the tip of his tongue. "I—I appreciate you. You're, um, you're a special woman." Keith shoved his passion down deep. Callie's expression was open, trusting. He wouldn't risk hurting Callie the way he'd hurt Adrienne and Vicki.

Although it had been almost three years since he stopped double-timing with his wife and girlfriend, Keith still didn't trust himself to treat a woman right. He thought about how Omar went behind his back to get to Callie first. One dirty turn didn't necessarily deserve another, especially when Callie's feelings were at stake. Suddenly Keith hoped that he hadn't tipped his hand. He needed to clarify things. "Omar is lucky to have you," Keith said.

"Thanks Keith," Callie said, her expression unchanged. Keith guessed that Callie had no clue of what he'd almost confessed. "Speaking of Omar," Callie turned and headed toward the telephone, "I need to make a call."

Keith roamed about the room, successfully avoiding hearing any part of Callie's conversation. His heart did a flip-flop when Callie hung up and asked him, "Would you mind dropping me at Omar's?" Keith had insisted on picking up Callie; he told her that since she was doing him a favor, the least that he could do was drive. Picking her up at her apartment had been a special pleasure, a fantasy semi-fulfilled. Driving her to her man's house wasn't part of his dream.

"So what will you guys be up to today?" he asked Callie on their way to Omar's.

"Oh, I don't know. We'll probably rent a movie, take it easy," Callie answered. Omar had actually been quite explicit about his plans to entertain Callie. When she'd hung up the telephone, Callie hoped that flushed feeling beneath her skin didn't show itself in her eyes. She could hardly wait to see Omar.

As he pulled up in front of Omar's building, Keith took in the drab mid-morning sky. His imagination working overtime, Keith thought about what he'd do with Callie if he were Omar. Keith's ideas didn't do a whole lot for his ego.

*B*AM! OMAR CAME down hard on the rim just as he remembered that if he bent another basket the school would ban them from it's court. He reluctantly let go.

"Come on Showboat," Keith chided him, but his tone was friendly. "You don't get extra points for tearing stuff up." Set laughed. In the four days since his first tutoring session he'd opened up a lot.

Omar bristled, but let it pass. He usually took Keith's jabs in stride. After all, talking trash was part of the game. Today the slightest comment from Keith scraped Omar's sensibilities like a Brillo pad. He wasn't pleased, not at all, to find that Callie had chosen to spend her Saturday mornings with Keith. Tonight she would be with Keith again, trying to help Set, with his illiterate ass, get his alphabets straight.

On the next play Omar drove hard to the basket and slammed into Keith in the process. Keith, caught off guard, was lifted off his feet and sent crashing to the pavement. His left knee was the first thing to connect with the unrelenting concrete. Every nerve in his body telegraphed the pain from his knee all the way to his jawbone. The other players stopped in their tracks. It was as though someone had counted to three, yelled, "Red light!" and then turned to point an accusing finger at anyone who dared move. Omar's aggression was clearly uncalled for, and the way he walked away without offering a hand to help Keith, who lay clutching his knee in pain, meant that the hit wasn't accidental.

Set walked over to Keith, who waved him away. Keith leaned, hands on his knees and breathed slowly, heavily. In. Out. In. Out. Keith wasn't catching his breath so much as struggling to control his anger. He didn't look at anyone or answer any of the, "you all right?" questions put to him by the guys. When Keith stood, he walked straight to Omar.

"What's the problem?"

"You got in my way," Omar responded and moved to walk around Keith.

Keith wasn't about to let it go at that. He blocked Omar's path. "Got in your way here? Or off the court?"

"You tell me." Omar's tone was thick with challenge. As he spoke, Omar took one step backwards and planted his feet, arms hanging loosely at his sides.

Keith had no problem going heads up with Omar. For the past several days Keith detected hostility simmering just beneath Omar's casual B-boy surface. Keith had his suspicions about what was bothering Omar, and he knew he'd hit pay dirt, when earlier in the day, Callie approached the two of them in the hallway and spent more time talking to Keith about Set than she spent talking to Omar. For the rest of the day Omar said barely two words to Keith, and now this.

Keith spied Set standing to his far left. He looked around and surveyed the rest of the young players, who were all watching expectantly. Keith knew that if he and Omar got into it on the court, this wouldn't be just another fight. It would be an example, a floor plan, of how black men, including professional ones, settled their differences. The idea of being a role model for black on black violence, even in an inconsequential basketball court squabble, held Keith's tongue in check. He decided to deal with Omar some other time.

"Let's play ball," Keith said.

"Why you let him dog you like that?" Set asked Keith later that evening. The incident had bugged him all evening. He didn't want to ask with Callie around, so he waited until she went to get a book from her car.

"It wasn't the time or the place to settle things," Keith answered. "Omar and I are grown men. Grown men have no business fighting in the streets."

"I don't know Keith; I think you should'a handled your business. Niggas think they can punk you; they be doin' it all the time."

"I thought about that. What would the other guys think if I backed down? Plus, I was angry. Even if no one had been there but Omar and me, I was still pissed enough to fight. Know what held me back?"

Set shook his head. He couldn't think of anything in the world that would've kept him from at least attempting to kick Omar's ass.

"Two things," Keith explained. "First off, Omar and I are normally pretty tight. I respect him and our friendship enough to try to find out what's up. That calls for a conversation, not a fight." Keith put his hand on Set's shoulder as he explained his other reason for walking away. "My second reason was you. The other guys, too, but mostly you. You say I should handle my business. I agree, but like I tell you all the time, there's usually more than one way to solve a problem. How can I tell you to walk away from a volatile situation if I don't have the will power to do it myself?"

Set didn't say anything. Keith could see that his mind was working, turning Keith's words over and over, pulling and stretching them to see if they were strong enough to serve a young brother growing up in the neighborhood. After several moments of silence Set reached a conclusion.

"Sounds like it takes just as much heart to walk away as it does to fight."

CALLIE'S FINGERTIPS ACHED. She picked up another envelope and shoved an invitation inside. *At least we have self-adhesive stamps* Callie thought as she tossed the invitation into the proper zip code stack. Callie sneaked a peek at her watch. It was almost two in the morning. Her early-morning companion seemed oblivious, he worked methodically, humming along with the slow jams that Monroe's overnight DJ was famous for. She scrutinized the unfinished boxes again. Another half-hour and just maybe they could finish stuffing, labeling and sorting the invitations to Monroe's 55th Annual Law Day Ball.

Law Day is actually a weeklong celebration observed by law schools throughout the country to emphasize the importance of our legal system. Events included lectures by famous lawyers, debates on hot topics and mini trials by gifted high school students. Then there was the Law Day Ball. As parties for middle-class folks go, it was an A-list affair.

Keith didn't care about the time. As president of the 1-L class, it was his job to see that the invitations were mailed. Until that was done, nothing was more pressing. As they worked in silence, Callie thought about how Keith changed when he was away from the other students. Not that he wasn't naturally friendly and a delight to be around in the law school setting; he was. Men sought him out as a friend, and, Callie noticed, several women, including a few who were about to graduate, coveted Keith's attention. His peers appreciated Keith's intelligence, his subtle, but unmistakable forcefulness and his caring, which is why they elected him 1-L president.

For all the ease that Keith displayed among his classmates, Callie thought she observed in him an underlying reserve, some emotion held back. She'd studied his face often; velvety black skin providing the perfect backdrop for his incredible, crooked little smile, wide, dreamy eyes and chiseled cheekbones that made one think of ancient African nobility. She always thought that his smile could be more open, his eyes more alight with life.

Around Set, Keith was still Keith, only better. He unleashed whatever it was that he usually kept locked away—put his whole heart into helping Set.

Callie, for all her acquired teaching skills, was no match for Keith. His ability to connect with Set was extraordinary. Keith's means of motivating Set changed depending on the circumstances. Callie had seen him use patience, compassion, even bullying—whatever it took to get Set to put one foot ahead of the other.

The young man responded like a long neglected grand piano that was finally receiving the fine tuning and polishing that it deserved. Callie realized that Keith wasn't merely helping Set improve his academic skills; he was giving him a lifeline.

As Keith sat there, long legs stretched out in front of him, keeping time to the music, Callie could feel his contentment.

"What are you thinking about?"

"What?" Keith laughed self-consciously and sat up in his seat.

"What's on your mind? You seem happy, like you could sit here and sing all night."

"Do I? Nothing in particular," he answered, "just enjoying the music and the company." Since his divorce, Keith had learned to control his idle thoughts, to never let his mind wander off on its own because unbidden, hurtful memories invariably shoved to the fore. Tonight his will to concentrate solely on stuffing envelopes deserted him. Pacified by Monroe's back-to-back D'Angelo tunes and a Maze mini-concert before that, Keith's stream of consciousness took over, retrieving thoughts that reflected his mellow mood. When Callie asked him the question, Keith had been thinking about her—how dedicated she was and how much he appreciated her help. That tidbit he wouldn't divulge.

"I'll bet I know where your mind is."

"Where?"

"On your boy."

"My boy?" Keith was confused. He'd thought a lot about little K. J. while sitting there, but Callie couldn't have known. He'd never talked to her about his family; she didn't even know that he had a son and an ex-wife.

"Set Shot."

"Oh. I guess he's crossed my mind in the last two hours."

"Just this moment, when I looked at you I could tell that you were thinking about someone you care about."

The way she said it, coupled with the peaceful melancholy that the music brought on, caused Keith to open up, partially, at least. "I do have a son, Keith Junior, K.J. we call him."

"In Atlanta?"

"Yeah, that's why I'm out of here every chance I get." Keith's face revealed a lot more than his words did.

Callie moved from her seat to sit on the arm of Keith's chair. She put one arm around his shoulder. "He knows you love him," she told Keith.

"How's it that you always say the right thing?"

"Not always, but with you it's easy. You're the kind of guy who…well, if you love someone, they can't help but know it."

Keith smiled. Did he seek out sweet, naïve women, or what? "There are a few folks in Atlanta who would take issue with that," Keith replied, as he picked up an empty envelope.

"K. J.'s mom?"

"Yes, her name's Vicki. We're divorced." He let Callie see his eyes, and added, "And one other woman." He went back to work and Callie returned to her own seat.

"But you know what," Keith said, breaking the silence. "If I ever have a good woman love me again, it's gonna be like you said. She'll know that I love her back."

"**E**-N-A-M-O-R," JANNA SPELLED and sat back, a satisfied look on her face. "That makes three games, Brett. You're a sucker for punishment."

"Not so fast. Doesn't that word have a -u- in it?"

"Not unless we're being British today."

"You're wrong Janna, check it out." Brett said. He tried to keep a straight face while Janna flipped through the dictionary. Brett knew that she spelled the word correctly; Janna always beat him at Scrabble. She was a board-game queen. It gave Brett pleasure to tease Janna, to watch her furiously flip through the dictionary, past the page she needed and then back again. For all her skill on the Scrabble board, Janna couldn't go straight to a word in the dictionary to save her life.

"Here," Janna thumped the page with her middle finger. "Enamor, e-n-a-m-o-r. 'To inflame with love.'" Janna seemed unaware that Brett was razzing her just so that he could see the earnestness mixed with triumph that she displayed each time she finally found the word.

"Okay. You win. What'll we play next?"

"I've beaten you at every game in this house. Let's do something different. How about pool? Or ice skating or miniature golf? There's got to be something you're good at."

Janna's suggestions, though casually put, addressed more than recreational options. Other than the rare out-of-the-way restaurant meal, Janna and Brett spent their time together in her home or his dormitory room. After months of playing the same board games, watching movies and listening to CDs, it was obvious to Janna that their staying inside wasn't by choice, at least not on Brett's part. For him it was a must.

Janna was sensitive to Brett's hesitance to jump head first into the interracial dating pool. The experience was new to her also; she knew that dating openly would be a challenge, especially in Dallas. Challenges didn't scare Janna—not being true to herself did. She and Brett shared a special bond; they clicked.

Janna and Brett had never made love. Deep kisses and strong, sterile hugs were the extent of their physical relationship. Unspoken between them was the fact that Janna could never be intimate with a man who wouldn't publicly acknowledge their relationship. She wouldn't let the light they created together be hidden beneath a bush.

The last thing that Brett did every night was to call Janna. He talked to her about a lot of things that he found difficult to discuss face to face. Janna knew Brett's life story, and he knew hers. She knew of his constant need to live up to his family's expectations and his feeling that thus far he'd failed. She even knew about Cyndi. Janna watched Brett struggle with the dilemma wrought by his caring for a black woman. She wished that she could help him, provide an easy answer or a balm to ease his confusion, but all that she could do was be patient. Her patience hadn't run out, but it was clear to her that they had reached a fork in the road. Brett had to choose between the seamless path paved by convention and the rugged, uncharted way dictated by his heart.

"Brett," she said, "what do you want to do?"

"Let's play Monopoly," he answered, deliberately ignoring the underlying question. As justification, Brett added, "We haven't played Monopoly in a long time, Janna. I'll bet I'm good enough to beat you."

Brett's flip dismissal stung. Janna decided that her patience was gone after all. Brett needed to make up his mind, and he needed to do it soon. Immediately.

"I've got a better idea, why don't we go price tuxedo rentals; you'll need one for the Law Day Ball." Janna said. Brett was so taken aback by the shift in conversation that he didn't notice the expression on Janna's face or the ultimatum in her voice.

"That's going to be a pretty big event. My dad told me that a colleague of his who lives in Houston is flying up for the ball." As he spoke, Brett tugged at his soul patch with one hand and ran his fingers through his hair with the other. "There are going to be lots of people there besides just the Monroe gang."

"Meaning what?" Janna asked. She didn't care that she sounded ready for battle. She was.

"Nothing. It doesn't mean anything." Brett tried to give Janna his 'please don't make me do this' look, but she wasn't buying. He tried another tactic. "I'd love to go to the ball, but honey, I just can't afford it."

"I'll pay for my own ticket, Brett. I'll pay for both our tickets. The only thing that matters to me is that we go to the ball. Together."

Brett walked over and lifted Janna from her father's easy chair. He embraced her and said, "I can't let you do that Janna. It's a man thing, you know?" He kissed her forehead and continued, "I promise you Janna, we'll do something special very soon." Brett was glad that Janna's face was buried in his chest. She couldn't see his shame. What he didn't know was that he couldn't see her tears.

RAVEN PINNED CALLIE'S hem and then took a step back to examine her handiwork. "That looks a lot better," Raven said. She picked up a half-eaten Hershey Bar from Callie's nightstand and finished it off in two bites.

Callie twirled in front of the full-length mirror on her bedroom closet door. "Yes, it does! I never thought that I had the legs to go this short, and I've never had the nerve."

"Well, the legs are working, believe me," Raven laughed. "Once you pull a couple of brothers with this outfit, the nerve will come naturally."

Callie sat on her bed, careful to avoid the pins along her waist and hem that gave her little red dress a tighter, shorter form. "Raven you don't have to do this. I can take it to a seamstress. I mean, look," Callie made a sweeping gesture, "this thing is lined. The whole dress will have to be taken apart and redone. It'll take you forever."

"Maybe it would take you forever, Callie, but I'll have this dress ready in time for next Saturday night. Plus, it'll fit better than if a professional seamstress does it. You'll be the best dressed woman in the house." Raven said. She made a shooing motion toward Callie, "Now take it off before you stick yourself to death."

Callie stood for Raven to unzip her. "Thanks for the compliment, but the dress you're wearing is going to leave everybody in shock for a week."

"The dress isn't the thing," Raven said. "Wait until they see my date."

Callie spun around, "No! Girl, you're going to the Law Day ball with Michael?"

"Why not? He's my man."

"But Raven, this isn't just some out-of-the-way gathering. Everybody from school will be there, not to mention politicians and lawyers from around the state. Keith told me that the Student Bar Association has already sold over five hundred tickets. You can't just bust off in there with a married man! That's tacky."

"Callie, by now you ought to know me well enough not to even talk about what I can't do," Raven said. *Who the hell does she think she is, making a morality call on me?* "As for tacky," Raven continued, "you'd better be glad I got hold of this dress before you decided to drag your ass to the ball." Raven stared at Callie without cracking a smile.

"Okay, I'm sorry. It's just that given Michael's position it's hard to believe that he's agreed to take you, that's all I meant," Callie said apologetically.

"I haven't talked to him about it yet, but he'll say yes." Raven didn't sound as confident as she usually did.

"Think about it," Callie took Raven's hands in her own. "This is something that Michael might not be able to do for you. He'd be risking everything. You're my girl, Raven. I don't want you to be disappointed if Michael can't come through for you."

"Michael loves me, Callie," Raven said defiantly. "If he loves me then he ought to be willing to do what makes me happy."

"If you love him then maybe you shouldn't put him in a position that will hurt him and his family." Callie said. "You're being selfish."

Raven looked at Callie as though she were a stranger. *Selfish? How the hell can Callie call herself a friend and not want what's best for me?* "Whatever," Raven said. "Let's finish getting you out of this dress." She tugged at Callie's zipper, which, like every other seam of the dress, was lined with straight pins.

"Ouch!" Callie arched her back and stepped away from Raven. "Watch it! These pins are sharp!"

"So I see," Raven answered. A slight smile played about her lips. "It looks like I drew blood."

CALLIE SAVED OMAR'S cotton sheets for last. She enjoyed the popping sound they made as she shook them out and whipped them straight. Callie stacked the cotton bedding next to two sets of satin sheets that had been stuffed into the bottom of Omar's laundry hamper. Her stomach did a tiny somersault as she looked at the two sets of expensive sheets, one royal blue and the other, a newer looking fuchsia set. She'd never seen the sheets before, never laid on them. Would a man sleep on satin sheets all by himself?

"Callie Stephens stop tripping," she said aloud as she placed the fresh sheets in the linen closet. She surveyed her handiwork for a final time. Omar's bathroom was strictly utilitarian, a man's bathroom. Still Callie thought, it looked good. The toilet gleamed, as did the floor. Callie spent a good hour on the shower stall, removing every speck of mildew and soap film. She'd gotten dizzy a few times, inhaling the fumes of strong cleaning solutions, but looking at the end result, it was worth the trouble. The glass door to the shower stall now gleamed as brightly as the mirror above the countertop did.

Omar's bedroom looked even better than the bathroom. Callie never would've guessed that a single man would own a sleigh bed, but Omar did and it fit him to a tee. The king-sized bed, made of heavy mahogany, set high off the floor, its dark color complemented beautifully by the deep-blue oriental rug beneath it, which in turn lay on cream-colored carpet. In Callie's view, Omar's bedroom was synonymous with safety. And a few other things.

The aroma of a slow cooking roast roused Callie and pushed her toward the kitchen. She had already prepared green beans and candied yams. All that Callie needed to do was bake a pan of cornbread.

There was German Chocolate cake, Omar's favorite, for dessert. Callie set off her old-fashioned spread with a slow jams CD and a good bottle of red wine.

The things one does for love. Callie had cooked for men before. She enjoyed the solitude, the time to think as she rolled homemade crust or seasoned a steak. The only time that she'd ever cleaned a man's home as thoroughly as she had Omar's was when the guy she was dating broke his leg while skiing. Callie's heart was generous, but she'd learned from experience to dispense her favors sparingly. Some men took kindness for weakness, turned a gift into a right.Everything was different with Omar. The intoxicating mix of strength and tenderness that she discovered in him on their trip to New Orleans drew Callie to Omar like a bee to honey. Callie was more than capable of taking care of herself; she'd been making her own money and her own decisions for years. Yet Omar gave her something more, something indefinable that she couldn't provide for herself. His presence in her life filled the hollow crevice that had been Callie's soul. Although she tried to hide the truth from everyone, including herself, Callie had been dangerously adrift since the day her father died. She went through the motions of living and sometimes, like when Raven made her laugh or when Professor Lenton rewarded her with a nod of approval, Callie almost rejoined the real world. Almost, but not quite. What family therapy accomplished for her mother and Trent, Omar provided for Callie. He turned her from the brink of despair and stood on the other side and caught her when she tumbled headfirst, into life.

Consequently Callie did her best to please Omar. She listened to and encouraged his dreams. If Omar mentioned that he liked something, Callie would do it or cook it or get it. She decided against cutting her hair because Omar preferred it long. In bed Callie extended herself, abandoned her innate reserve and let the sensuality that Omar mined within her take her wherever Omar wanted to go. Callie accepted Omar's murky explanations for the middle-of-the-night telephone calls that sometimes caused her to be left alone in the giant sleigh bed while he retreated to the living room for privacy. Occasionally she loaned him money.

Callie didn't mind opening her heart to Omar because he did the same for her. This night, for example, Callie expected to receive much more than she gave. Had Sonny been alive, the following day would've been his fifty-fifth birthday. Callie had avoided her mother all week, coming up with a variety of excuses why she couldn't stop by or talk on the telephone for more than two minutes. Cordelia wanted to reminisce about Sonny and the huge birthday celebration that would've been. The therapist told her that it was healthy to remember the good things about him. Callie couldn't face her mother's inevitable tears, or the nightmares that plagued Callie whenever she privately dwelled on her father's mysterious life and unsettling death. Yet as she watched her mother and brother heal, Callie admitted to herself that perhaps she too should voice her unresolved feelings about Sonny. Omar would listen.

When Omar walked through the door warmth engulfed him. Home. The fullness of those four simple letters embraced Omar whenever Callie spent time at his condominium. Her presence, her special touch, made Omar feel that the fifteen hundred square feet he inhabited was his refuge from the rest of the world, his castle. Callie was Omar's queen; regal and strong in her own right, yet mindful of his every need. She was what he wanted, respectable and smart in public, pliant and willing behind closed doors. Omar was glad that the other brothers at Monroe didn't know the fire that burned beneath his woman's mellow veneer.

Omar was afraid that Keith might make a move on Callie. Omar was never one to allow his love interests to share friendships with other men because he didn't believe in platonic relationships; every man was always on a mission to get some. He knew that Keith wanted Callie. Tutoring Set was bullshit, a ruse to get close to his woman.

As Callie came out of the kitchen to plant a warm greeting on his lips, Omar knew one thing for sure. Keith's game would have to be tighter than tight to push up on Callie.

Dinner was good, and it wasn't just the food that made it so. Something about Callie, something delicate, stood out. After dinner they lay on the sofa, bodies entwined, not a word passing between them.

Ten minutes into the quiet, Omar asked, "Are you ready to tell me?"

"Tell you what?"

Omar kissed Callie's forehead and said, "I know you Cal, you're a part of me. When something's going on with you it's happening to me, too."

"Ummm," Callie sighed. She wanted to open the flood gates, release all her anguish and anger. She couldn't do it.

Omar felt Callie withdraw. He tried again.

"You're hurting me, Cal."

"Hurting you?"

"You say you love me, but you're shutting me out. I'm new at love, but I know it's about honesty between two people. Always. You're not being real now. That hurts."

"Omar." An endless pause. "It's bad."

Bad. Omar's mind raced. *Disease. Pregnancy. Keith. Shelly.* "I can deal with bad."

They listened to Will Downing's latest CD in complete silence. Then, for the first time ever, she said it.

"My father committed suicide."

O MAR DIDN'T GET the full story until the next morning. That night he held Callie—all night, while she cried. Cried and rocked in the safety of his arms.

All that Omar knew about Sonny Stephens came from people other than Callie. She never mentioned him unless it was to respond to a compliment from a lawyer or professor. By all accounts Sonny Stephens rivaled John Reese as a mentor for the city's black lawyers. Reese knew the Monroe crowd and the few black students from the law school across town who had the luck to find out about Reese's Bookends.

Sonny Stephens, on the other hand, knew everyone. Cross the threshold of the state district court buildings and Sonny Stephens knew you, knew your story. Judges in both civil and criminal courts fought over Sonny's services; each wanted him as their bailiff. Sonny knew how to run a courtroom. He knew more about court procedure than most lawyers, so it went without saying that he knew more than the judges.

Sonny knew about other things too: the stock market, real estate, venture capital, government contracts, and he shared every bit of his knowledge. The ones who paid attention, like Senator Michael Joseph, became millionaires. Omar assumed that since he'd done so well for others, Sonny left a saddened, but wealthy family behind. Omar knew that he loved Callie, but the money didn't hurt.

Not that you could tell that she had it like that. Callie lived comfortably, but her taste wasn't as starkly expensive as Raven's. She was no match for Shelly when it came to gift-giving, but she'd bought

Omar a few nice things. Callie had loaned Omar money twice. To his mild surprise, the money really was a loan, not a gift. He didn't mind repaying her; Shelly kept Omar's pockets filled, and he was no slouch at saving and investing himself. Omar's income from two years of playing for the Chicago Bears, and his stock in Winslow Computers lasted and multiplied. Besides he like the fact that Callie had money and the sense not to throw it into the wind. If he decided to make her Mrs. Callie Faxton, Callie's inheritance would take care of them both. He would be taken care of by a woman who was lucky enough to have his genuine love.

Then Callie told him about the real Sonny Stephens.

"Suicide?" he asked her as the first shafts of morning sun peeked through the blinds.

Callie simply looked at him, her eyes wide, but dry. The night before she'd cried nine months worth of tears. Callie almost hoped that more tears would come to moisten the dry, thorny words she needed to speak. But the tears were all gone. She forged into her private desert of hurt without them.

"It was the end of July," she began. "Hot. A beautiful, wonderful day." Callie flashed a smile so brilliant that Omar's heart skipped a beat. She wasn't smiling at him, but at an ideal Sunday afternoon forever branded into her memory.

"Trent and I spent the entire weekend hanging around my mom and dad. I don't know why. Something drew us there and held us. You know?" Callie shook her head and repeated in a small whisper, "I don't know why."

My mom was so happy. I hope you get to see her like that one day. Daddy was mellow, introspective, I guess. Trent and I were used to Daddy peppering us with questions, but this time he didn't. He just sat in his lawn chair and watched everybody—watched my mom barbecuing, Trent and me playing cards. But Daddy watched mama the most. When I think back on it, it was like he was memorizing her."

He asked Trent about his girlfriends. Told Trent which one he liked, which one Trent would be better off without. Out of the clear blue, Daddy's telling Trent what to look for in a wife! Trent laughed it off. At twenty-two, settling down wasn't on his mind."

Daddy always pushed us to do our best, and with law school just weeks away, I expected him to give me some of what we called 'SS words of wisdom,' because he always gave advice to everybody. He'd talked to me all summer about how to study, keeping my confidence, stuff like that. That evening he didn't talk about those sorts of things. He talked to me about accepting setbacks, dealing with disappointment, being strong in the face of adversity."

Callie stopped. The words hurt again, so much so that she could imagine blood mingled with thorns trickling down her throat. "In all my life, my daddy never talked to me about failure. Never."

Callie finished her story. "Daddy loved my mother's barbecue, but that night he barely touched it. For a solid hour, from eight until nine that night he didn't say a word. Not one word. He watched the sun set. And he watched mama some more.

"At about nine my dad got up from his lawn chair. He kissed Trent and then me. Nothing odd about that. But when he got to my mom, he pulled her from her lawn chair and held her, held on to her. It was intimate, but not in a sexual way. It was like—it was a true love hug, you know? The love Luther sings about. I think mama knew something then. My father was an affectionate man, but God, this was so different!

"My dad went inside. Ten minutes later we heard the shot."

Callie shivered. Her fingernails dug into Omar's arms so deeply that he found tiny scars later that day. Her skin, layered with goose pimples, was icy cold. Omar gazed outside at the fine spring morning. All that he could do was let Callie continue to hold on.

Tears that Callie thought were all gone started to flow again.

"I'm the one who found him."

OMAR CHECKED HIMSELF in the mirror. Damn he looked fine in a tuxedo! His broad shoulders trim waist and long, powerful legs all subtly made themselves known beneath the soft black material. Looking at himself didn't bring Omar the thrill that it usually did. He felt moody, a little depressed, but for Callie's sake he would put up a good front. Tonight she would be smiling, looking beautiful on the outside while going through inner turmoil that only he knew about.

Omar straightened his bow tie and thought about Sonny Stephens. After he killed himself, Callie and her family found out that Sonny, was, at his core, nothing more than a weak, pathetic man. Sonny killed himself in his study. He was quite particular about his study. No one, not even Cordelia, was ever invited to get comfortable there. In the days following his death, the locked drawers of his huge, beautiful desk revealed Sonny's ugly stories. An old Polaroid snapshot and a binder of papers pained his family's collective heart as much as the fiery crack of a single gunshot did.

Omar understood Sonny leaving the papers behind; that alone was reason enough for him to put a hole through his heart. Omar recalled the disgust in Callie's voice as she told him about the papers.

"My dad stopped following his own investment advice once his stock portfolio climbed to nine hundred thousand," she'd told him. "Bit by bit, he sold off the blue-chip stocks, and replaced them with high-risk tech stocks. Because he was good at picking them, my dad did well. Very good. His portfolio exploded; within two years his investments tripled in value."

Evidently that wasn't fast enough for Sonny, so he picked up the pace, and bought more shares, maxing out his margin account and every credit card that he could get his hands on. Then the technology bubble burst, and Sonny lost everything within a year. By the time he placed the .357 to his pitiful chest, Sonny had gone from two point seven million in the black to three hundred thousand in the red.

A different piece of paper, a letter from prison, summed up the photo and explained the likely reason that Sonny killed himself. The letter was from Jason Cook, a seventeen-year-old boy who, at the time he wrote it, was one week into a twenty year prison term for armed robbery.

Omar thought about the stricken look in Callie's eyes as she'd told him about the letter. "Evidently Jason's mother begged my dad to spend more time with Jason and his sister, but he wouldn't. Once he got tired of her, he left the three of them on their own."

Jason's letter to Sonny was long and bitter.

"I don't blame Jason for being angry," Callie had said. "Even when he got into trouble, my dad still wouldn't help."

Omar agreed with Callie that Sonny's failure to aid Jason was his most despicable act. Sonny had known every top-rated criminal defense lawyer on a first-name basis, but he'd valued his reputation over his illegitimate son's life.

Callie told Omar that the photo showed an attractive woman in her late twenties holding a baby girl. A fortiesh Sonny, smiling like he was the luckiest man in the world, stood with one arm around the woman and the other resting on the shoulder of a boy who looked no more than five.

"Looking at that picture of Jason was like looking at myself, dressed as a boy," Callie said. "Our smiles are identical."

Omar surmised that Jason's smiling days were over. According to his letter, during his first week in prison he'd been beaten and raped twice.

"Why didn't we see him for what he really was?" Callie had whispered. "It's bad enough that he betrayed my mother, but to treat his outside children like dirt? I'll never understand it. He was always there for Trent and me."

"I don't know. People have secrets, Cal."

"Not like that," said Callie, unwilling to accept that simple explanation.

"How's Jason doing now, how's he coping?"

Callie stiffened in Omar's arms, and wouldn't look at him. "I don't know."

"You mean you haven't seen—"

"No," Callie said. "He's in Huntsville. What's that, about two hours from here? But I can't bring myself to go, or to write." She finally looked at Omar and said, "What to know the worse part? I'm doing just what my dad did, abandoning Jason. When people would say that I looked like my dad or acted like him, I used to be so proud. Now it just makes me sick, because I figure they're right."

Callie said of her father, "I hate him for what he did. I swear to God I do. And I hate myself for not doing right by Jason."

As Omar held Callie, part of him wished that he could take every ounce of her suffering for his own. That would've been better than watching her struggle with a burden so huge and awful that it almost broke her.

Still, old habits die hard. Lurking beneath Omar's empathy, unbidden thoughts roused themselves like wicked gremlins and made their way to the fore of his consciousness. The longer Omar stared at his dapper image, his mind on Callie and Sonny, the higher the little miscreants climbed. *Callie doesn't have a damned thing*, they whispered as they ascended. *She hid her past until she thought she had you hooked. A good woman wouldn't do that. You probably have more than she does.*

He tried to fight it, but there was no denying the truth. The old Omar was rising.

*T*HE MEN ALL PAUSED. That's what happened when Raven stepped into the Rambling Hills County Club ballroom. Omar looked at her and wondered how a woman could send the message that she could and would lay any man she wanted, while looking like the very definition of class. Keith, who hadn't had sex since his Thanksgiving tryst with Vicki, felt himself stiffen. Raven wasn't the type of woman he would take home to his mother—but still! Brett ran his fingers through his hair and smiled shyly at his date.

Senator Michael Joseph gagged and almost spilled his drink down the front of his wife's dress.

She was a vision. The top of Raven's strapless evening dress was liquid gold lame. The dress hugged and lifted her lush breasts and was long-waisted enough to show that her stomach was tight and flat. The dress was backless, all the way down to where her spine gave way to her beautiful round rear. It was almost indecent. Just far enough above Raven's pelvis so as not to make her curvaceous hips appear wide, her dress became kerchiefs of soft, ivory chiffon. When Raven walked, smooth silkiness caressed her thighs, making an almost inaudible whoosh. Yes, the men all paused, and they thought about caressing Raven with their hands, their lips, their tongues—the way her silken scarves did.

Raven glided into the room and dispensed glowing bits of her aura casually, greeting this person, returning that man's eye contact. Her cool attitude masked her mission. She had to find that son-of-a-bitch Michael and let him know, *school* him on the real Raven Hollo-way. For him to pull some crap like this, she'd obviously waited too long. How *dare* he set her aside for his whiney wife? Michael didn't know who he was messing with.

"Brett Milstead." The man paused in front of Brett and his date and extended his hand in greeting.

"Yes sir," Brett's voice took on a colorless, corporate tenor that he hadn't used in months. "You must be Arnold Grawl," Brett said.

"Good to meet you, son. Your dad and I go back a ways." Arnold Grawl scanned the room and said, "This is quite a turnout, more than last year. Your dad thought I'd be able to spot you right off, thought you'd stick out like a sore thumb." Arnold Grawl wagged a finger at Brett, "But like I told him, 'Andrew, Monroe has plenty of white students and supporters. If all Brett and I have to go by is that we're both white, we'll never find each other.'" Arnold Grawl laughed and deliberately looked at Brett's hair. "Fortunately I'd know a Milstead head anywhere."

Brett also laughed. He usually liked his father's friends. It seemed to Brett that his old man picked easy-going pals to offset his own rigid personality.

Brett turned to his date. He couldn't remember whether her name should be accented on the first syllable or the last one. Maybe it was the middle one. What the hell.

"Mr. Grawl, I'd like you to meet Andrea Harris," Brett said, coming down hard on the first *a*. The lithe young woman extended her hand and said, "Andre*a*. Good evening Mr. Grawl."

Quicker than Arnold Grawl could respond, the color drained from Brett's face. He began to cough. Coming toward them, looking confused and pleased all at once, was Janna.

"Brett, you came! I'm glad." Janna moved toward Brett, who knew what to expect. He stepped away, closer to Arnold Grawl than to Andrea, and turned his cheek to receive what was meant to be a kiss on the lips from Janna.

"Hi, Janna. I'd like you to meet Mr. Grawl and Andrea." He gestured toward Janna. "Folks, this is Janna."

Janna, her smile more genuine now, nodded toward the man. "Mr. Grawl," she said. Finally Brett was introducing her around. She turned to the woman who was a younger version of Hillary Clinton. "Andrea…Grawl…?" Janna said, a question tugging at the corners of her smile. She didn't know whether Andrea was wife, date or daughter.

"Heaven's no," Arnold Grawl spoke up. "I'd give anything for a daughter, especially one this beautiful. Andrea is Brett's date."

"Nice to meet you," said Janna, following through with her greeting, but her voice was no longer friendly. "Pardon me if I don't stay, but with us both here, Brett's got one girlfriend too many on his hands."

When Janna turned to Brett daggers sprang from her eyes. "If I'm too good for you, you should've said so. You didn't have to try to hurt my feelings. But you know what? It's okay." Janna's voice trembled, but there was no doubting her conviction. "You're going to miss me a lot more than I'll miss you." She slapped Brett, hard, and told him, "Don't ever speak to me again."

Janna walked away. Brett, his face stinging with both pain and embarrassment, could tell by the set of her slender shoulders that she was gone for good.

"RAVEN—*GIRL!*"

"Girl yourself. You're looking good."

"You're responsible for that," Callie admitted. She was relieved at Raven's warmness. Since their tiff over Senator Joseph, Raven had been distant and it hurt. Callie spotted the Senator and his wife as soon as she entered the ballroom. She silently resolved never to tell Raven I told you so. Callie glanced up at Omar who was by her side, as he'd been all night. "Omar can't get over this dress. I've gotten compliments all night," she told Raven.

"It's not the dress Callie. You have the look of a satisfied woman." Raven turned to Omar. She had to admit he did look yummy. "Why is Callie looking so good?" she asked pointedly. "Have you been surgically enhanced?" Omar was still on Raven's payback list. She zapped him whenever she felt like it.

"Not me," Omar said as he sucked his teeth and fixed his gaze just above Raven's head. He wasn't in the mood to be played with. Shelly and Winslow were in the house. Shelly was looking plenty fine, and filthy rich. She hung onto her tubby hubby like he was Tom Cruise. Omar shot a zinger right back. "I see that Joseph's wife has him tonight. Bet he picks up another three inches at just the thought of not having to deal with you."

"Omar!" said Callie.

"Haa!" Raven's laughter was loud and carefree. It made Omar feel that she'd won their verbal skirmish, even though he'd taken the last shot. "Callie, you sound surprised. You'd better learn what you're dealing with." Raven tossed Omar one last, dismissive look, heaved her gorgeous breasts high and said, "Now to find my Senator, extra three inches and all."

Raven was glad that Omar tried to piss her off. She needed a razor-sharp edge, draped in chiffon, for her confrontation with Michael. She eagle-eyed the ballroom. No Senator and Mrs. Joseph. Raven's heart pounded. Had she missed them? It would be just like Michael, the slug, to duck out early to avoid a confrontation. Just as her blood lust started to ebb, Raven's eyes swept past the ballroom doors. There the lovely couple stood, in the lobby. Fine Michael and his plain-Jane wife, greeting Mr. and Mrs. John Reese.

Raven swept through the doors of the ballroom. She smiled at the couples and glanced briefly, but directly, into Grace Joseph's eyes while brushing almost imperceptibly against Michael. *Did that girl deliberately bump into my husband?* Raven saw the question in Grace's eyes and knew that Grace didn't know the answer, and that she cared. A lot.

Raven positioned herself near the men's room and waited, never looking at the foursome. Moments later Joseph strode into the men's room and as he passed her said, in his most senatorial voice, "Back off, Raven!"

Rambling Hills Country Club is lavish, opulent. Even the men's room has a sitting area. Raven sat down and watched as the men slowly became aware of her presence and, one by one, scurried out. Michael alone didn't move. His face played between revulsion and fascination. One never knew what to expect of Raven. After the last man zipped it up and moved on, Raven locked the door behind him. She wasn't surprised that the door locked from the inside. In elite settings men sometimes need to be alone.

Michael's disgust turned to wariness and an unfamiliar unease, yet his fascination held tight. Michael's shirt collar suddenly felt two sizes too small, even the sweat forming there didn't give him wiggle room. *Maybe she knows karate or something; maybe she can kick my ass,* Michael wildly thought. He'd never seen Raven fail at anything she attempted, and right now she was like a lioness closing in on her prey. His irrational panic left as quickly as it seized him. *Raven is just a woman—my woman, at that.* Now was as good a time as any for her to be taught her place.

"Now, Raven…" Michael began, his index finger stabbing the air.

He shut up when Raven reached down and gathered the chiffon scarves of her dress to her waist. Beneath it she wore lacy stockings that gripped her thighs. That was all. Michael's shirt started choking him again.

Still holding her scarves Raven walked slowly to Michael and kissed him full on the lips, pressing to him as she did so. Abruptly she stepped away and moved towards the marble basin countertop.

"Take your pants off," Raven commanded.

Michael did as he was told. Then somehow—he didn't know how—couldn't reconstruct the scene afterwards to save his life, Raven perched above one of the basins and he was inside her. When she felt him shiver, Raven introduced Michael to her index and middle fingers, and she wasn't too gentle about it either. Michael arched his back and would've screamed, if Raven's other hand hadn't been clamped on his throat like a vise. As much sex as he'd had, Michael got a glimpse, at that moment, of what really turned him on.

Raven pushed him away and gracefully hopped from the countertop.

"Raven," Michael pleaded, reaching for her. "Raven, please—I've never—please, just once more. I need more. C'mon baby."

Raven ignored Michael until she finished washing her hands and tidying herself. Then she turned to him.

"I need some things, too. First, I need that summer internship."

"But I've already hired...."

"That's your problem, not mine. Fix it. Two, I need, or rather I don't need, to see you in public with that bitch ever again."

"Wait a minute, Raven," Michael began. "You're overstepping...."

But she was gone.

Grace Joseph offered up one more glazed smile before again craning her neck toward the ballroom entrance. "I wonder what's keeping Michael," she said to John Reese and his wife. Grace pivoted and took one step toward the entrance. "Maybe I'll...."

"No. I'll go see" said Reese, stopping her. *That damned Michael!* Reese didn't know where Michael was, but he had an idea who he was with. Better for Grace not to see.

Michael was too far gone to think of what Grace or anyone else might see. Just as Reese opened the ballroom doors, Raven swept past him. Michael was so close behind her that, had the scarves of Raven's dress been longer, Michael would've tripped them both. Michael's arms, his whole body, pleaded for Raven to stop, turn around.

Reese gripped Michael's upper arm and yanked him back. Reese, his words masked by a smile whispered, "Remember where you are."

Reese didn't know if Grace saw Michael; he was afraid to look in her direction, but plenty of other guests noticed the senator.

Michael snapped far enough out of his trance to still his feet, but he kept his eyes on Raven until she disappeared into the throng.

"Let's go be with our wives," Reese ordered.

"Well," Michael said, as they approached the women, "anyone care to dance?"

Grace smiled, but her eyes were dead. She took her husband's arm, and they headed to the dance floor.

Mrs. Reese cornered her husband, "What was that all about?" she snapped.

"What was what? Honey, you sound like I did something wrong, I…"

"John, who do you think you're talking to?" Mrs. Reese cut him off, "Maybe you didn't do anything, but you know what's going on! I'm warning you John, you'd better talk to Michael. I don't know how much more of his foolishness Grace is going to take."

Grace was ill at ease for the rest of the night. She still did the Senator's Wife thing, could do it in her sleep, but Grace kept her eye on the young woman who had entered the ballroom just before Michael and Reese. She knew that Michael saw other women, but this was the first time in a long time that Grace actually crossed paths with one of them. Someone told her the woman's name, Raven Holloway. She was beautiful, but that wasn't what bothered Grace. It was the way the young woman carried herself, as though she feared nothing and owned everything.

After Michael pulled to a stop on the circular drive of his and Grace's austere Oak Cliff home, as was his custom, he went around to open his wife's door. Grace sprang from the car and slammed the door. Michael thought, *she's tearing up my ride*, but all he said was, "What's wrong, honey?"

"You smell like that tramp, that's what! Her perfume is all over you." Grace's chest, heavier since the birth of their second son, heaved like she'd just run home instead of being driven there in a Benz. "How dare you embarrass me like that!"

Grace stomped toward the front door. For the second time that night, Michael found himself on a woman's heels, begging. In the weeks and years that followed he would become intimately familiar with that position.

"RAVEN YOU PACKED like you're going to Europe for the summer. Five, excuse me, six evening outfits? I doubt that summer interns have much use for formal wear."

Raven took off her sunglasses and winked at her friend. "It depends on the intern." She flipped onto her stomach and unhooked her bikini top. Raven picked up the sun screen lotion (even deep chocolate women need protection from the rays) and handed the bottle to Callie. "Do my back, please."

"You don't know Texas; Austin isn't Paris or New York or San Francisco. It's Austin," Callie said.

"So? Am I supposed to stop being me just because I'm surrounded by a bunch of hicks?" Raven raised her head from her folded arms, the ends of her hair catching a bit of the lotion that Callie spread liberally about Raven's shoulders.

"Guess not. How did you get Michael to give in?"

"First I took the normal route. Grades, resume, references, so Michael knew that I was qualified."

"You're capable, but not qualified. At least not according to the rules." Callie blurted.

"I'm top of the class; I do outstanding work, plus Michael hops into bed with me every chance he gets. Add those up and what do you get? Qualified." As she spoke Raven turned onto her back and placed her bikini top on the table next to her lounge chair.

"Someone's gonna see you!" Callie whispered. She couldn't believe that Raven would go topless at an apartment complex pool.

"Who?" Raven asked, scanning the pool area. "No one's out here but that little bald man over there. He looks like he could use a good look at a beautiful body." Raven, hands behind her head, leaned back and closed her eyes. After a moment she opened one eye and fixed it on Callie.

"What's wrong? Bottle empty?" Raven sighed and snatched the lotion from Callie. "Probably don't even touch your own breasts, unless you have to."

Raven gave herself a slow, sensuous massage, while she told Callie, "The regular route didn't do me any good. It rarely does."

"He was stuck on the fact that you're just finishing first-year?" Callie surmised.

"Right, plus he'd already awarded the internship to Gerald Foley."

"I've heard that Gerald's pretty smart. He worked like crazy to earn that internship."

"Gerald's no smarter than me, and no way has he worked harder on this thing than I did. He's just lucky enough to be second-year."

"But getting Michael to take it away from him and give it to you. Everybody's talking about it, Raven. That job's always been reserved for a second-year student."

"Let them talk. Who cares? Besides, Gerald will find another internship," Raven paused and then laughed, "or he won't."

"So how'd you get the job?" Callie asked as she covered her own arms and legs with lotion. Michael's already getting what he wants from you, what was his incentive?"

"Michael wasn't getting what he wanted from me; he didn't know that, but I did. So I turned him out."

"Whaaat…," Callie perched on the edge of her lounge chair, knowing that she sounded simple, but she was intrigued. Raven had a way with men, and Callie knew that it was more than Raven's looks at work. Some women went without a real relationship for months or years; even sisters who supposedly were a complete package: looks, personality and high-paying profession. Most women were like Callie; men came their way, but there was no guarantee how things would go. Then there were the Raven's of the world—women who always had the man of their choice.

"Raven, give it up. What did you do to Michael?"

"What I did was no big deal. It was the timing that counted."

"What do you mean?"

"There's a time when a man wants a particular woman. He might have a half-dozen women who are finer, more willing. But it ain't about that, it's about him conquering that one woman, staking his claim, planting his flag, pissing on his fire-hydrant. Whatever."

"Okay," Callie said. Nothing profound there.

"During that split-second, which could literally be just seconds, or maybe it'll drag on for weeks, a man will do just about anything to get that woman. And I'm not talking about just bedding her. He's got to own her, have her allegiance, her mind."

"So it's not a sex thing?"

"Sure it is. Sex. Control. There's no difference."

Callie considered this. She thought about Omar and the way he'd been at the time of their New Orleans trip. He was still attentive and loving, but she couldn't get the late-night telephone calls and new satin sheets out of her mind. Had her split-second with him already come and gone?

"The key to a woman running the relationship," Raven continued, deeply into her subject now, "is that she has to recognize when that moment comes along and take full advantage of it."

"That's the problem, Raven," Callie interrupted. "It's too hard to see this time you're talking about; otherwise more women would have things their way."

"The typical woman is so busy running around trying to do everything she can to keep a man, she overlooks the fact that he's sitting there, like a hairy dog in the middle of August, begging for a cool drink from her fountain. Sisters forget that they control the spigot."

"I don't see most men as being that weak for sex."

Raven gave Callie her best, *dummy, please* look. "It's not about them being weak, it's about them being men. You've never listened to R. Kelly?"

Raven massaged her lightly muscled arms as she continued. "And you're right, sex isn't the main thing. For Michael it isn't the only thing, but it was a major weapon in my arsenal."

She moved her attention from her arms to her shapely chocolate legs. "So a woman's got to recognize the moment, know what the man gets off on: adoration, abuse, a surrogate mother, whatever he needs. Then she's got to work her stuff."

Callie was again intrigued. "What stuff?"

"Your stuff. Knowing what you've got and how to use it!" Raven looked at Callie as though she were a six year old. "Knowing the exact power of what you've got, never under or overestimating it."

Callie couldn't bring herself to utter another stupid *what?*, but thankfully Raven kept going.

"Take me, for example," Raven said as she pointed two perfectly manicured index fingers toward her breasts. "I've got these and all the rest that goes with it. That's serious stuff, but that's not it."

Callie no longer cared about appearing naïve. "I don't know what you mean."

"There are plenty of killer black women out there, tons of them. Twenty years from now, when I'm in my fifties, it's not gonna be this body that keeps Michael holding on," Raven laughed and shook her thick mane from side to side. "Or maybe it will be. Who knows?"

Callie thought about the fact that Raven expected to be with Senator Joseph long term. Two months ago, Callie would've bet that Raven had no chance of snagging him. Now she wasn't so sure.

Raven leaned forward and spoke slowly. "Now Callie, listen to this. Even though my body isn't my ultimate drawing card, not my royal flush, it's at least a four-of-a-kind. I never forget that."

Raven went on to explain that for some men she'd known, sex was enough. Others needed more.

"Take this one guy in our class," she said, thinking of Omar. "He was crazy about me, but he knew I was too much for him. He needed his ego stroked more than he needed sex. I'll boost a man's ego—I do it everyday with Michael, but this guy wasn't worth the effort. I blew him off and he settled for someone less exciting than me." Raven admitted only to herself that the problem with Omar was that he didn't want her enough to give up running his game. It would've taken her a while to find his manipulation button and give it a long, hard ring, but she could've done it. Raven knew that Callie, with her big, dairy cow innocent eyes, didn't have a clue about Omar, about what made him tick.

"Who's the guy?" Callie asked.

"Doesn't matter."

"So what is it that you've got, Raven?" Callie asked at the end of the mini-lesson on men.

"Balls."

"Huh?"

"People think that I'm good at everything I do, and I am, because I've got the nerve to try anything and the patience to perfect it," Raven said.

CALLIE WAS OFFERED summer internships in Dallas, Houston and Chicago. She chose to stay in Dallas, although the other two firms offered more money and prestige. Since telling Omar about Sonny's suicide, Callie was slowly dealing with Sonny's legacy, except she still couldn't bring herself to visit Jason. Trent dealt with his grief by taking off for Europe with little more than a knapsack and his American Express card. Callie stayed in Dallas so that Cordelia wouldn't have to retrace the last months of Sonny's life all alone.

When she wasn't at work or with Cordelia, Callie spent her time at Reese's Bookends—she, Keith and Set, studying history, working algebra problems. Callie realized how attached Set had grown to Keith and her. Sometimes after they finished up, the three of them would go out for ice cream, or ice skating at the Galleria.

Keith had begun working part-time at Reese's Bookends—charity on John Reese's part. During the summer, traffic in the bookstore was light; Reese could handle it by himself. But he'd liked Keith since day one, admired the quiet way he went about helping Set. Reese saw in Keith the same potential he'd spotted in Michael Joseph twenty years before.

Not that Keith needed charity. Several firms in Atlanta wanted to hire him, and he'd decided to accept one offer, until Vicki, who'd planned to spend two weeks in the Bahamas, started changing her plans to accommodate him. He didn't want to be the cause of Vicki putting her life on hold, so he stayed in Dallas, splitting his time between a legal aid clinic and Reese's. He went to Atlanta every other weekend, to spend time with K.J. Keith thought about having K.J.

spend time with him in Dallas, but he rejected the idea. If K.J. stayed for more than a few days, he'd meet Set and Callie, and Keith didn't want the boy feeling like he and his mother had been replaced.

Keith's public story was that the Atlanta job fell through and that he needed a break from tedious research and writing. Privately, Keith took John Reese's measure as a man and decided that Reese could teach him the things that he needed to know better than some silver-tongued law partner. Keith needed to know how to recapture his life after what he'd done to Vicki, K.J. and Adrienne.

One particularly slow day, while he and Mr. Reese sat in the back room eating barbecue, Keith told Mr. Reese his story.

"Son, you're walking around with enough guilt, so I'm not going to get into the wrong of what you did," Reese told him, "but let me say this." Reese picked up a rib and finished it off before he said another word. "Even though marriage vows talk about God putting two people together, ninety-nine percent of the time it us putting ourselves together, whether God says the same or not. We don't always make the right choice. Get what I'm saying?"

Keith nodded yes.

"Now here you were, young, married to your high school sweetheart, probably never knew any other woman before you married her."

"I didn't," Keith agreed.

"I'm sure she's a lovely girl; they probably both are, so I'm not saying anything against your wife or the other one. It's just that before you knew enough to build a fence around your marriage, you fell in love with someone better suited to the man you'd become," Reese said. "I know, because it happened to me."

"Mr. Reese, you're a good man. No way you've done the things I've done!" Keith said.

"Who told you that good men don't make mistakes? I've made plenty, but stepping out isn't one of them. I don't share this with many people, but it was my wife who had the affair. So while I've been through it, I was on the other end."

Keith was stunned. He'd met Mrs. Reese and she acted like a good woman who loved her husband. Although Vicki had given him another chance, Keith didn't know if he would've taken her back if she'd been the one who got caught. A woman's cheating was somehow worse, in Keith's mind.

"My wife and I are happy now, but it was tough going for a while. I tell her all the time that she's my second wife, because the mistakes she made with me during that time, and the mistakes I made with her, we put behind us," Reese said.

"I won't get a second chance." Keith said. He felt sorry for himself.

Reese started clearing away his place at the table, signaling the end of the conversation, "Yes you will, but not with either of those two women," he told Keith. "There are lots of lovable women out there, Keith. The next time you fall in love, and you know it's right, build a fortress around your relationship. Don't let any love seep out and don't give any outside love a chance to get in."

Keith thought about Reese's advice every day, and every day he lived more in the moment than in the past.

Brett went home for the summer. He spent his days working in his father's firm and his evenings doing the socially required things with Cyndi. Brett tried to reach Janna the day after the Law Day Ball, but she'd left her recorder on. He chose not to leave a message, no point in setting himself up to watch a phone that probably wouldn't ring. He wrote Janna and told himself that she didn't write back or call his father's law firm (the number was right there on the letterhead) because she was accustomed to keeping their relationship low-key. *Relationship* was how he thought of them now. Before, Brett was always careful to use the word "friends," just friends.

Each day Brett awoke to cool Minneapolis mornings and his first thought was Janna. *Janna.* Just her name. At night his last vision always was of Janna—her beautiful braids cutting the air like so many martial arts blades, as she turned and walked away from him at the ball.

🍁   🍁   🍁

Omar spent sixty of the one hundred days of summer on some of the most exclusive beaches that the states and the Caribbean have to offer. Little St. Simons Island off the Georgia coast, La Jolla, California. Nevis and St. Barts in the Caribbean. Winslow Huffmeyer planned to take Shelly himself; something told him that his marriage needed a little R&R, but at the last moment, Huffmeyer had to go to South Africa on business. No sense in traveling fifteen thousand miles and not taking in the sights, so he scheduled a safari hunt and a few other adventures and was away for most of the summer. Omar pinch hit for Winslow in the R&R department.

The few days that he was in Dallas, Omar spent with Callie. He loved life with her, loved languid Saturday afternoons they spent exploring Dallas and Saturday nights spent exploring each other. Omar gave up going to church when he found out about his mother, but now he went to church with Callie and Cordelia, whom he'd taken to calling "Mama C." Afterwards they went to Cordelia's for dinner.

Omar hadn't gotten over the fact that Callie's family didn't have big money, but he came to realize that lacking an inheritance didn't pose a problem for Callie. Omar could tell from the way she fielded questions from their professors—calmly, expertly, as though she'd been arguing the law for years—that she had the potential to become a first-rate, well-paid litigator. Callie had no student loans, because even at his worst, Sonny left his children's educational funds intact. When Callie left Radnel, she sold her stock at a handsome profit and designed her own modest well-performing portfolio. Inheritance or not, Omar considered Callie a financial asset, and she was so good to him that he decided to forgive her for misleading him about her family's wealth.

One night, while making love to Shelly beneath the stars on a secluded stretch of beach in St. Martin, Omar decided to marry Callie. They would do it the summer following their second year. He strained his brain beyond what Shelly was doing to him and concentrated on recalling the day's date. July 17th. He and Callie could marry exactly one year later. No need to wait until they graduated, Omar didn't want Callie to enter the working world and come into contact with other men before he had his fix in.

He knew that Callie would say yes. What's more, he'd find a way to keep Shelly. Omar's salt and pepper mix would keep his palate satisfied. His only doubt, and it was a fleeting doubt at best, was about Callie's growing friendship with Keith. She talked about him way too much.

Omar opened his eyes to look at Shelly moving above him, her face mysterious with ecstasy. He and Callie would come to St. Martin for their honeymoon, and he'd let her do to him what Shelly was doing now, in this same spot. The feel and sight of Shelly, mingled with thoughts of Callie made it so good that he screamed. Too bad he couldn't get them together in real life.

Raven spent her summer turning Austin and Senator Michael Joseph completely out, just as she said that she would.

*T*HERE IS A saying in law school: the first year you're scared to death, second year worked to death, and third year, bored to death. *The second year has definitely begun* Callie thought as her pen raced across notebook pages to keep up with Professor Lenton's rapid delivery. It was deja vu, except this time the subject was a 2-L course, oil and gas.

"That's it for today," Professor Lenton said and flashed a friendly smile. The class didn't smile back—Lenton had just assigned over one hundred pages of impossible reading. All business again, she looked directly at Callie and commanded, "Ms. Stephens, be in my office in ten minutes."

"First day of class, and you're in trouble already, Cal," Omar teased. Omar sat to Callie's left; Raven to her immediate right. Keith and Brett sat directly behind her. Omar stood and let out a silent, muscle rippling yawn. His body already in excellent condition, seemed to have become even more perfect over the summer. He was toasted golden, the hair on his forearms bleached almost blond. As Callie scooted past Omar, lightly brushing against him, a distinctly non-scholarly thought crossed her mind.

Callie felt great. The day following the one-year anniversary of Sonny's suicide, she woke up feeling like a new woman. She'd lived through Sonny's death, and she'd find a way to deal with the Jason issue. This would be her year. No matter what Lenton wanted, it wouldn't disturb Callie's groove.

When the door opened Callie expected to see Lenton's usual larger-than-life self. Instead they were eye to eye. The great one wasn't wearing shoes.

"Ms. Stephens, please come in," Professor Lenton said. "I'm not as imposing when you chop off two and a half inches, am I?"

"No, no…I just…I'll just come in," Callie sputtered. So much for composure.

"Would you like some coffee? It's an Ethiopian dark roast," Professor Lenton offered as she paused to pour herself a cup.

The deep aroma filled Professor Lenton's office, and, coupled with the mellow crooning of Toni Braxton coming from the sound system that sat next to Lenton's coffee maker, made the office feel more like a soulful coffee shop than the chamber of torture that Callie was certain it was.

Callie remembered a negotiating tenet from her days at Radnel: Never be the first one to utter the word no. Her stomach already churning with anticipated agony, Callie smiled and said "Yes, I'll take a cup. Thank you."

Once they settled in, Professor Lenton got directly to the point.

"Are you on work study?"

"No. I saved enough money before coming to law school to pay my way." *What was this about?*

"So, you don't work?"

"No, I don't. I interned for a law firm this summer, but that's it."

"Would you consider working for me, being my research assistant?"

Callie, who had been perched on the edge of her seat, sat back and sipped her coffee. She could enjoy it now.

"Yes, I would, but I don't think that I qualify for work study."

Professor Lenton swiveled around in her chair and poured herself another cup of coffee. "Then you'll have to be on the school's regular payroll. That'll take some doing, but I'm sure that I can arrange it."

"Professor Lenton, I have to ask, why me? I'm sure there are plenty of second-year students who've been given work study and would jump at the chance to be your RA." Callie wasn't sure about that last part, but she knew that getting her onto the payroll would be a bigger headache than Lenton let on.

"That's not the point," Lenton said. "I want you Ms. Stephens. You're intelligent, not just book smart, but all around bright. When you speak, you breathe life into the law, into legal concepts that are hundreds of years old."

"Thank you." Callie hoped that her voice sounded even, that it masked her surprise and delight.

Professor Lenton didn't stop there, "You're going to be a very good lawyer, probably a litigator. Your feeling for the law is innate. That's why I want you."

"But my grades–"

"Are good, I've already checked. Being at the very top of the class means that a person is the best test-taker. I don't want a test-taker. I want a lawyer."

❧   ❧   ❧

When Callie got to her locker she found a gossip hungry trio waiting.

Omar spoke first. "So, what did Lenton want?"

Keith looked as concerned as Omar. Raven wore her usual inscrutable expression.

Callie pushed her way through her friends and began working her locker combination. She took her time to dig out her marital property book. Figuring that she'd squeezed the last drop of drama from the moment, Callie turned to the three and announced, "I'm going to be a lawyer."

"Hell, I hope so, considering all the time and money you've spent," Omar dryly said. "Now tell us what happened."

"Lenton wants me for her RA." Callie tried to keep a lid on her jubilation. She disliked the little girl gleefulness that she sometimes took on when she was happy.

"You?" Raven blurted. Keith smiled. This time it was Omar whose expression was unreadable.

"Yes, me."

"Why you?" Raven demanded.

"What do you mean, *why*?"

Omar spoke up. "Cal, that's great. It's just Lenton's reputation…well, the word is that she always picks the best student in the second-year class to be her RA."

"Lenton thinks I'm the best, Omar. She told me that I've got the makings of a real lawyer, not just a test-taker." Callie realized too late that she may have offended her friends. Raven, Omar and Keith all made better grades than Callie.

"Oh, so now grades don't mean anything? I guess this is the new affirmative action," Raven snorted.

"I don't think…," Callie started.

"Lets you know how the white boys feel," Omar interrupted.

Callie was stunned. Maybe they were right, maybe Lenton lowered her standards when she chose Callie. Her self-doubt would've mushroomed, were it not for Keith.

"I can't believe y'all," Keith spoke up. "If Lenton always picks the best, then that's what she's done this time. Sounds like hatin' to me."

"Whatever!" Raven said. "Good luck Callie, You'll need it." She smiled and added condescendingly, "working for the queen bitch, I mean."

"Yeah, congratulations, baby," Omar added. He realized that Callie's feelings were bruised and felt a little miffed at himself for setting up Keith to come to her rescue. But hey, what did Callie expect, flaunting her selection for a job that they were all better qualified for? Still he didn't want his woman to be in a funk. They planned to spend the night together; Omar didn't need anything interfering with his flow.

"Why don't you two go to class," Omar gestured toward Callie and Keith. "We'll wait for you, and we can all go to Cantina de Carlos to celebrate Callie's new job."

As they waited for marital property to begin, Keith told Callie that she had to develop a thicker skin and a defense strategy. "You need to put Raven in check more often," he advised. "Learn how to get her off you."

Callie sighed. "I know. She's my girl, but sometimes…." Callie thought a moment and then asked, "What about Omar?"

Dump him. "I can't tell you what to do about your man," Keith replied.

Raven and Omar sat on the law library steps as they waited for their friends.

"You want some?" Raven asked Omar as she unwrapped a Dove Bar.

"No, we'll have dinner in an hour." Omar couldn't get over how much she could eat and keep her body tight.

"A foursome for dinner," Raven said as she leaned onto the steps behind her. She bit into the rich candy and chewed slowly. "You know Callie's pissed about what I said. What are you thinking, setting up a dinner?"

Certainly not about you Omar thought, but he didn't feel like fighting so he said something else. "You guys are friends. Sure Callie's a little disappointed to find out that Lenton gave her special consideration, but she'll get over it."

Raven sat upright, her Dove Bar forgotten, "So you think I'm right?"

"Of course. All our grades are better than Callie's. I can see Lenton not choosing Keith; they got off to a bad start, remember? But there's no way she should've skipped over you and me."

"Omar Faxton and Raven Holloway agree on something. Amazing," Raven said. She resumed her relaxed position and finished her candy bar.

"No it isn't," Omar turned to Raven and, for the first time in a year, looked at her in a way that excluded the rest of the world. "Beneath the skin, you and I agree on a lot."

CANTINA DE CARLOS always put Callie in a good mood. Callie realized that Omar was sorry about his tacky comments. He planted so many light kisses on her lips, and caressed her back and shoulders so often that Callie almost felt embarrassed. But with no one but two of their closest friends present, she figured there was no need for shyness.

Keith averted his eyes each time Omar touched Callie. He was discomfited by his blunt attraction to Callie because of what it made him see in himself: selfishness and disloyalty. First he ruined his marriage by taking from a woman on the outside rather than giving more at home. Now, instead of finding his own woman from among the many beauties at Monroe, and all of Dallas for that matter, he was craving his partner's woman.

Keith didn't want to wreak havoc in Callie's life, but his self-chastisement didn't make looking at Omar's over-the-top display of affection any easier to take. He decided to bring up the one topic certain to divert Omar's attention.

"What do you guys think about the upcoming Mock Trial competition?" Keith asked.

Omar backed away from Callie's ear lobe. "Nothing to think about man, we're in," Omar said to Keith.

"With Dean Burthood as the trial judge? Better you than me," Callie said.

"Oh, you're doing it, 'Ms. I'm Gonna Be A Lawyer,'" Raven said. She hadn't fully recovered from her pique over the Lenton thing. "I signed us up this morning."

"But this is a wide-open competition, 3-Ls even get to enter," Callie said. She looked at her friend, who at the moment was starting in on a third basket of chips, having finished off the first two almost single handedly. How could Raven be so calm about entering one of the most grueling competitions that law school had to offer?

Mock Trials, as the name implied, pitted students against one another to try a fictional or 'mock' lawsuit. The jury would be composed of some of the best litigators in the state. The judge would be, as tradition dictated, the head of the law school, Dean Thaddeus Burthood. The saying was that Burthood was so tough, he made Lenton look like a doting mother, loving wife and best friend sister, all rolled into one.

The things that happened during Mock Trial competition became the talk of Monroe. Brilliant performances might get kudos for weeks, but it was the major blunders that became law school folklore. There was the guy who perspired so hard that he left a puddle on the floor. The girl who came up after him slipped in the sweat and broke both arms, so they said. Years back a woman, whose name no one remembered, started passing extremely aromatic gas, and couldn't stop. Burthood's fault. Tears were not uncommon to Mock Trials, quivering voices and nervous stomachs the rule. Ironically, no one was forced to participate in the competition; it was voluntary. The better, competitive students flocked to it.

Omar was up for the challenge. He goaded Raven. "Maybe you and Callie will be knocked out in the early rounds, then you won't have to take a real beating from Keith and me."

Raven laughed. A good dare always lifted her mood. "Man you must be crazy!" she replied. "Your girl here," Raven said, without malice, "is an ace litigator. And you know me; I'll fight you to the end."

"Fight!" Keith, who last semester decided that Raven wasn't his kind of people and only hung out with her because of Callie, couldn't help but tease Raven. "You two cuties won't have a chance against us."

That sparked a spirited debate that lasted until Cantina de Carlos closed for the night. The foursome seemed an enviable group—young, beautiful, intelligent and friends for life.

"HAVE YOU SEEN the Mock Trial problem?" Omar asked as he took his turn at the free throw line.

"Yeah, it looks tough," Keith replied. He waited for Omar's shot to lazily circle the rim and then go through the basket, before grabbing the ball and putting it up.

"We must not be talking about the same problem," said Omar as he laughed, scooped up the ball and passed it to Brett, who took his turn at the line. The three men spent some of their best time together taking turns at the free-throw line while waiting for their young friends to trickle onto the court.

"No matter how hard it is, I'm signing up. One of you guys want to be my partner?" Brett asked. His shot bounced off the backboard without getting anywhere near the basket.

"Brett! Set Shot's gonna eat our lunch today, you keep putting up bricks," Omar said. Since second-year started, Brett's game had been way off. Omar suspected that it had to do with Janna, who as far as he and Keith could tell, had sentenced Brett to a womanless existence.

"Why are you asking a stupid question like that?" Keith chided Brett, but also spoke the truth. "You know me and my man already hooked up. You've gotta find someone else."

"Yeah, like Janna," Omar said. He connected with the basket without looking at it. Unlike Brett, Omar seemed to have improved his game over the summer. Relaxation made him a better athlete.

"Janna's still got me on ice," Brett confessed. When he lost Janna, Brett also lost the shame that caused him to deny his feelings for her in the first place.

"Can you blame her?" Keith wanted to know. "That was hard, the way you did her at the ball."

"Yeah, player. School Brett on the pitfalls of letting two women cross paths. You're an expert on that." Omar said.

Brett glanced at Keith and saw his friend's jaw muscles flex. Omar was cool with Brett and other guys, but lately, his banter with Keith had taken on a machete edge. Omar low-rated Keith about his opinions, his car, and not having a woman. But his favorite topic was what Keith told Brett and Omar in confidence about Keith's screw-up with Vicki and Adrienne. When the high school boys were around, Omar's jabs descended to even lower lows.

The rigid set of Keith's jaw told Brett that a confrontation wasn't far off. He guessed that Keith let Omar off the hook because Keith still felt guilty about his past, but if Omar ever brought up a sensitive topic, like Keith's son or the miscarriage, Brett expected Keith to put Omar in his place. If they got into it, Brett couldn't guess which man would come out on top and he didn't want to find out. Time to change the subject.

"What makes you think that the competition won't be hard?" Brett addressed Omar. Was that a look of relief on Omar's face? Although Omar stayed on Keith, Brett didn't believe that Omar was one hundred percent sure that he wanted to tangle with Keith.

"The trial problem is simple," Omar explained. "Old gal's flying high making that paper, chooses not to pay her taxes, gets popped for tax evasion. She pleads guilty and comes out with a hefty fine and a probated sentence."

Brett picked up the ball and the story. "The government promises to keep things hush-hush, but next thing you know, the woman, her husband and her dog are all over the evening news."

"She sues the government," Omar finished. "Keith we're representing the government, right? Baby, we ain't got shit to do! She pleaded guilty; it's part of the public record. A person can't sue Uncle Sam for something that anybody can find out with a trip to the court clerk's office."

Keith thought for a moment and then said, "Good argument, but I think the issue goes deeper than that. How about the statute that says that tax return information can't be disclosed without a taxpayer's permission? That might be the real issue."

"What grade did Lenton give you in case analysis? An F? Your opinion sucks, 'cause you're screwing up the analysis of this problem...." Omar said, then stopped his tirade mid-sentence when he looked at Keith. *Step off.* At least that's what Brett saw in Keith's eyes. Omar must have seen it, too. The tension of unspoken words weighed so heavily in the air that it's a wonder the ball continued to slice easily toward the basket, but it did.

The young players idolized their elder counterparts and as a rule the law students' attitudes set the tone for the game. The edginess between the two would've ruined everyone's game were it not for Set's incessant exuberance. His awe of Keith and Callie was uncontained, and being a kid he couldn't stop talking about them, especially Callie.

Robert, the cool guy who used to ruin plays by acting like Snoop Dog with a basketball, was in love. "Gina's fine. Tasha Hill told me that Lashaun told her that Gina told her that she thinks I'm cute. I'm telling y'all, Gina's gonna be mine."

Little Cory and the rest of the young players envied Robert. Gina Taylor was off the chain.

Set had a different opinion. "Gina's two steps from being a hoochie, with all that make up and pasted-down hair," he said, teasing Robert.

"So?" Robert, dribbling like a real player, made a faultless pass to Omar. "Add in her straight nasty attitude and skin-tight dresses and

I'd say she is a 'hood-rat hoochie. I'm seventeen, what do you think I'm looking for? A hoochie!"

Everyone fell out laughing. Keith looked around the court and felt proud. The energy, creativity and camaraderie on the court were palpable. For the thousandth time he wondered why the average American was scared stiff of young black men.

Set who laughed as hard as the rest, good naturedly continued the conversation. "I don't want a hoochie," he said as his eyes roved for an unguarded space from which he could take care of business. He got off a shot before talking again. "My woman's gonna be just like Callie, sophisticated and sweet-talking."

"What can you do with a sophisticated girl, take her to the opera?" Little Cory chided him. "And why would a girl like that want your thuggish ass?"

"That's all right," Set said. He beat his chest with one fist. "I got to be tough, but my honey, she'll be a pretty brown angel with a killer smile and a sweet…disposition." Set tried out the latest addition to his vocabulary and looked to Keith for approval. Keith winked back, his protégée had come a long way.

Encouraged by Keith, Set laid out his fantasy for the rest of the guys. "My girl's gonna be from right here in Dallas. We're going to Monroe together."

"Oh, so now you're college material?" interjected Omar.

Set's smile faltered, but, Keith was proud to see, he didn't stop. Not long ago, Omar's comment would've guaranteed Set's silence for a whole week.

"She's going to have at least two degrees," Set said, sounding as though getting more than one degree was a new concept that he was introducing to the rest of the world. "She'll become a doctor or a lawyer—something like that."

"Shut up and play ball," Omar said. He bumped Set's shoulder and snatched the ball from him. Set could have called a foul, but instead he kept on talking.

"My girl's not going to think she's all that, just because she's smart. She'll give back to the community," said Set, dropping a phrase that he heard on BET talk shows all the time.

"Sounds boring to me," Richard said. "I need a fun gal who knows what's up. Only weak brothers go for the type you're talking about."

"Keith's not weak and his woman is just like that," Set said, defending his position. "Tell them about Callie, Keith." Set didn't know anything about his tutors' private lives, but he recognized the look in Keith's eyes each time Callie walked into a room. Set assumed that they were a couple.

"Set we're not…," Keith started, but he got no further.

Omar slammed the ball against the chain link fence surrounding the court and like lightening, got in Set's face.

"There are some things you best recognize, you little borderline retarded asshole," Omar said to the startled boy. "First, Callie is *my* woman! You got that? Second, a woman like Callie won't ever look at your punk ass!"

Set tried to take a step backwards, but Omar's hand shot out and grabbed the child by his jersey, holding him in place.

"The only reason Callie bothers with you is because she feels sorry for you, you little no reading motherf—"

"Stop." Keith, his voice calm, clamped his hand over Omar's. He didn't say another word, just squeezed Omar's hand. The three stood there—Keith and Omar with their hands at Set Shot's neck. The boy seemed to shrink. He blinked once, twice. Set's eyes glistened, but he didn't cry. All the guys froze in place. Brett stood directly behind Omar and could see the cold violence in Keith's eyes.

Omar let go.

Keith stepped in front of Set and without looking at him, used one hand to push the boy back.

"Put your hands on him again," Keith whispered with controlled rage, "and we'll see who's the motherfucker."

"Fuck you," Omar hissed. "If that little bitch mentions Callie again, I'll kick his ass, and yours, too."

Omar's hot fury fully matched Keith's icy rage.

Brett could only shake his head. He knew then that if there were ever a physical confrontation between his two friends, so similar in passion and unassailable strengths yet so different in character, there would be no winner.

※   ※   ※

The sketch of Callie that Omar began during their first semester was a work in progress. Whenever he uncovered another layer of Callie's personality, Omar returned to the portrait, and as a result it became more complex and beautiful with every new stroke.

The evening after his standoff with Keith, Omar propped a chair in front of the easel and sat there, staring at his woman's image. His eyes probed the charcoal streaks for some hint of deceit. Was Callie making time with Keith? Set certainly thought so.

When Omar found out about Sonny Stephens, he assumed that he'd found the answer to the riddle locked behind Callie's eyes. But maybe her deepest secret wasn't about Sonny, maybe it had to do with Keith.

Omar wondered whether he'd been wrong about Callie. Women, even the ones who played the good girl role, were master cheaters, especially the ones who acted like they were perfect ladies, Shelly was a prime example.

"Shit!" Omar jumped up and slammed his chair to the floor. The portrait's revelations unsettled him. The depth of his love for Callie showed itself in every stroke, and that scared him as much as the thought of Callie getting with Keith. He knew better than to give his whole heart to a woman.

This wouldn't do. Omar had to regain control of the situation. He paged Shelly, then he changed his bed linen. It was going to be a royal blue satin night.

"AFTERNOON MR. REESE," Omar said as he ambled up to the checkout counter with an armful of books.

"Good to see you, son. How was your summer?" Reese asked. He looked at Omar's strong bronzed arms. "Didn't know a guy could get a tan like that from library lights."

"You can't," Omar laughed. He gave Reese the sanitized version of 'How I Spent My Summer Vacation.' While in college, Omar spent one summer working as a lifeguard for the YMCA. His supervisor, a Y man for seventeen years, had been around the world helping the organization to develop swimming programs. Whenever Omar needed to explain having dropped out of sight, he adopted the man's story, with modifications.

Omar told the truth about his island hopping but changed the locales to places less exotic, like Jamaica, the Bahamas. And his mission, rather than slaying Shelly, was to help underprivileged island kids, all in the name of the YMCA.

"That comes to three forty-nine, ninety-six," Reese said. He placed the books in neat personalized bags that had "Reese's" printed in Roman script between two giant marble column bookends.

"I guess you know Thomas Eastman?" Reese continued as he swiped the credit card that Omar handed him. Reese knew without looking that the card said Shelly Huffmeyer, not Omar Faxton. During the first week of classes the year before, Omar came into Reese's with a beautiful, friendly young white woman. She introduced herself, pulled out her driver's license and her VISA and told Reese that Omar would be using her card frequently. Reese saw that sort of thing all the time, but the purchaser was rarely as eye-catching as Shelly.

"Thomas Eastman..." Omar repeated the unfamiliar name. "Who's he, a student at Monroe?"

"No. He's one of the top-ranking blacks in the YMCA. He's based in Chicago, comes through Dallas all the time," Reese answered.

"Oh yeah...yeah, Tom Eastman," Omar nodded. "Sure, I know Tom, great guy."

Reese said nothing. *Liar.* No one, not even Eastman's own wife, called Thomas Eastman, Tom. Whatever Omar did over the summer, it didn't involve the YMCA. Why make up an elaborate lie in response to a simple question? Reese knew the answer. Some people couldn't help themselves; they would lie about which day of the week it was, if they could get away with it. Omar was one of those.

As Reese handed Omar his bag, airy, laughter filled the bookstore. Reese's eyes lit up and a smile curved Omar's lips, as Callie bounded up to the counter.

"Hi, babe," Callie said as she tiptoed to place a light kiss on Omar's lips. "This is a pleasant surprise."

"Yes, it is," Omar replied. With one arm, he pulled Callie to him for another kiss. He used his free hand to pocket Shelly's credit card.

"Law school's driven you crazy, girl," Reese teased, "laughing all by yourself." As he talked, Reese studied Callie, marveling at the change in her. She'd looked good the year before, but this year she looked absolutely vivid, like a flower in full bloom.

"Hey, Mr. Reese," she said leaning forward a bit with Omar still holding her tight, to give the older man a peck on the cheek. "Keith's the one who's crazy. That guy...," Callie erupted into more laughter before finishing. "He's parking the car."

Omar's lips flat-lined, and his eyes hardened. Callie didn't see it, but Reese sure did. Reese didn't know about the run-in on the basketball court days before, but when Keith walked in, Reese could tell that Callie was a wedge between the two men. Reese couldn't decide which man to empathize with. Callie was Omar's woman, Keith ought to respect that; maybe he did, but he obviously had it bad for Callie. As he ambled up to the counter, Keith's eyes zeroed in on Omar's arm wrapped possessively around Callie's waist. Keith looked away—too late, though, to hide his feelings. Callie, as happy as Reese had ever seen her, chattered nonstop. She didn't know.

Reese didn't count either Omar or Keith weaker for their jealousy. Callie, with her easy, giving personality and subtle sexiness, was as desirable a woman as Reese had ever seen. Still, Omar and Keith covered their hunger for Callie with a surface layer of cool. Reese watched the young bulls warily circle one another.

"Omar, what's up? Didn't expect to see you here," Keith spoke first.

Omar took an extra long, intimate look at Callie, then confronted Keith with his eyes. *What the hell are you doing with my woman?* "So I see," he responded. Omar's tone dared Keith to say more.

Keith ignored Omar. "Mr. Reese, I just came by to drop Callie off and to say hello. I'm headed out," Keith said as he turned toward the front door.

At that moment Reese knew where his sympathies lay. He'd been looking forward to seeing Keith do some snorting and hoof-stamping of his own.

"Oh yeah," Keith turned around, his words sounding like an afterthought. "are we still on for this evening?" He spoke only to Callie, as his eyes gripped her as securely as Omar's arm did. Keith's message to Omar was clear. He shared a bond with Callie that excluded her man.

"Sure," Callie answered, unaware that the testosterone level in the room was jacked up to a suffocating level.

With that, Keith pivoted and strode out of the bookstore.

"Why were you riding with him?" Omar demanded.

"My car gave out on me last night. We just had it towed from the library parking lot, Keith thinks it's my starter," Callie answered.

What's wrong with Omar? she thought. "Keith was at the library so he gave me a lift last night, and this morning."

"Why didn't you call me?" Omar asked, already knowing the answer.

"I did. Last night and this morning." Now Callie was the one sounding suspicious. "You didn't answer."

Omar had unplugged his telephone and spent a steamy night with Shelly, their second one within a week. He'd felt good about it too, until now. Callie was the one who was supposed to feel threatened, not Omar. Seeing as he didn't have the winning hand, Omar decided to smooth things over.

"I'm sorry," he said, kissing Callie on the cheek. "Next time you need help, I'll be there."

He started to ask what Keith meant about that evening, then thought better of it. They were probably meeting to tutor Set.

"Mr. Reese, you mind if I study in the backroom with Callie?" Omar asked. He wanted to keep Callie close to him for the rest of the day, charm her in ways that Keith couldn't.

*K*EITH HAD NO PROBLEM bumping heads with Omar over Callie, but he lost some respect for Omar over how he treated Set. When it came to their studies, the guys moved their squabble from the basketball court to the library basement. For weeks, Keith and Omar haggled over how to present their mock trial argument. All of the students participating in the competition were given the same set of fictitious facts. Some were assigned to represent the plaintiff, aptly named Ineda Loya, and others were assigned as lawyers for the defendant, the Internal Revenue Service.

The facts were deceptively simple. Ms. Loya, the most powerful woman in Dallas, was the longtime head of the Dallas City Council. Late one evening she was visited by two IRS criminal agents, who told Loya that they received a tip that she hadn't filed her tax return for the preceding year. They asked Loya several probing questions, and numerous mundane ones, like the ones asking for Loya's full name, occupation, birth date and home address. Three days later, the local United States Attorney, Rusty Spike informed Loya that his office had information that she'd filed false tax returns for the past eight years. Spike's office planned to bring charges against her. Spike told Loya that her hustle was up in Dallas, but that if she pleaded guilty right away, his office would keep the information from the media. Loya could move, to Houston maybe, and get a fresh start. A week later, Ineda Loya, her attorney and Rusty Spike stood before a federal judge in an otherwise empty courtroom so that Loya could enter her guilty plea. Loya was Ineda's birth name. To help conceal her identity, the judge allowed her to use her married name and her initials. Loya's plea agreement named her as I. L. Thomas.

The next day, the headline for the Dallas Morning News read, "LOYA A TAX CHEAT." The article stated that I. L. Thomas who, on April 15th, pleaded guilty to eight counts of tax evasion, was Dallas' own Ineda Loya, head of the city council. The writer gave Loya's real age (the most scandalous revelation as far as the public was concerned) her home address (she actually lived outside the city limits), and the fact that she would be required to pay back taxes and penalties. Loya sued the IRS because, she said, the agency agreed, via Rusty Spike, not to disclose any information about her.

Omar and Keith were assigned as attorneys for the government. Callie and Raven were Loya's lawyers. Omar didn't feel sufficiently challenged. He and Keith had a hands down win as far as he was concerned.

"Loya has no case," Omar told Keith for the umpteenth time. "The IRS didn't tell the newspaper anything private about her."

"That's not the point," Keith argued. He was as sure of his interpretation of the case as Omar was. "The IRS has a statute that prevents it from disclosing tax return information, some circuit courts give it a liberal interpretation, but the one that includes Texas isn't one of them."

"Loya didn't even file returns, so there can't be any return information! Listen to me Keith. This is a procedural question. Our position is that Loya's case should be dismissed for failure to state a cause of action."

Keith shoved all the papers on their library table to one side. "Okay, Omar, let's see what we've got. I believe that we've been given the losing side of a legal issue. That isn't what the mock trial is about; it's about being able to identify the issues. The side that does the best job of identifying the issues will be the winner, irrespective of whether, in real life, they would've won the case."

Omar folded his arms. "I disagree."

"I know you do," Keith interjected before Omar could go on. "So let's say my view is the worst-case scenario. Hope for the best, but prepare for the worst, right? I think that the issues go like this: one, is the statute prohibiting disclosure of return information applicable?"

"No." Omar sounded exasperated. "No tax returns."

"If you'd read the statute, you'd think otherwise. The definition of return information includes information gathered by the IRS to determine whether tax is owed. Nowhere does it say that a tax return has to be filed. The information that the criminal agents got from Loya, her name, address–"

"That's crazy, Keith. All that information is common knowledge."

"Not all of it, but that's not the point. The point is the source of the information; it was gathered during a tax investigation and shouldn't have been disclosed."

Omar made what he knew was a solid counter argument. "Even accepting your position, once this information was disclosed to the judge in open court, it became public information."

"Good point," Keith said. This felt like old times, he and Omar engaged in debate. Maybe working together like this would help heal their differences. "I think that as long as we recognize disclosure as an issue, we win, at least in part."

"How can we win on that? It's too simple!" Omar humored Keith by even discussing the argument, but he didn't believe for one minute that Keith was right.

"It's not that simple, there's a split among the circuits on whether the public information rule kicks in. You know that that's what mock trials are designed to test, whether we've done enough research to argue both sides of the case. But something else has been bothering me about this whole thing. If we can figure out that one of the issues is whether disclosure in open court changes things, Callie and Raven will figure it out just as easily." Keith said, pausing, too preoccupied with the idea forming in his head to notice Omar's mocking expression. "I'm thinking that the other, almost hidden, issue is whether all of the information is considered return information."

"What do you mean?" Omar asked.

"I'm talking about the information regarding the charge against Loya and the fact that she has to pay back taxes and penalties."

"If you're right about how the statute should be interpreted, then I'd say yes, all the information is return information, which means our side is screwed from the beginning," Omar said.

Keith reached for one of the books that he's shoved aside earlier. "I found a case that says that information about what a person is charged with and about the legal penalties for the charge isn't considered return information."

"That's illogical!" Omar was tired of listening to Keith. "It doesn't make sense that giving Loya's name and address would violate the statute, but telling what she was charged with would not."

"We can argue that the court should find that the statute calls for an illogical, wrong result, but the point is, we must raise the issue." Keith did his best to bring that point home to Omar. If they didn't raise the issue in their trial memorandum, they wouldn't be allowed to make the argument during the trial.

"I know you're working your way around to something. What is it?" Omar asked.

"You're convinced that our argument should be that the case should be dismissed for failing to state a cause of action. I'm not down with that, but I could be."

"Provided?"

"Provided that my argument about disclosure in open court is included in the memorandum."

Omar nodded yes.

"And the argument that the IRS has every right to disclose the charge against a taxpayer and the penalty imposed by the court," Keith added.

"It's your show," Omar said wearily. He stood up and began gathering his books.

"I'll make the changes to the memorandum tonight," Keith said as Omar walked away.

The next morning Keith handed Omar a copy of the revised memorandum. "Tell me what you think," Keith said. By that afternoon Omar still hadn't given Keith any feedback on the memo.

Keith tracked Omar down on the parking lot. "We've got to get this thing turned in tomorrow. Does it look okay?"

"Yeah, it looks good. I found a few typos though."

"If you made the corrections on your copy, give it to me. I'll make the changes tonight."

"I don't have the memo with me," Omar said. "Tell you what, e-mail the memo to me. I'll make the corrections on my computer, print all the copies we need, everything."

"Good deal. We're scheduled to put on our argument at three o'clock, right?" Keith said.

"Right. I don't plan on coming here until it's time for us to go before the court, but I'll e-mail the corrected copy to you first thing in the morning," Omar replied.

Keith liked the idea of getting the memo early, via computer, but he had one other concern. "Don't you think we need to get together, to practice, I mean? We've both got to be fully prepared to make all of the arguments, because we don't know which one of us the court will call on first."

"You want to meet in the library basement, say around noon tomorrow?" Omar suggested.

Keith agreed.

That night Omar poured himself a glass of Hennessy, settled into his sofa and read the memo for the first time. Keith was an excellent writer, Omar would give him that, but his arguments about the statute, disclosure, all that shit, were so obvious, so typical. *If these arguments were so on point, I would've thought of them, not Keith.* If Keith would only follow his lead, they wouldn't only win, but win in a big, dramatic way. The team of Faxton and Dawson would be the only one to ignore the petty stuff and cut to the heart of the issue.

Omar walked over to his computer. He zoomed straight to the part of the memo that he didn't like (there were no typos, not one) and began blocking paragraphs. Keith's asinine argument was five pages long! Omar resumed his place on the sofa, finished his drink and thought about his options. As far as Omar was concerned, Keith's argument was wrong from beginning to end, tinkering with it wouldn't help. He started to take another sip of cognac, and stopped just as the snifter touched his lips.

Omar took his seat before the computer again and looked at the pages that he'd blocked. He removed the block command and placed the cursor at the beginning of the argument that discussed whether it was proper to release information about the charges against the taxpayer. Omar began blocking again. He sat back and smiled. Keith's nothing little argument within an argument was only three quarters of a page long. Omar pressed the delete button.

Then he went back to the part of the memo that argued for dismissal of Loya's case. Omar edited the argument, making it roughly three quarters of a page longer. He spell checked everything and then printed six copies.

Omar went back to his Hennessy. Things were working out fine.

*K*EITH SHOOK HANDS with Raven and then Callie. He wondered if they could see behind his smile, whether they had an idea of the magnitude of the headache that was promising to crush his skull.

"Where's your partner?" Callie asked. She hadn't spoken to Omar the night before. She and Raven stayed at Reese's until almost eleven, late for them, going over their trial presentation. She assumed that their opponents had done the same thing.

Excellent question for which Keith had no answer. When Keith woke up that morning he went straight to his computer. No e-mail. He telephoned Omar. "Hey man," he said when the recorder picked up, "I didn't get the e-mail. Try it again."

Keith spent the morning going over his presentation, especially the argument about dismissing the case. It would be his luck that the judges would make him address that issue, the one he didn't believe in. He still hadn't heard from Omar by the time he was ready to head over to Monroe. But he wasn't worried, typographical corrections were no big deal.

But here it was, two forty-five and no Omar. Keith felt like a mother whose seventeen-year-old son had taken the family car on a Saturday night and was two hours past his curfew; he didn't know whether to be worried or pissed. Lockhart Dees, Chief Justice of the Honor Court, and the only student allowed to help the professors organize the Mock Trials, approached Keith.

"Mr. Dawson, we don't have your team's trial memorandum." Dees looked bored, but he wasn't. He enjoyed denigrating Mock

Trial students. It was like fraternity hell week; he went through this when he was second-year, and so would they.

Before Keith could give an excuse, someone spoke. "Chief Justice Dees, here you go—the original and three copies." Omar handed over the memos. He turned to Keith, "Ready partner?" He handed Keith a copy of the memo.

"Sure, everything okay?" Keith asked as he and Omar took their seats at defense counsel's table. Omar gave him a thumbs up. Keith let his irritation go, he couldn't afford to expend his energy on anything but the trial. He flipped through the memo—it looked good, pretty much the same as it had when he gave it to Omar. Keith felt himself relax, he was going to enjoy this.

"All rise!" Dees, who acted as the bailiff, called out. Everyone in the courtroom stood as the judges filed in. Next came the jury. Omar's pulse quickened as he examined the jury, four men and two women, who were among the best litigators in the city. All heavy hitters, one juror was, in actuality, a federal judge. After today, Omar could name the job he wanted.

Dean Burthood was the Chief Judge of the Mock Trial. He made a few perfunctory remarks and then got right to it. "The defendant has raised failure to state a cause of action as an issue. Before we take any witnesses, let's deal with that." He looked at Omar and Keith. Dean Burthood had an option, he could let them decide which one of them would present the issue, or he could decide for himself. Burthood saw Omar button his coat, he saw the glint in Omar's eyes.

"Mr. Dawson, we'll hear from you first," Dean Burthood said. He loved his job.

Omar felt the wind go out of his sails. Damn, now they were screwed for sure!

Dean Burthood leaned back as Keith began his opening statement. This was a bullshit argument, but he'd give the guy a chance. Soon Burthood was sitting erect, his bored expression gone. Several members of the jury were leaning forward, hanging on Keith's every word. Keith was on. He divided his attention between the jury and the judges, talking to each in a conversational tone, as though he was one of them. No one could tell that he agreed with Dean Burthood. Keith's forcefulness, his complete command of the facts and the issue, made the argument sound plausible. Only Omar seemed unimpressed; the moment was rightfully his, and Keith had stolen it.

When Keith finished, there was whispered approval from the audience. Dean Burthood turned to the plaintiff's table. "Ms. Holloway, the plaintiff's response, please."

All eyes were on Raven as she stood and moved from behind the desk. She was beautiful, confident. Everyone knew that she was the top ranked 2-L, and they couldn't wait to see her in action.

Raven turned toward the jury box, she looked directly at Senator Joseph, who tried to keep the lust out of his eyes as he met her gaze. He needn't have worried about it, because Raven's look, for the only time since the day he met her, didn't turn him on. Raven's eyes were flat, beady stones. Her lips, normally inviting, were fixed in a rigid, puffy line. She tossed her head to one side, flipping her thick hair over her left shoulder. *Raven looks a bit like a horse*, Joseph thought.

Raven never looked at the jury again—she addressed the judges, calling Keith's motion to dismiss stupid and misguided. She pranced around the courtroom, like a high strung filly, flinging barbs at Keith that bordered on nasty.

When Dean Burthood had seen enough he interrupted her. "Ms. Holloway, you've fully vented your righteous indignation at Mr. Dawson, what this court wants to know is your legal basis for objecting to the motion."

Raven flipped her hair and fixed Burthood with her mega-watt sex smile, and flipped her hair again, this time using her hand to brush it away from her face and over her shoulder.

Burthood couldn't believe what he and everyone else in the room was witnessing. He enjoyed eyeing a fine student just as much as the next professor, but this overt flirting on Raven's part was too much.

"Is something wrong, young lady? Are you having some sort of fit or something?" the dean bellowed.

"No—I'm sorry Dean, I–" Raven stuttered. Joseph stared at Raven. She actually looked scared. Raven sputtered on, "I believe that the rule–"

"What rule!" Burthood spat at her.

"Well, you know, the one about—the one that says–"

"Ms. Holloway, this court has no idea what you're talking about. Unless you can cite some legal authority for your position and I mean right now, then please take your seat!" Burthood said. He was thoroughly disgusted. How could this shallow woman be a—correction—*the* top 2-L student?

Raven stood there for a moment, half expecting for Burthood to change his mind or for one of the other judges to come to her rescue. She looked at Professor Noah Small, her Administrative Law instructor. Freaky little fool, had he forgotten about the little treat she gave him in his office just two weeks ago? The professor averted his gaze. Raven didn't bother to hide her feelings; she stomped to her seat, cursing under her breath. Several members of the audience tittered.

Callie didn't say anything to Raven or even look at her. She was stunned. What happened here? Callie figured that when put to the test, Raven's arrogance and coldness stood out; she didn't know how to connect with people.

Dean Burthood banged his gavel, bringing the room to order. "Although plaintiff's counsel has fallen short of explaining why defendant's motion to dismiss should be denied, this court is bound by the law, and on this point the law is clear. Defendant's motion is denied. Plaintiff's counsel, please call your first witness."

Examination of the witnesses, 1-L students who took on the roles of Ineda Loya, Rusty Spike and the IRS agents, went smoothly for both sides. Give and take with witnesses isn't so nerve-wracking for lawyers because the spotlight is on the witness. Raven struggled a bit, but she didn't embarrass herself again.

Standing alone, making an oral argument to the judges, and being challenged by them at every turn, is another matter. Keith and Raven had already had their turns, and after the witnesses testified, Omar and Callie were center stage.

"Let's hear the disclosure argument. Mr. Faxton." Dean Burthood said.

Omar stood. He didn't say a word until the room was completely silent. "May it please the Court," Omar began, smoothly, profession-ally. "Ladies and gentlemen of the jury, we know that you sympa-thize with the plaintiff, Ms. Ineda Loya, but the truth is the Internal Revenue Service didn't disclose anything to the public that a trip to the federal clerk's office wouldn't have revealed."

Omar had everyone's attention. He was good, born to the court-room it seemed. He talked about the disclosure statute and explained why it didn't apply. Callie scanned Omar's memo, he covered every single point. She was so proud of Omar that she forgot her own ner-vousness, and before she knew it Dean Burthood was saying, "Ms. Stephens, the plaintiff's reply?"

Callie's mind went blank, her stomach churned. "May it please the Court," she said in a shaky voice. Callie started out hesitant at first, but it didn't take her long to become absorbed in her argument. She assumed the role of a thoughtful leader, taking the judge and jury on an interesting journey toward the correct conclusion. She was the only one of the four to elicit a laugh from the jurors. Senator Joseph leaned back and crossed his legs. Like a lot of legislators, Joseph was a partner in a law firm on the side, and he got the idea that Callie would fit nicely there. He wasn't the only juror thinking that way.

When she finished, Dean Burthood invited Omar to make a rebuttal argument. He hadn't asked Keith to make one because Raven didn't say anything worth countering.

"A moment, please your honor," Omar said. He leaned toward Keith. "I think we're pretty much done, what do you think?"

"Callie made all the right points, but we've still got the winning hand, go ahead and make the argument about the charges and the penalties not being covered by the disclosure rules."

"But I don't think–"

"Mr. Faxton," Dean Burthood interjected, "do you have a rebuttal?"

Omar sighed and stood up. "Yes, your honor. Assuming arguendo that the plaintiff is right about the disclosure statute, the government's position is that it does not apply to all of the information that was released to the newspaper."

Excellent, every judge and juror thought in unison. They had been listening to Mock Trial arguments all week, but this was the first team to realize that another issue existed.

"Go on," Dean Burthood said.

"The charges against Ms. Loya and the penalties that she has to pay are not return informa–"

Callie didn't wait another second. She stood and said, "Objection, this argument has not been properly placed before the Court." Callie picked up her copy of the defense memo and held it high, "The argument isn't here."

"Mr. Faxton?" Dean Burthood asked. Callie had the heart for the game, Burthood had to give her that. He hadn't completely read the defendant's memo—no one had, since it was handed in at the last minute. Keith and Omar were sharp, the argument had to be there.

Omar coughed. "Well, your honor, uh–," His mind raced, looking for a way out.

Keith saw Omar freeze. Omar didn't have the memo in his hands, he'd left it on the table. Keith stood. "Your honor, if I may," Keith said apologetically. "The argument is in our memorandum, my co-counsel just doesn't have a copy of it in his hands." Keith flipped through the memo as he spoke. "May I direct the court's attention to–." Keith looked for the argument. *Where the hell was it?*

Omar still didn't say anything, yet Keith didn't give up. "Your honor, the argument should be on page 46, just before we begin our conclusion. Does your copy have–"

"No it does not," Dean Burthood said wearily. He was disappointed. How could they make such a simple mistake? "Mr. Faxton, for future reference, all arguments that you want to make in court must be set forth in your memorandum or your brief. Please be seated."

OMAR MECHANICALLY JABBED his hand toward those outstretched to shake his. His well wishers were few, who offered insincere compliments and moved quickly on. Omar tried to hold them longer, to seem attentive; but the throng gathered around Callie and Raven overpowered the shallow conversations he tried to maintain.

Quickly Omar was alone. The crowd across the room had thinned a bit, at least he could see Raven, her head bobbing up and down in unison with her handshake. Raven's smile was broad and no doubt beautiful, if you didn't know her, but Omar saw that it was an ice cold killer smile.

Raven was pissed, and Omar knew why. The attention directed at Raven was a mere side effect of being Callie's partner—Callie was the star of this show. Seeing Raven's anger made Omar feel better. He watched Senator Joseph give his lover a quick handshake and politician's kiss before making a beeline toward Callie.

Raven turned and looked directly at Omar. Her expression mirrored his thoughts: *How dare Callie upstage me?*

"Excuse me, I just want to say congratulations."

Omar looked down at the petite, attractive girl standing before him. He'd noticed her before; she was new, a 1-L, too fresh to have any knowledge of the law or trials. She had no idea that Omar had let loose one apocalyptic turd of a performance. He'd had enough of this stuff—time to say a final thank you and go home. As he shook her hand Omar noticed the girl's expensive Swiss watch and tasteful tennis bracelet. Nice.

"I'm Tanisha Malveaux." Omar detected a Louisiana accent, which, if a women didn't rush her words, was quite appealing.

"I know you guys lost, but, you were so,…great," Tanisha gushed. Her eyes, which at first looked gray to Omar, flashed a brilliant bluish green. That was nice, too. Omar decided that he didn't need to head home just that minute.

"Tanisha," *a woman likes to hear a man say her name*–"thank you," Omar said and meant it. "I've seen you around. How's first-year treating you?"

Tanisha Malveaux tried to be cool, she'd seen Omar, too. He was a living god, a butterscotch colored, living god. The idea that this man had noticed her, well, it was almost too much. He probably thought she was pretty, at first glance—some people did. Maybe he thought she was smart because she attended the competition.

"Tanisha?" Omar spoke her name again.

"Oh, sorry, first-year is okay, except there's this one case, *Pennoyer…*"

Omar laughed so hard that tears came to his eyes. At first Tanisha looked confused, then she laughed with him. Right now, laughter was just what Omar needed.

"Despite what you saw today, I'm pretty decent at civil procedure," Omar said at last. "Explaining *Pennoyer* just happens to be my specialty."

Tanisha's exotic eyes flashed again, and Omar saw something in them besides academic admiration. He looked toward Callie and her worshippers. His plan had been to take her out after the Mock Trial and massage her hurt feelings over having lost, but he was the one who needed soothing and where was she? Omar looked back at Tanisha.

"If you have time, we can talk about *Pennoyer* right now. Are you up for having dinner with a loser?"

❦   ❦   ❦

Senator Joseph wanted to take Raven and Callie out to celebrate, but Callie begged off. She and Omar agreed that the winner would treat the loser to a quick dinner, followed by a lingering session of TLC. Callie knew that Omar would be a disagreeable dinner companion—he hated to lose—but she would coax him out of his foul mood once they were all alone.

Callie looked to where Omar stood just a moment before, evidently he'd stepped away, probably to the men's room. Callie waited for twenty minutes in the empty mock trial courtroom, then phoned his home and cell numbers. After another twenty minutes passed, Callie called his cell number and left a message. "Omar, honey, where are you?" she said after the beep. "I'm waiting in the courtroom." Once Callie started calling Omar, she couldn't stop. She placed five calls in one hour.

As a last resort, Callie called Keith. "Is Omar with you?" she asked.

Keith chuckled. "No Callie, this is about the last place your boy would be right now."

Callie hesitated. She knew that without Omar's grandstanding, he and Keith might have won the competition.

"So, how are you?" she asked her friend.

"You know how it is—knife stuck in your back—it itches," Keith answered.

"I'm sorry," was all she could say. Callie moved to hang up the receiver, then said, "Keith, if you do talk to Omar, please don't tell him that I called."

A full two hours after her triumphant law school moment, Callie went home. Alone.

⁂   ⁂   ⁂

Maybe my losing was fate. Omar sipped his wine and considered the possibility. If he'd won, he wouldn't be having dinner with Tanisha Malveaux.

Malveaux. Just the name excited Omar. It normally wouldn't have; Malveauxes were a dime a dozen in Texas. Tanisha, however, was a Baton Rouge, Louisiana Malveaux—that was different.

Omar's new friend was as pedigreed as the descendent of slaves could get. Her great-great-grandmother, Victoria, had been the octoroon mistress of Philip Malveaux, a French speaking, Louisiana planter. The old man, more French than American in his ways, lived openly with Victoria and when he died, he left her his sugar cane plantation. Victoria was only twenty-two at the time, but she'd learned enough from her lover to keep everyone—the State of Louisiana, neighboring planters, the Klan—from grabbing her property.

At forty-four, Victoria gave birth to her only child, a boy, who, unlike her, had brown skin and curly hair; only his green eyes carried his mother's imprint. Victoria named the boy Philip Malveaux.

The Malveaux family prospered and rehabilitated their lineage so that no member was darker than one part coffee, five parts cream. Still, they were black, and proud of it.

The Malveauxes diversified their business and, when the time was right, entered politics. Tanisha's mother, Marie Gaston Malveaux, was mayor of Baton Rouge; her father, Philip III ran the family's businesses.

Omar watched Tanisha as she emerged from the restroom. A lover of all types of women as long as they were good-looking, Omar found Tanisha's light skin and green eyes as arresting as Shelly's blonde hair and Callie's smooth chocolate complexion. Tanisha was about five-three, shorter than Omar preferred, but every inch of her petite frame was packed tight. She wore jeans, a simple sweater and Cole Haan loafers. Tanisha's hair was wavy, thick and untamed,

Omar didn't much like the look, but he knew that between his fingers her hair would be soft.

Tanisha's face would've been ordinary, if not for the two jewels on either side of her nose. Omar didn't appreciate the effect that his own translucent brown eyes had on the opposite sex until he looked into Tanisha's. Her eyes were fire, green one moment, gray or slightly bluish the next. They were sleepy-sexy looking and set off by perfectly arched brows. Tanisha, whether she was serious, tired, playful or even depressed, possessed eyes that sent one message: I want you to do me.

Omar stood and helped Tanisha into her seat. Bzzz–! Omar felt his cell phone vibrate. He shut it off without looking down, Shelly could be persistent, but this time she was overdoing it. On second thought maybe something was up, maybe Winslow was sending his wife on another quickie vacation alone. Better check it out. Omar ordered a second drink for Tanisha then excused himself.

"You have five messages," a recorded voice informed Omar. "Press 1 to listen to the first message."

As Omar listened intently, a smirk started at his eyes and, by the time he listened to the last message, spread across his entire face. The messages were all from Callie! He especially liked the last two, she sounded slightly panicked and very disappointed. The natural order of things was being restored.

SENATOR JOSEPH LOWERED his head—it would do no good for Raven to see his frown. Being with her during the week following Mock Trials had been like walking barefoot on shards of shattered glass. So far he'd managed to keep up the happy face routine; otherwise Raven's temper, more lethal than jagged glass, might direct itself toward the senator and carve his eyes out. *I wish I'd never met her* was becoming his constant lament. When the feeling passed, he again looked into Raven's eyes and pretended to pay attention to what she was saying. Joseph didn't need to listen, her tirade was so familiar to him that he could have mouthed the words in unison with her.

"And you, Michael! What the hell was that! You barely acknowledged me—"

"Honey, let's order now, okay? That'll calm you—"

"SHUT UP! Don't tell me to calm down, and don't fucking interrupt me again!" Raven leaned across the table and got menacingly close to the senator's face. She could see beads of sweat on his upper brow, could smell his anxiety.

Senator Joseph glanced self-consciously around the dining room. It was bad enough that he was being seen with Raven again, but a public outburst would be too much. He'd carried on affairs right under his wife's nose—including a spicy three month fling with her first cousin—for at least eighteen years, more if you counted the years before they married. But never had his stuff been as open as it was with Raven. For now, Grace was riding out the storm, but who knew how long that would last? Joseph thought about all the divorce court judges who would enjoy an opportunity to crucify him.

Once Grace found out that Raven was his summer intern, that he'd dumped another student for her, Grace set out to stake her claim. She'd done it before—fly to Austin and flaunt her position as Mrs. Michael Joseph. Grace couldn't stop her husband from fooling around, but she could certainly let his tramp know that she, Grace Joseph, was, and always would be the top show dog in Joseph's little kennel.

Grace showed up one day thinking she would work her routine with Raven. Joseph was in meetings from eight in the morning until late that night, so he didn't get to see what took place. In fact, he didn't see Grace at all; she took an early afternoon flight back to Dallas.

When Joseph called home that night, he expected iciness or reproach. But Grace didn't even mention Raven—she spent all her energy trying to keep the fear out of her voice.

About two weeks later, Senator Joseph went home for three days of meetings with the Dallas City Council.

"You look wonderful," he told his wife when she opened the door to greet him, "I didn't know you like Donna Karan." Raven was the one who'd taught Joseph about designer clothing, but Grace let it slide; she was just glad that he noticed. In addition to her new wardrobe, she'd lost ten pounds (a nervous stomach being the only good thing that came from her meeting with Raven) and colored her hair.

That night Grace put on a Victoria's Secret outfit and waited for Joseph to come to bed. He walked into the room, took one look at her, and retreated to the kitchen for a glass of water. Grace followed him. She stood in front of him, encircled him with her arms and pleaded, "Honey, come to bed. Please, Michael." Grace kissed her husband and pressed herself to him, but he wouldn't part his lips, and his body didn't respond.

Joseph sighed and stroked his wife's hair, "Grace, you look great—and you're a wonderful woman, a good wife, but right now isn't a good time for me. Go on to bed, I'll be in soon." But Joseph never came, he slept in the guest room that night and every night thereafter. Joseph's body belonged to Raven—he was beyond expending feelings on Grace, and he couldn't wait to get away from home and back to his woman.

Since summer, things between Raven and the senator had moved at fast-forward speed, with Raven's finger on the button. For every new thing about her that he'd come to love, Joseph discovered two things that repulsed him, or should have. For example, the night after the Mock Trial competition, Raven slapped him—twice!" He was shocked at her violence and sickened by the instant hardening it brought to his groin.

Now, as they sat in a crowded restaurant with Raven calling him every slimy bastard in the book, the senator only thought about how good her perfumed breasts, which were thrust repeatedly into his face during her tirade, would taste right about now. He hated himself.

"Do you want Callie? Is that it?" Raven demanded.

"No!"

"Then why were you all up in her face?" Raven mimicked her lover, "Callie, that was a fine argument, you were outstanding. OUTSTANDING!" Raven yelled.

"I didn't say…"

"I know what I heard, you lying, sorry piece of SHIT!" Raven's voice, hit such a high, violent note that other diners began to stare.

Senator Joseph sat back and sipped his drink. What was the point? Raven wouldn't stop until she whipped herself into the highest level of fury possible. Right now she was little more than halfway there, so he might as well settle in for the bumpy ride.

For Joseph it wasn't so bad—Raven's way of winding down after one of her tornado tantrums was to have rough sex. A smile tugged at the corner of his mouth: if he were lucky, maybe she'd choke him. He wondered how she would vent her anger with Callie.

CALLIE CLUTCHED HER pillow and deliberately tried to make her breathing sound even and deep, though she was actually wide awake—nowhere near the dreamless, deep sleep zone that she usually experienced after making love with Omar. But that was the catch: What just happened between them wasn't making love. Omar was much more sensuous than Callie; he could linger over her body, reveling in its taste and touch until she became the aggressor, urging him into her, but not tonight. Tonight as Callie had laid on her stomach, half asleep, waiting for Omar to finish his shower, she was brought fully awake by the weight of Omar pressing himself onto her back. Without so much as a word, kiss or caress, he quickly satisfied himself, dismounted her and went to sleep.

Things had been this way for the past month and a half, since the Mock Trial competition. At first Callie didn't think much of it; Omar was a bit self-centered, and she knew that it hurt him to embarrass himself in front of the entire student body, not to mention the outside bar. She took Omar's aloofness as a temporary condition; he needed time to get over it.

But she couldn't continue to deny that things between them had changed. His quickie sex move just now was the most intimate they'd been in the past two weeks. They'd always spent Tuesday nights together since Wednesday classes didn't start until ten, but lately Omar seemed inconvenienced by their standing Tuesday date, and the week before he skipped it altogether—said he forgot. Their conversations had become as stilted as their sex, no spontaneity, no delight.

When she asked if was something was wrong, Omar said no, he just had a lot going on. But Callie knew him, it would take more than a hectic schedule to keep Omar away from a woman.

Tanisha Malveaux. Even her name, for Callie, was a witch's hex. Tanisha was the one who kept Omar so busy these days—he tutored her. Callie had seen Tanisha around school but met her for the first time Saturday.

Callie thought about what a fiasco Saturday had been. She and Raven hopped into Raven's car early Saturday morning for a day of outlet shopping in a pleasant little town about ninety miles outside Dallas. The week's weather had been a dog—thunderstorms made moving about dangerous during the day and at night, kept the sky bright with lightening. The rain made Callie miss her Tuesday night with Omar even more; committed lovers never missed a good storm. But Saturday was an Indian summer day. Raven let down the top on her Boxter.

Callie leaned back and let the wind do what it would with her hair. The only reason she hadn't cut it was because Omar liked shoulder length hair, and on days like today she was glad that he insisted that she let it grow. Raven hadn't had much to say beyond good morning, and Callie assumed that it was because she too was enjoying the beauty of the day.

"Nothing hits the road like this car. I love it." Callie commented.

"Just because my car is nicer than yours doesn't mean we have to wear it out," Raven snapped.

Callie let it pass; the truth was that Raven always offered to drive. The few times they rode in Callie's new silver Honda, Raven commented, with a laugh of course, that no one noticed them.

At the outlet they shopped at all the women's stores: Saks Off 5th and Ann Taylor took the hardest hits from Callie. Raven's needs usually dominated their shopping excursions, but this time she wouldn't try on a single thing.

Callie picked up an empire-cut wisp of a dress that would look perfect on Raven.

"Raven, try this on. This is you."

Raven's 'bored with it all' attitude faltered for a split second. She could do that dress justice. But it pissed Raven off that Callie tried to flaunt her own Little Miss Innocent facade by making Raven look just the opposite.

"How come everything you pick out for me is whorish, naked stuff?"

"This isn't–"

"Is that what you think of me, that I'm a tramp?"

"No, I didn't–"

"Let me tell you something," by now Raven was pointing her finger in Callie's face. "I may not be Professor Lenton's pet or the Mock Trial Queen, but I'm the topped-ranked second-year student in the entire school!"

"Raven!"

"I don't need a dress like that to get attention! I can put on any of that cheap junk hanging in your closet and stop traffic."

Callie hung the dress on the nearest rack, turned and walked out of the store. She was slow to anger, but Raven had gone over the line. She called Omar to pick her up.

"Baby, I wish I could, but I've got my tutorial at noon, can you wait until about three?"

"Omar, I'm stranded! It's only eleven now, why can't you rearrange your session with Tanisha?"

"I've never asked you to change your plans with that little punk you tutor, and besides, Tanisha's test covering *Pennoyer* is tomorrow. She's counting on me."

"I'm glad someone's able to!" Callie shouted and pushed the end button on her cell phone. Once she'd calmed down she called Keith.

"No problem. I'm on my way," Keith assured her.

When she saw Keith drive up, Callie felt a weight lift from her chest. He hurried from his car to grab her packages and help her into the front seat.

"Callie, what's this all about?"

"I don't want to talk about it."

Other than thanking him for picking her up, Callie said nothing during their drive back to Dallas.

"Have you eaten?" Keith asked as they entered Dallas city limits.

"No."

"I'm taking you to Cantina de Carlos."

As Keith reached to open the restaurant door, it was pushed open from the inside. Out came Omar, smiling ear to ear, and he wasn't alone. A girl, with eyes like fire and soft, untamed hair, was with him.

Keith, his voice dry as saltines, spoke first, "What's up?"

Omar was too startled to respond to Keith."Callie, what are you doing here? I mean—I—are you okay?"

Callie's eyes, her whole body felt hot. She looked from Omar to his companion, then back at Omar. *Bastard.*

Callie turned to Keith. "Let's eat." She stepped into the restaurant and never looked back.

Callie knew that their run-in on Saturday was the reason she found herself in Omar's bed tonight. Callie didn't have anything to say to Omar for three days. He'd hounded her nonstop, explaining that he and Tanisha were merely taking a lunch break. Whereas he was too busy for her before, now Omar was ubiquitous. But Omar hurt Callie by setting her aside for another woman, even if the other woman was his little trainee. Plus, Callie wasn't sure that was all there was to it.

On Tuesday after class he caught her off guard—kissed her at her locker, a gentle, lips only kiss. Now, Tuesday night, she watched his sleeping form and wondered: What can I do to make things right again?

"THAT ARGUMENT HAS no merit!

It's rooted in prejudice! What's the public interest that needs protecting?"

"A society has a right to say that certain values ought to be upheld. We've got to draw the line somewhere. What's next—pedophiles marrying little boys?"

Professor Wiley crossed his arms and leaned against the blackboard, adding another layer of chalk to his already dusty black suit. He loved it when they got like this—passionate and agitated by what they saw as their fellow classmates' rabid intolerance or feel-good liberalism. Soon enough he would bring them back to the real questions: Do individual states have the right to ban gay marriages? How does the United States Constitution impact the question?

Professor Wiley signaled for the class to calm down. He nodded, acknowledging Brett Milstead's raised hand.

"The idea of two men or two women being married is distasteful to most of us because we don't personalize the issue. But what if it were your brother or your sister?" asked Brett, who was seated near the front of the classroom twisted in his seat so that he could be heard by the sixty other students in the room.

"It's like the miscegenation issue of the fifties and sixties, nobody liked it, in part because they didn't have a relationship with a mixed-race couple." His eyes locked onto Janna's. "A couple who loved each other enough to set aside other people's opinions."

What the hell, go for it, Brett thought, and found himself standing, speaking to the class, but looking only at Janna. "Take me, for example. You know me, most of you think I'm all right, for a white guy." Brett took his eyes off Janna just long enough to see a few of his classmates nod their heads. Even Nathan Lewis, who'd given Brett a hard time the year before, nodded in agreement.

"And take Janna...uh...Ms. Taylor," Brett said, using her last name, as students and professors did while inside the classroom. "She's a beautiful woman. Wonderful. Everyone loves Ms. Taylor."

Omar put down his pencil and instinctively looked at Keith, with whom he hadn't exchanged more than a chilly hello since the Mock

Trial. Though Omar and Keith were on the outs, Brett was still their boy, their friend.

Professor Wiley walked halfway up the classroom stairs so that he could see Brett's face.

Brett smoothed his soul patch and cleared his throat. "Now suppose…no, take it as a fact, that I love Ms. Taylor more than I love anyone or anything else. That I love her the way a man loves a woman."

Everyone, including Professor Wiley turned to look at Janna. She was stone, her expression blank. Was Janna looking at Brett, or straight through him? No one could tell.

Brett kept going. "And suppose you take it as a fact that I want to marry her." Brett cast a defiant glance around the classroom. "Would anybody have a problem with that?"

The classroom was silent.

Nathan Lewis looked at Janna, still frozen, and then took in Brett, slowly from head to toe.

"I might be a little jealous," Nathan deadpanned, "fine woman like that. But otherwise, no problem."

The class started clapping and laughing, coming alive, but Brett wasn't finished. He held up his hand for silence.

"Ms. Taylor, do you have a problem with that?" Brett's voice was strong, confident.

"A few," she replied. "But maybe we can talk about them."

Brett and Janna talked, then they set their wedding for the Saturday after Thanksgiving. Their story was the talk of the law school for a full week. The most popular version had Brett on one knee and Janna crying so hard that she choked. Professor Wiley provided a modestly embellished description to the faculty members, who couldn't get enough gossip about students' private lives.

By the next week Brett and Janna's story was old news, eclipsed by a juicy, tawdry, tale of unrequited lust.

THE GUY'S NAME was Prince Lucious Anderson Washington. He was from Palestine, a small town with little more than a caution light, deep in the piney woods of east Texas. Many a farmer's boy or chicken factory worker broke from the country life and made fresh starts in Dallas or Houston and Prince Anderson Washington was determined to be in that number. By the time he arrived at Monroe Law Center, he had, after trying two or three other names, decided on and legally become P. Anderson Washton.

Washton hit Monroe with a bang—gold front gleaming, this nigga go hard, high cap attitude in place. Always looking for a hookup, Washton approached Mr. Reese the first week of school and asked to pay for his books with hot merchandise. His conversations with his classmates, be they male or female, centered on which "bitch" he knocked off the weekend before. Sometimes he talked about fashion.

He was as much a fool inside the classroom as he was outside it. The adage that there is no such thing as a stupid question didn't apply to anything Washton asked. Ignorant of both history and current events, Washton knew nothing beyond what he saw on black television sitcoms.

Behind his back Washton's black classmates complained that he was the sort of black man who made it hard for everyone else. How did Washton get into Monroe? Hell, how did he make it through undergrad? Embarrassed black students from Jasper, Longview, Nacogdoches and other East Texas towns referred to him as, "Nigger Wash."

Only one student cared about Washton, Summer Phillips—a big-hearted, big-busted 3-L—who managed to see something good in everyone. The woman tutored Washton in the subjects he was in danger of failing: torts, civil procedure, contracts and property. In other words, everything.

After just two weeks, Phillips complained to the dean of student affairs that Washton sexually harassed her. She said that while she tried to explain the law of perpetuities and property rights to Washton, he would just sit there, chalky tongue roaming full brown lips, talking about his own ability to last in perpetuity and the length and diameter of his most personal property. At some point, every half-way-decent looking law student, male and female, gets propositioned. Summer wasn't upset that Washton tried to get with her. But one day he touched her.

The Honor Court charged Washton with harassment. Made up of both students and faculty, the Court heard cases of student misconduct and decided on the appropriate remedy. The court's disciplinary power ranged from private reprimands to dismissal.

Washton was an idiot, but he understood that the court would happily dismiss him; most everyone felt that he had no business at Monroe anyway. Washton needed a sharp, well-respected advocate to represent him before the court. He didn't attend the Mock Trial competition, but he heard about it. Washton wanted Callie Stephens.

Since her argument with Raven, Callie studied in a carrel in the library's basement. She preferred Reese's backroom, but Raven acted like the space belonged to her. Mr. Reese didn't like what was going on; if one of the women had to go, let it be Raven. Reese told Callie as much: "Just say the word and she's out." But Callie, sick of fighting, took to the library.

Two weeks before he was scheduled to appear before the Honor Court, Washton slid into Callie's cramped study carrel, cocked his head to one side, licked his lips and said, "What's up, Ms. Stephens?"

"Criminal procedure, what's going on with you?" she answered. Callie noticed that Washton's form blocked the small panel window pane that was the only way to see into the carrel.

"You know what's up. I need some representation, girl."

She swiveled her seat around so that they were face to face, looked Washton square in the eyes and asked whether he sexually harassed his tutor. Washton struck his best homie pose, right arm extended just so, thumb distanced from the rest of his fingers, his arm mobile only from the elbow down.

"Naw, I was just doing my thang and shit."

"Doing your thing includes assaulting women?" Callie looked at Washton like he was a pile of garbage and then turned back to her outline.

Washton dropped all pretenses then and told her that, yes he'd been attracted to Summer Phillips, and let her know how he felt. His approach wasn't appreciated by the city girls. He understood that now. But honestly, how was a brother supposed to know his game was too strong?

"Besides I wouldn't push up on no gal if she didn't want me to. I got five sisters, know what I'm sayin'?"

She knew what he was saying all right. Things were very confused on the sexual front. During her junior high school years, it never dawned on Callie that "pulling a train" was another name for gang rape. None of her girlfriends had thought of it as gang rape either. Trains were just something that occasionally happened to some airhead who didn't know that skipping school to hang out with four or five guys from the football team was asking for it.

Callie realized that everyone didn't snap to the new code of sexual conduct at the same time. She asked Washton to explain exactly what happened between him and his tutor. They sat there for four hours—Callie probing, Washton hesitant, embarrassed and sometimes angry. But the bottom line for Callie was that he seemed sincere and his story made sense.

That night she told Omar about Washton's case.

"What do you think, should I get involved?" she asked.

They lay, fully clothed, across Omar's giant bed. Omar unpinned Callie's hair. He thought: Her hair is pretty—thick and healthy—but not as soft as Tanisha's.

"Do what you want to do," he replied.

"Omar, I know I can do what I want, but I'd appreciate your opinion."

"Burthood's in charge of the Honor Court, right? You'll win," Omar said as he stroked the hair at the nape of Callie's neck. "Damned girl, you need a perm," he added.

"Quit it," Callie said and slapped his hand playfully. She was so intent on talking about Washton's case that she didn't notice Omar's frown. Tanisha never pushed him away, not even in jest.

Callie wanted to talk about Dean Burthood. "What does his being in charge have to do with anything?"

"Obviously, he likes you. Wendell Roberts will probably be the prosecutor, you're the defense counsel. There's no way a man can win against you as long as Burthood is the judge."

Callie propped up, facing Omar. "What's that supposed to mean? The case will be decided on the facts!"

"The case will be decided on how sexy you look to Burthood," Omar said, an odd smile touching his lips. "Just like during Mock Trial."

Callie shoved Omar's hand away and scrambled off the bed. Omar didn't move, just lay there, relaxed.

"You can't accept the fact that I beat you!" Callie shouted. "You've been in a funk ever since the Mock Trial. I'm sick of it, Omar."

He said nothing.

Callie calmed herself and then sat down next to Omar. She tilted his chin up to her.

"Look," she said softly, "you know I love you, but I can't take much more of this. I need you to treat me the way you used to."

Omar's heart melted. He missed her, missed them. If she did her part to put things back together, Omar decided, then he'd stop spending so much time with Tanisha, put her on the back burner with Shelly.

Omar said, "Baby, all I need is an apology. I guess you didn't mean to—not consciously anyway—but the way you shook your ass and carried on in front of Burthood and the other men. Admit that's how you beat me."

"I can't believe you said that! You're crazy!"

"You haven't seen crazy," Omar lashed out. "Keep trying to play me, and you will!"

"Oh, so now you're threatening me?" Callie threw her hands up. "Forget this, I'm not taking this from you. I'm out!" She stalked out the bedroom door, "Have a good life."

RAVEN THUMBED THROUGH the latest issue of *Essence*, her unseeing eyes skimming the glossy pages. She wondered: what's an untold juicy secret worth? Not much. Raven excelled at keeping things to herself, but this time she felt like sharing. She shivered, imagining the shock, the questions, her chance to replay the details.

Raven picked up the phone. "Hello Jacqueline," Raven said when her mother answered.

"What's wrong? What's happened now?"

"Nothing." It never took Jacqueline long to annoy Raven. "Why do you ask?"

"It's six in the morning, Raven." Both Raven and Jacqueline knew that Jacqueline hadn't been asleep. She'd become an insomniac when her toddler son died and rarely slept during the early morning hours. She'd lie awake, tormenting herself—*how did he get into the bleach? Wouldn't the smell alone have warned him off?*

"I'm calling with good news." Raven said.

"Oh?" replied Jacqueline. She took a deep breath and willed the pounding in her chest to subside, though she doubted that any news from Raven could be good, per se. At least it wasn't disastrous.

"Michael and I are getting married."

"Isn't he already married?"

"And your point is?" Raven snapped. "Unlike Dad, some men have the guts to get out when a marriage has run its course."

"Or gets run off its course." Jacqueline shot back. "So his wife won't make a fuss?"

"She'll end up with two cute kids and a nice house. She might complain about having to get a job because I'll be damn if she's going to get Michael's money," said Raven.

"But isn't Texas a community property state?"

"Jacqueline, *you know* that if I say that his wife isn't getting any money, then she isn't getting any money."

Jacqueline did know, and she didn't care, at least not about that part of the deal, but she did need to get through to Raven about something else. "Raven, what about the children? You know that you can't be around small children."

"I can do whatever I want, but just so you know, Michael's boys are almost into their teens. Michael's done his part and he'll pay child support. There won't be any reason for us to see much of them."

Cruel as it sounded, Jacqueline hoped that Raven was right. *At least they're old enough to tell someone if something goes wrong* Jacqueline thought, but she didn't share her that with Raven. Instead she said, "I hope that you don't expect for your father and me to pay for your wedding."

Raven hung up in Jacqueline's face, which was the usual way that their telephone conversations ended. She wondered why she'd bothered to call. Jacqueline long ago ceased being awed by or interested in her daughter's life.

Raven needed naive, easy-to-shock Callie. Raven missed her. Callie always lifted Raven's spirits with compliments about her appearance, her brains or her attitude. Ever since Callie pissed Raven off, there was only Michael to buoy Raven's ego. Michael was damned good at Raven worship, but he had no choice, so it wasn't the same. Callie's admiration, which didn't have a sexual price tag attached, kept Raven aware that she, Raven Holloway, was the ultimate It Girl.

Why hadn't Callie apologized yet? Raven stopped being angry the moment Callie stalked out of the dress store. If Callie hadn't acted so superior for weeks after the damned trial, Raven thought, she wouldn't have had to tell her about herself.

Raven never said she was sorry to anyone, for anything. She couldn't and still uphold her twisted code of personal conduct. But sometimes practicalities called for a departure from principle.

Raven threw her *Essence* to the floor. She needed Callie and knew how to make amends without too many words. Raven stood, stepping square onto the face of a sensuous doe-eyed model on the cover of the magazine, and headed for her closet.

      ❦   ❦   ❦

The doorbell rang once, then again. Callie glided to the door, her silk nightgown clinging to her, her hair soft and mussed in a sexy-sleepy way.

"Who is it?"

"Cal, it's me! Omar!"

Callie opened the door. Omar stood there, wickedly good-looking in a tuxedo. He held two dozen red roses. He placed the flowers at Callie's feet and lifted her–

Bzzz–!

Callie snapped awake. Her heart heavy, she realized that she'd dreamed of Omar. Again.

Bzzz–! That really was the doorbell. Callie groped for her slippers and robe. She glimpsed herself in the mirror. Wrinkled T-shirt beneath a terry cloth robe. Hair a mess. *So what* Callie thought, still half caught up in her dream world: *Omar's seen worse.*

Callie looked through the peep hole. It was Raven, wrapped in London Fog.

"What are you doing here?" Callie asked as she opened the door.

"Hey girl," Raven breezed in. "Let me show you what I've got."

Raven unbuttoned her coat and twirled it over her shoulder. She wore the dress that Callie picked out for her at the outlet store.

"Callie, you know me better than I know myself." Raven spun round two times, letting the silk layers of the dress catch the air. "This was made for me!"

Raven didn't wait for an answer. She dug into her oversized bag. "I've got something else." She handed a gift-wrapped box to Callie. "For you."

Callie opened the box and stared at a pair of pearl earrings. Coming from Raven, Callie knew that they were high-quality cultured pearls.

"I know I'm not supposed to give you these until after, but I couldn't wait," Raven chattered.

"After what?"

"My wedding!"

"Wedding?" Callie's anger, still intact when she let Raven in, gave way to curiosity, happiness and guilt. It had to be Michael, or did it? News of love triumphant usually thrilled Callie, but this time the cost, the breakup of a family, was too high.

"We have to wait a while; Michael has some legislation he's got to push through first. A divorce in the middle of things would be too distracting." Raven plopped onto Callie's sofa. She added, "Distracting for the legislature, not for Michael."

Callie wanted to ask the when, where, why questions, but she crossed her arms and waited. Raven knew that Callie wanted an apology. Forget that. Wearing the dress was apology enough. She had to get Callie into a friendly mood without saying she was sorry.

"Got any coffee?" asked Raven as she headed for Callie's kitchen. Raven put four spoons of sugar in her coffee and microwaved two cinnamon rolls. Watching Raven consume sugar fascinated Callie. Raven knew it so she took a third cinnamon roll. Callie shook her head and smiled. Apology accepted.

"Tell me about it," Callie said.

Raven licked sticky sweetness from her fingertips. "Michael thought that I was seeing someone else," she smacked.

"So you made him jealous, made up some stuff about another man."

"I didn't make it up. You know that when I make a move, it's for real. I wasn't into the guy, not the way Michael thought, just getting my freak on, you know." Raven looked at Callie. *She looks downright nasty*, Callie thought.

"Who was it?"

"Now that Michael and I are getting married, that situation's dead. No need to name names."

CLIMAX

"**M**ICHAEL," REESE SAID, "you may as well get to it."

Joseph stood in front of a print of Norman Rockwell's famous painting of a little black girl striding into school, guarded by federal marshals. Courage: folks back then had it. He'd read a story about the girl in the picture. She was grown now, about the same age as Joseph. According to the article, she was a civil rights activist—still had her passion. He'd been like that. Never thought he'd get derailed by bullshit.

"Yeah." Joseph smiled. He looked like a crying clown. "I may as well." Joseph spoke without facing his dear friend, the man he vowed back in law school never to disappoint. "I'm leaving my family, John."

"For what!" Reese felt pounding in his ears. Damned blood pressure. A penetrating hurt started in Reese's stomach and spread to his chest. Hurt, but no shock.

Michael abruptly turned from the picture of the little girl. "You know why."

"Maybe I do, but I want to hear you say it."

Michael emitted a dry, heavy sound. "It's Raven. She's got me, man."

"Is she pregnant?"

Joseph shrugged. "I can't even claim that as an excuse. That girl…." He shook his head and turned to the picture again. "She's something else, that's all. I can't explain it, John, but I have to be with her, all the time. I can't live unless I own her."

"You're kidding me! You're going to break Grace's heart, abandon two kids who idolize you, because you've fallen in love?" Reese grabbed a rag from beneath the counter and began scrubbing some offending spot that was invisible to the naked eye. It eased his urge to punch Joseph.

"Love?" Joseph looked surprised and let go a genuine laugh. "Love!" He pinched the bridge of his nose and laughed some more.

"John, I don't even *like* her. Love doesn't have a damned thing to do with it." He looked confused. "At least I don't think so."

Joseph looked Reese square in the eyes. "I'm not proud of it, but here I am, a forty-seven-year-old man. Wealthy, well-respected and semi-famous within my own world and I've been turned out by a thirty-two-year-old slut."

"Okay, okay, I can understand that," Reese said, although he didn't. He hoped that by sounding compassionate, he could talk Joseph into keeping Raven on the side. After a while, Joseph would tire of her.

"The girl's still got a year and a half of law school left. Why don't you just leave things as they are, wait and see what happens?" Reese suggested.

Joseph was a politician and naturally hard to shame. His ears turned red and beads of sweat formed on the tip of his nose. "Because she's seeing someone else. Either I'm going to marry her or kill her." Joseph didn't smile. "I figure marriage is less complicated."

Reese didn't ask, but Joseph volunteered, "She's screwing Callie's friend, Omar."

TO HIS CREDIT, SLEEPING with Raven wasn't Omar's idea. He thought it was something that just happened. Omar didn't know that Raven's actions were never controlled by coincidence.

The Mock Trial debacle caused Raven and Omar to develop a limited camaraderie. They'd run into each other in the hallway or in a quiet corner of the library and exchange concerned whispers about how much Callie had changed. Raven's line was: Callie's my girl, but she's become a self-centered, smug, pain in the ass. Omar would agree and recite his own part: I care for Callie, but she can't be trusted. All that sweetness she throws off is just a front."

Late one evening they ran into each other on the law school's parking lot. It was cold, but Omar didn't have on a coat, just his trademark jeans and sweatshirt. Raven listened to him dog Callie for ten minutes, nonstop. Talking about Callie angered Omar, made him seem mean and dangerous. Raven didn't interrupt him, just hopped from one leg to the other and continuously rubbed her gloved hands together as she watched Omar's clenched jaw and flashing eyes. Something Omar said brought Joseph to mind. Raven had the same problem with Joseph that Omar had with Callie: Raven and Omar controlled their relationships on a superficial level, but deep down Callie and perhaps even Joseph still had enough self-respect to walk away. She knew Joseph wanted her, but he didn't want to divorce Grace and he definitely didn't want to leave his boys. Neither Callie nor Joseph was completely broken.

She studied Omar, his arms akimbo, legs wide apart, unaffected by the mid-November evening wind. Raven shivered when she first walked onto the parking lot, but now she felt hot inside her heavy coat. Suddenly she knew exactly how to bring Joseph to his knees.

"Where's Tanisha?" Raven asked.

Omar looked around the almost empty parking lot. He'd been wondering the same thing; Tanisha was usually on his heels. It was a little irritating; he'd become accustomed to Callie's ways—Callie treated him well, showed him in a hundred little ways that she loved him, but she wasn't into hero worship. Sometimes when Tanisha focused her wild, sexy eyes on him, Omar imagined pushing her into a muddy puddle or shaving half her head while she slept—crazy stuff, anything that would get the girl out of his face for a day or two.

"I don't know, probably somewhere looking for me."

"Sounds like you could use some space."

"No, having a woman around is nice," Omar said. "It's just that Tanisha's so young…" Omar voice trailed into the darkness. The cool night did remind him of Callie. He pictured them, last New Year's Eve, walking along the banks of the Mississippi river in New Orleans. Callie had pressed herself to him and held both his hands for warmth. Cal. Wonder what she was doing tonight?

"Missing Callie, just a little bit?" Raven said. She reached out and touched Omar's arm in sympathy. Even through his sweatshirt, Raven could feel muscle.

"Hey, I've got an idea," Raven said quickly, before Omar could answer her question. "Let's finish this conversation over a pitcher of margaritas." Since he and Callie broke up, Omar hadn't had a good sit down with anyone. He and Keith didn't speak, and Brett was busy with wedding plans. If talking to Raven was as close as he could get to old times, he'd take it.

The next thing Omar knew, he and Raven were in the back room at Reese's. She claimed it was just a quick stop on their way to Cantina de Carlos. Raven tore the room apart looking, she claimed, for a lost diamond earring.

Then she started to cry.

"What's wrong?" Omar couldn't stand a whiney woman, but with all that talking and thinking about Callie, he felt almost tender-hearted.

"I'm sorry," Raven sniffed. She took off her coat and threw it onto a nearby chair. Raven wore a rose-colored cashmere dress, secured by five big black buttons that ran straight down the front. As usual with her clothes, the dress gripped everything Raven had. "Being here makes me think about Michael. I don't know if Callie told you, but he and I spend a lot of time here." Raven had been looking down, but now she fixed Omar with a watery eyed, imploring look. "I'm scared that it might be over, I think he wants somebody else," Raven lied.

"How could he want someone else?" Omar asked. He sat next to Raven and took her hand. "Look here, you and I have had our differences, but you're an exciting woman, in every way. The senator's no fool, he knows that."

She scooted next to him so that their hips touched. "I know I've got the body," Raven said between sniffles. "But maybe he likes his women different, prettier than me."

"Raven, please. Ninety-nine percent of the women in this city can't touch you. You know that." She smelled good too, but Omar didn't say so.

"But still, look at what you've done. You traded in Callie for Tanisha. I'm more on Callie's style—dark skin, full lips. You guys might play with our type for a while, but when it comes time to be serious, you go for the light skin, long hair."

Omar looked down at Raven and smiled. It was crazy, but being close to her made him feel close to Callie. Raven and Callie didn't look alike, but they were cut from the same cloth and then fashioned into unique, stunning garments—one soft and delicate, the other daring and demanding. "Please Raven, you're a modern woman who dates modern men, I know you don't believe what you just said. Besides, different doesn't mean prettier, it's just different. That's not why Callie and I broke up."

"Remember that date we went on, to De Longchamp?" Raven asked. "The way things turned out, I assumed that you don't think I'm attractive."

"That wasn't it. You're a handful, Raven." Omar felt himself opening up, being sincere, the way he used to with Callie, and it felt good. "I wasn't in the market for a woman like you, and you weren't looking for a man like me."

She leaned back. Her hair brushed Omar's hand. Raven, who'd tried every seduction technique known to mankind and invented a few of her own, would never know that it was the simple feeling of her hair against the back of Omar's hand that made him do what he did next.

He kissed her. Closed his eyes, grabbed a handful of Raven's hair and pretended that he was kissing Callie.

From that point, Raven took control. They didn't go to Cantina de Carlos for drinks. Raven timed things so that they left the backroom at just before midnight.

As they walked to Raven's car, she stopped in the middle of the parking lot and pulled Omar close to her. "Look, I know this shouldn't have happened, but I don't regret it. Thank you, Omar." She kissed his lips, his cheeks, his ears.

As they drove away, Raven adjusted her rearview mirror. Sure enough, Senator Michael Joseph's black Mercedes was parked at the curb across the street.

THE WEDDING WAS the Saturday after Thanksgiving. Janna wore white. Her braids, fashioned into a towering crown, were embroidered with pearls and rhinestones. Even Brett's father's eyes reflected appreciation as his soon to be daughter-in-law walked down the aisle.

Brett—flanked by his brother Drew, Omar, and Keith—was too mesmerized to make a move toward his head or his chin.

Once Brett asked Janna to marry him, he moved forward with a deliberateness that surprised everyone. "I'm sorry that I was afraid for so long," he told Janna. To prove his sincerity, Brett insisted that he and Janna go everywhere together: to movies, ballgames, even to church. Dallas isn't big on interracial dating, and the couple endured a few hostile stares and comments, but Brett always handled the situation in a way that made Janna know he loved her.

His parents, especially his mother, balked at first. They put Drew on a plane to Dallas; he'd always been able to reason with Brett.

"It's like going to a little hamlet in foreign country and marrying one of the locals. I'm sure that Janna's great in her own environment, but once you get back to the real world, she won't fit," Drew told his little brother.

"The world Janna and I live in is real, Drew," Brett explained. He wasn't defensive or nervous the way Drew expected. "You can tell mom and dad that any place where she isn't welcome, then neither am I."

On his flight back to Milwaukee, Drew couldn't stop thinking about Janna. For the only time he could recall, Drew actually envied Brett.

Brett gained not only Janna's love, but claimed his family's respect. As he stood at the altar, accompanied by three men he'd always felt inferior to, Brett was easily the happiest, most confident person in the room. As much as Janna loved him and wanted to be his wife, even her elation at that moment couldn't match Brett's.

But Brett could have been an unwilling groom looking for the first opportunity to bolt from the church, and he still would've been less miserable than some of the witnesses to his wedding.

"The ring?" the minister asked.

Keith reached into his vest pocket and handed Brett the modest gold band that Janna insisted on.

Keith heard his own voice saying earnestly to Vicki the same words that Brett was now saying to Janna. Why had he allowed it all to become a lie?

Callie sat with Raven and Senator Joseph. Two rows in front of them, her gigantic hair almost blocking Callie's view, sat Tanisha. The only member of the wedding party who Callie had a clear view of was the one she didn't want to look at. Omar. He kept looking in her direction, but Callie knew it was Tanisha he was seeing, not her.

In fact he looked at them both. Omar remembered that night on the beach with Shelly and how it had made him decide to marry Callie—too bad she wasn't the woman he'd believed her to be. Omar thought Callie was a manipulator, indecent enough to use her sexuality to sway the Honor Court, even if it meant embarrassing the guy she supposedly loved and she was about to do it again, getting Washton, a guy who was practically a rapist, off the hook. *Maybe if she were roughed up by a man, she'd have more respect for the system*, he thought.

Callie and Omar made eye contact. He intentionally hardened his gaze and then slowly let his eyes rest on Tanisha. The way Omar looked at Tanisha sent pain through Callie's entire body.

Tanisha was something to look at. She wore a mint green little dress with a bolero jacket sporting rhinestones on the shoulders. Callie had seen Tanisha come into the university chapel and even from a distance of ten feet or so, it was apparent that the little girl from Louisiana could be a showstopper when she put her mind to it. *I'm so plain compared to her*, Callie thought. The winter-white suit trimmed in blue looked fine when Callie put it on at home, but not here. No wonder Omar looked away.

Callie wasn't the only one with her mind on Omar. Raven bullied Senator Joseph into attending the wedding by mentioning that Omar would be there, but not with Callie. Joseph didn't know about Tanisha, but even if he had, there was no way he would let Raven get a chance to be alone with stud boy. Looking at Omar's handsome face and athletic body made Joseph want to puke.

As the newly pronounced Mr. and Mrs. Bretton Milstead took their stroll down the aisle and stepped into a waiting limousine, Raven turned to Callie and asked, "Do you want to ride to the reception with us?"

"No, I won't be able to stay long so I'll take my own car," Callie said. Her eyes darted to the floor as Omar passed her pew.

"Good idea. I'm sure Michael and I will shut the place down," Raven giggled. She was thrilled to be in a church, at a *wedding*, the ultimate commitment date, with Joseph.

Outside the chapel Callie waved to several friends, but never slowed her stride toward the parking lot. She'd decided to get to the reception quickly, say her congratulations and leave. Callie didn't want to go at all, but Keith made her promise to show.

Callie figured that she could arrive early and come achingly close to Omar in the receiving line or make a late entrance and risk watching Omar romance Tanisha the way he used to do her. She thought about her first date with Omar, at Janna's house party and the way he held her when they slow danced. Nope, couldn't take seeing him with Tanisha. Better to arrive early, give Omar a fake two second smile and go home.

Callie relaxed a bit when she spotted her car, then stopped in mid-step when she realized that she'd left her purse in the chapel. Callie hurriedly reweaved her way through the thinning cluster of wedding guests still standing on the chapel lawn. Most people had already headed toward their cars. Callie didn't want to get stuck in the receiving line with a bunch of nosy classmates. There was already enough gossip about how Omar had dumped her for a wealthy, sexy young girl.

During the ceremony Callie had been too miserable to appreciate her surroundings, but now the chapel whispered to her, insisted that she slow down. Callie took in the vast white columns lining the broad windows that looked out onto gardens filled with roses of every description. She stood in a dark corner at the back of the chapel and faced the altar. The retreating November sun cast a beam of sunlight across the altar. Callie could hear her own heart beat. She closed here eyes and let the serenity surrounding her seep into her soul. *Ahhh.* She felt herself start to do it: Let go and let God have his way.

Murmuring voices roused Callie from her meditation. She stared, not willing to comprehend what she saw at the altar. Omar, his face distinct in the sunlight stood facing Tanisha, holding her hands. He said something, and Callie having memorized his every gesture, knew that he was serious and insistent. Tanisha didn't say anything and Omar spoke again, leaned down to Tanisha, tilting his head just so. Intense, intimate and wholly irresistible. Whatever he asked, whatever he wanted, Callie realized, Omar was about to get.

Tanisha shook her head. Yes. Omar pulled her to him and kissed her.

You've got what you want; how does it feel? Omar tried to block out the voice, to lose himself in Tanisha's kiss. Still his mind wouldn't shut off. *How does it feel?*

"What was that!" said Tanisha as she backed away and jumped. She could be a mousy thing sometimes. They both looked toward the heavy oak chapel doors, which were slowly closing.

"I guess we had a witness," Omar said. He looked up at the skylight. The sun was gone. "Hey, we're going to be late for the reception."

On their way out of the chapel, Omar answered the voice in his head. He felt like the old Omar. Like nothing.

❧   ❧   ❧

After seeing Omar and Tanisha in the chapel, Callie skipped the reception and went straight to the library to work on Washton's case. She reviewed the typed, double-spaced direct and cross-examination questions that she'd finished two nights before. Without Omar in her life, Callie had plenty of time on her hands and she poured most of it into preparing Washton's case, so much so that she risked overworking it. Callie read a question, crossed it out and rewrote it. She read the new version and then scratched it out. "Great," she said, "I've gone from bad to worse."

"Bad. Worse. Two words that'll never fit anything you do."

Callie turned to find Keith in her study carrel doorway. "Good enough words for a pity party," Callie replied as she motioned for Keith to sit.

"I don't know how you feel right now, but you look good to me," Keith said. Callie had looked frustrated and worn when Keith first saw her. He was pleased that as soon as she heard his voice and turned to him, she immediately relaxed.

Keith and Callie sat for two hours and talked about everything and nothing. Everything, that is, but law school, Omar, and Keith's marriage.

$\mathcal{T}$HE MOOT COURT auditorium filled to capacity for Washton's trial. None of the spectators were well-wishers because Washton hadn't managed to make any friends. They were there to witness his last humiliating Monroe moment.

Omar and Tanisha sat at the back of the auditorium. He leaned over and whispered to her, "The case with me was a fluke, Callie's about to get knocked on her ass."

But Omar was wrong, Callie was spectacular, even better than before. During her cross-examination of Summer Phillips, Callie probed and pulled until Summer agreed with her that perhaps she'd misinterpreted Washton's advances. When Callie finished her closing argument, every person in the audience who believed that even the least among us deserves justice also believed that Washton's conduct, though crass, didn't meet the standard for harassment.

Washton entered the auditorium without friends, and he left the same way—he was his normal buffoonish self during the trial. Callie, on the other hand, emerged with a reputation for legal acumen that bordered on mystical. Her defense of Washton was nervy, and brilliant, a virtual case study on how to win a hopeless case.

The day after her Washton victory, Callie stayed in bed until she woke naturally. She skipped her two morning classes, didn't turn on the television or the radio, and she didn't read the morning paper. Callie simply sat and absorbed what had taken place the day before. She knew that getting Waston off meant that her litigation skills were rare and awesome and that once word got out to the legal community, she'd become one of the most heavily recruited law students within the state. She needed time alone to get used to the fact that her future was a lock before she dealt with more congratulations. And it wasn't just praise that Callie set her mind for, she didn't forget that a few students, especially some of the woman, might demand that she justify her defense of the odious Washton.

As she sat, Callie thought about Omar and for the first time in weeks she didn't feel heaviness in her chest. No one told her that triumph was salve for a broken heart, but it seemed to be.

When Callie reached Monroe she managed to get into the building and onto an already crammed elevator without running into anyone. She felt a tap on her shoulder from someone behind her.

"Congratulations," she heard Raven say. It sounded like she meant it.

"Thanks." Callie said.

Raven pushed her way to the front of the elevator so that she stood next to Callie. She hugged her best friend and said, "I'm so proud of you. After all the gossip today, I wasn't sure how you'd handle all this."

"I haven't been around today. I knew that people would be talking about the trial, so I stayed away until it was time for Lenton's class."

"Oh, I'm not talking about the trial, I mean the *big* news. It's so exciting!"

"What news?"

"Haven't you heard?" Raven showed every tooth in her head. "Omar and Tanisha are engaged!"

"*I* HEARD ABOUT what you did to your girl on the elevator; you're pretty hard, Raven." Omar wasn't surprised that Raven showed up, unannounced, at his front door. It would've pissed him off any other time, but he was eager to get a first hand account of how things went down.

"Monroe runs on rumors. I didn't do anything to Callie."

"Oh yeah? I heard different. I heard that you busted her with the news about Tanisha and me, right in front of everybody. I heard that Callie was practically in tears when you finished with her." Omar didn't even try to conceal his satisfaction.

"That's what I mean about rumors. No way was Callie about to cry, bet she wanted to though."

Raven took two steps toward Omar so that it was difficult for him to look directly into her face. From where he sat, Raven's small waist was all that he could see and, Raven knew, the perfumed body lotion that she rubbed all over her thighs and between her legs every morning had to be driving Omar nuts. Raven's vantage point was a lot better than Omar's; he sat with his legs open wide, his feet on the outside of the chair's legs. She looked at the flatness of his crouch and bet herself a slice of pecan pie that she would get a rise out of him within thirty seconds.

Raven fixed her eyes on Omar's lap just long enough to be sure that he could feel her giving him the once over. Then she continued, "Your woman, or rather your *ex*-woman, is stronger than you know Omar. She's confided in me about some of the awful things that you've said to her and it hurts her, but she'll never let you know that.

Callie's as determined to keep her emotions under control as she is to be the best litigator that Monroe ever produced."

Raven looked down again and saw that if she played fair with herself, she wouldn't be having pecan pie that night. But she decided to give herself a break and another thirty seconds to get next to Omar. She inched closer, so that her legs almost straddled Omar's left knee.

"Given all the time you and Callie spent together I thought you would know that. I thought…" Raven said, as she decided that maybe pie wasn't the only satisfying thing she wanted, "that you knew women a whole lot better than that." She slowly sank down on Omar's knee and looked him square in the eyes.

Omar felt his testicles crawl into his stomach. The time he'd done her before, he'd wanted Raven only because she'd reminded him of Callie. But today Raven was too much like him, too aggressive and carnal, to hold his interest. Still, he sensed that Raven was primed to give up valuable information if she could get what she wanted.

"Raven baby, I'm just a man, I don't try to understand women. I just try to be what they need when they need it." Omar looked for flecks of imperfection in the whites of Raven's eyes—it was a trick that he perfected in undergrad to maintain that deep, soulful eye contact that women liked.

"Well, I'll tell you a secret Omar, everybody's got a weakness," she placed her right hand on the inside of Omar's thigh. "Even me, no matter how in control I seem to be, push just the right button and I lose it. Callie's that way too."

"I take it you know Callie's weakness."

"Sure I do. You know it too, Omar, your male ego has just caused you to go in the wrong direction. It's not the love of a man, I can tell you that. Heartbreak Callie can get over, some other things wouldn't be so easy."

"What things? Tell me."

Raven squeezed Omar's leg with her thighs. "What will you do for me?"

Omar used both hands to grasp Raven's hips and pull her all the way up his leg. He thought about what it would feel like to yank her hair hard until her clear eyes lost their confidence and became tearful and begging. It worked. He kissed Raven softly and made sure that her knee pressed into the heaviness of his crotch. "I'll be what you need, when you need it."

After Raven left, Omar poured himself a drink, turned on his Earth Wind & Fire compact disc and studied his sketch of Callie. For the longest time he saw nothing, and then it just popped out at him. How could he have missed it?

"*H*EY." OMAR OPENED the door before Callie could knock. "I've been watching for you. I thought maybe you changed your mind."

"No I didn't," was all Callie managed to say. To her own ears her voice sounded small and shy. She tried to sound more at ease. "You're right, I'll need those notes for next semester, that's the only reason I'm here." But the minute she looked into Omar's face she knew that she was lying. The look in Omar's eyes said that he also knew it.

He rested one hand on the top of the door and without breaking his gaze said, "Come on in." As Callie ducked beneath his outstretched arm she thought of polished leather.

The house was a mess, books and day-old dishes covered the table. A pile of unfolded laundry filled the chair that Callie, in planning her quick entry and exit, had decided to sit in—if sitting became absolutely necessary. Omar's workout mat and dumbbells were in the middle of the floor. It seemed that every inch of the place was filled. Omar removed the newspaper strewn over the sofa and motioned for Callie to sit down.

"I haven't been in much of a mood to clean lately," Omar said as he snatched up a pair of briefs lying on the arm of the love seat and headed toward the bedroom. "Make yourself as comfortable as you can. I'll be right back."

Callie unbuttoned her jacket and laid it across the arm of the sofa. She went into the kitchen and used the only clean glass in the cabinet to get a drink of water. *Evidently Tanisha isn't as good a housekeeper for him as I was. Smart girl.* Although she tried not to, Callie remembered all of the cozy evenings that she and Omar spent at his place, cooking dinner, studying and making love afterwards. *All that's over now.* She decided to glance over the paper while she waited for Omar. She read a story about a dog that won two thousand dollars for performing stupid pet tricks and scanned another one about a boy who lost his right eye to infection because his parent's didn't have health insurance. *Whole world's gone crazy.* Callie set aside the paper and fingered the neck of her wool sweater. She got up and switched the thermometer indicator from heat to air just as Omar walked into the room.

"It's a little warm in here; I turned on the air," Callie said as she moved toward the love seat. Suddenly, standing before Omar, Callie felt very self-conscious. She wondered whether Omar noticed how nice her legs looked in the short black skirt. Omar looked at the thermometer and then peeked through the mini-blinds. "It looks like snow. It has to be forty degrees outside."

Callie studied Omar. As much as she willed herself not to, she noticed the way his biceps flexed when he lifted the blind. His T-shirt was tucked into his jeans, leaving no doubt that he had a washboard stomach and a firm athletic rear. Callie forced herself to think about the wedding—how humiliated and alone she'd felt.

Omar turned and walked toward Callie. He looked at her hard for a moment, hung his head and looked at her again.

"I miss you."

"Omar please, that's not why I'm here."

"I know that Callie. This isn't what I thought I would be saying to you right now, but it's what I'm feeling."

"What *you* feel! What about what I've felt Omar, since you took up with Tanisha? How do you think it feels, to have everyone looking at me, feeling sorry for me, because my man's got someone new? The last thing I want to hear from you, Omar Faxton, is how you feel!"

Omar looked down at Callie. Seeing her excited, whether in happiness or anger always turned him on. His mind flashed back to the first time he ever saw her that way, jumping up and down, flinging popcorn all over his living room. Boy that turned him on. It was like that with most women, but his reaction to Callie was always quicker, more electric. Omar felt the beginning of an erection as he sat down beside her.

"Callie, we've been over this before. Things between us weren't good, baby you know that, I know that. All I'm saying is I miss you. We've been through a lot together, spent a lot of time together at school, on this sofa and in there," he said nodding toward the bedroom. "Do you think that the way I feel about you has changed so quickly?"

"Yeah, I do. You're with someone else now."

Omar leaned in so closely to Callie that he could smell her perfume. His light brown eyes glistened, but his tone was smooth and sure. "Look, I would never deliberately hurt you, what I'm doing is dating someone else, Cal. You've said yourself that toward the end, we were like oil and water. I'm trying to accept that and move on."

"Since when is being engaged the same as 'just dating'? Raven told me...."

"Raven?" Omar interrupted in a tone that one would use with a small, tattling child, "Baby, you know that the last person you ought to listen to is Raven, especially if the topic is our relationship."

He inched closer to Callie. Part of her wanted to move away, but she just sat there. Omar gently touched her chin with his forefinger and tilted her face toward him. He measured each word. "I...miss...you. You will always be special to me. Cal, you know what I'm saying is true."

Callie felt her stomach start to churn. She closed her eyes and tried to block out Omar's words, his hand, which was gently caressing the side of her face, and the memory of what they were like together. She envisioned he and Tanisha standing at the altar, holding hands and kissing. And even though she summoned the vision in order to strengthen her resolve, instead it made her feel like crying.

"Look," she said and took a deep breath in order to hold back the tears. "I can't talk about this right now, I can't. Please give me the notes, and I'll get out of here." She tried to stand, but Omar suddenly wrapped her in his arms. His grasp was gentle yet strong and masculine at the same time. The sensation of leather, the smell and the smooth feel of it, enveloped Callie.

"Cal, please don't do this," he said in such a soft voice that Callie could barely make out the words. "Don't leave like this." Omar loosened his hold on Callie but still held her with one hand, stroked the nape of her neck with the other and planted small kisses on her lips, then her throat and her cheek. His full lips were warm and smooth against her skin and the neck of her sweater.

"Cal please, we've never lied to each other. I want you," he whispered before pausing to nibble at her ear lobe. "I can tell you want me, too." Omar's touch was so smooth that it was the instant hardening of her nipples rather than his caress that made Callie aware that his hand had moved from her face to her breast. Her heart racing now, Callie realized that her rigid posture of a moment before had given way. She'd actually shifted her body to accommodate his touch. Callie made a feeble attempt to push his hand away. Omar, who to Callie always seemed to have the appendages of an octopus, clasped her hand with one of his, placed it between his legs and held it there. He leaned away from her so that they were again face to face. When he spoke, his voice was husky and indescribably sexy.

"Let me love you, Cal." he said as he kissed her again. This time it was a deep penetrating kiss.

All of the emotions that marked Omar and Callie's tumultuous relationship—passion, regret and most of all the clash of two strong-willed individuals merged into their coupling. Callie always enjoyed Omar's special mixture of forceful toughness and tenderness. Tonight his masculine edge was dominant; he seemed to drive and drive, caressing her at just the moment that his touch became slightly uncomfortable. The entire time that they held each other Callie felt herself near tears, wanting to cry one minute for being so weak-willed and the next to cry out at the sweet, deep feelings that Omar stirred within her. Their lovemaking was difficult, vaguely disturbing, but Callie didn't want it to end.

Soon they were bathed in Omar's perspiration. For Callie this had always been their physical relationship's only turnoff. Omar always used his big hands to smooth the sweat from Callie's face so that he could plant soft, small kisses on her eyelids, and nose and lips. Trouble was, he swept the sweat straight back into her hair. She had to wash it every time they were together.

But tonight Callie look forward to Omar's little ritual. It would be something familiar, something to allay the feeling that nibbled at the edges of her confidence in his feelings for her. *I guess it's not over after all,* she thought to herself as she caressed the small of his back.

When the end came, Omar didn't hold her close and bury his face in the crook of Callie's neck the way that he usually did. Instead he pulled away from her, letting the waves sweep through him in solitude.

Callie opened her eyes the slightest bit and looked out the window. The snow had begun to fall. Suddenly she felt warm and safe. She enjoyed the moment, with no thought of the past or the future.

Her serenity was interrupted by tiny droplets of salty sweat. Sweat stung her eyes and blurred her vision. Callie raised a hand to shield her face.

"Hey, honey don't do that. I'm wearing my contacts." She wiped her eyes and looked up to find Omar suspended above her, his feet and arms balanced on either arm rest of the love seat. Omar looked her straight in the eyes and shook himself again, the way a dog does when it's being given a bath.

"Come on, Omar, quit it."

He looked at her again, still stretched out above her. For the first time Callie noticed that the soft gaze he wore only moments earlier had been replaced by the steely glint that she'd come to know so well during the last couple of weeks.

Omar's sometimes beautiful lips curled into a snarl as he said, "I've finally been blessed with a good woman, and here I am fucking around with you. I must be crazy."

Omar looked into Callie's face savoring her shocked expression. *Now's the time, choose your words carefully,* he thought.

"You think you've got most people fooled, but you don't. Always trying to act like you're all that, and here you are giving it up to me, knowing that I'm about to marry someone else. You ain't shit," Omar smiled and slowly delivered the bombshell that he'd practiced all morning. "Perfect on the outside, and nothing but an insecure fuck-up and a fraud *and* a whore on the inside, just like your dad."

Omar collapsed onto Callie, almost knocking the breath from her. He got up and walked into the bathroom. He didn't look at her again.

Omar emerged from the shower twenty minutes later. Callie was gone, as he knew that she would be. Omar chose a Mary J. Blige CD and bathed in the sounds of anguish that only a beaten-down woman knows and can express. Damned, life was good.

⚜   ⚜   ⚜

Callie lay, curled into the fetal position, in the middle of her bed. She was dimly aware that she was cold—the temperature dropped another ten degrees while she was at Omar's—but Callie didn't adjust the thermometer or cover herself. She was afraid to move from her place on the bed, afraid that the slightest shift from her narrow comfort zone, and she would lose control. Rather die than lose control.

Sonny Stephens lost control, and in the end what had he been, but a whore and a fake?

After Omar said what he did, Callie thought she would die. For a full minute after he abruptly left the room Callie lay there, stunned, trying to convince herself that she'd misunderstood. But there was no mistaking the facts, he was engaged to Tanisha, just like Raven said.

"TRY IT AGAIN, Set," Keith insisted.

Set Shot didn't move. He just kept on chewing his bottom lip, his hooded eyes angrily cast toward the door.

"I said try it again!"

Set grunted and went back to his struggle with a W. E. B. DuBois essay. "If I strive as a Negro, am I not per...per..."

"Perpetuating," Keith broke in, not waiting for Set to unlock the word on his own.

"...perpetuating the very cleef–"

"No, it's cleft!" Keith interrupted. "You should know by now–"

Set shoved his book toward Keith and shouted, "Well I don't! You know everything, you read it!" He added, "Who wants to read about some fool talking about *Negroes* anyway."

Keith was embarrassed; he'd never lost his temper with his protégé. "I'm sorry Set, I'm just trying to help."

"You ain't trying to do nothing but make me look stupid." Set slumped in his seat. Teenage funky attitude saturated the air. He eyed Keith condescendingly and said, "Callie's the only one who can help me unlock words."

"Callie's not here."

"News flash! Somebody better call BET," Set retorted. The young man's tongue was sharp, but his face was miserable. He didn't say anything else for a while and neither did Keith. Then Set asked, "How come she's not here? This is the second time in a row."

Keith stood and went around to Set. The kid needed a hug, and so did Keith. Keith hadn't spoken to Callie in four days, which was a break from the norm since they'd gotten into the habit of talking every day. When he called, she never picked up and she wouldn't say more than hello when they saw each other at school. It was killing him. Keith roughly massaged Set's shoulders. The only good thing that came out of their tutorial session was that Keith found out that Set could be pushed only so far. He was such a sweet, eager-to-please guy that sometimes Keith worried about him.

Keith told Set, "Callie's going through some changes."

"You helping her out?"

"I haven't even tried."

* * *

After the tutorial Keith went straight to Callie's apartment. He knew that she was depressed about Omar's engagement. It took everyone by surprise, including Keith and Brett. "I wonder what he told Callie, and that other woman, Shelly," Brett had mused. Keith had no idea how Omar had handled his business and didn't want to get involved.

Callie answered her door wearing sweats, no makeup at all and a messy ponytail. Keith didn't know what to make of her, except that she looked very young and very, very vulnerable.

Callie hugged him, held him tightly. "Keith," she said, "it's so good to see you. Come on in."

Keith had been to Callie's place before, but never alone. Her apartment was spacious and bright, but right now it felt intimate, about the size of a European elevator. Callie motioned toward the sofa. Keith scooted into a chair. No point in getting too close.

"Set sent me to apologize," he began.

"For what?"

"For whatever we did to run you off." Keith watched Callie, her elbows on her knees, chin propped in her palms. She was an angel, a slim, sensuous seraph. Except angels didn't have paste on smiles and eyes that hurt.

"I'm the one who should apologize. I've just been…," she paused, her lips puckered oddly, "I've been tired."

"He hurt you," Keith heard himself say. He'd vowed to steer clear of saying anything about Omar. Who was Keith to criticize a man for switching women?

Callie's eyes brimmed. She unashamedly wiped her eyes with her palms. "Everything happened so fast. One minute we're together, the next, he hates me, doesn't even respect me." Callie stifled a sniffle and served up a weak smile. "I'll get through it."

"Just because Omar's seeing someone else doesn't mean he hates you, Callie," Keith said. He didn't want to defend Omar, but this whole thing reminded him of Vicki. So this was how she felt—worse even, because of the years, the marriage and K.J. "Omar probably feels like a dog because of what you're going through."

"Yeah, right," Callie scoffed. She didn't want to tell anyone how Omar humiliated her, but she had to let it out. "Something happened Keith. I got with Omar. I know I shouldn't have, but I did." Callie knew from the way that Keith's eyes darted away from her that he knew what she meant.

Keith didn't want to hear any more, and he knew that Callie wouldn't say another word unless he let her know that it was okay. "Want to talk about it?" he asked.

"Afterwards, and I mean *immediately* afterwards, he told me some things, things about what he thinks of me, that I can't repeat, even to you. Then he did that Mike Tyson thing—wouldn't even walk me to my car."

Before he knew what he was doing, Keith found himself on the sofa beside Callie, holding her hands in his. He spoke urgently, his voice an odd mixture of rage and tenderness.

"Omar and I have had our run-ins, but still, I wouldn't undercut the brother. I'm just gonna tell you the truth."

Callie looked at Keith and noticed, not for the first time, how handsome he looked when he got serious.

"Omar was lucky to have you, and he knew it. You're hurt now Callie, but I'm telling you, losing Omar ain't losing much. I hung with him, I know."

"But he said—"

"I don't give a damn what Omar said!" Keith couldn't completely hold his temper. "You're *everything* a man could want." With no hesitation, he added, "If you were my woman, my only goal would be to make you happy."

Keith released Callie's hands and hugged her. It wasn't sexual, just strong and comforting. He kissed her forehead and whispered, "Callie, don't let Omar break you. Don't give him the satisfaction."

❧   ❧   ❧

The Christmas holidays were weird for Callie. One day she would be way up, ebullient, the next day she'd crash. On New Year's Eve Callie cried all night. On January second, she woke early and jogged two miles—she'd get up to six before school started. She went to the gym three days a week, got a facial and treated herself to a steamy bubble bath every night. Callie reread her favorite book and bought three CDs that she'd always wanted but never got around to getting.

On the Saturday before classes began, Callie went to Cynthia's Hair Palace and told Sharon K, her stylist, two words: cut it.

Callie, Keith and Set studied, shot pool, and generally had a good time. By the third week of January, when the spring semester began, Callie was more *Callie* than ever.

$\mathcal{P}$ROFESSOR LENTON SUPPRESSED a smile while she watched Callie try to make sense of her latest paycheck. It was the first Friday of the spring semester, and to Lenton, Callie looked like she'd spent her winter break at a high-priced spa. Her skin glowed, her eyes were bright and rested. Callie's new hair cut set things off—with her hair out of the way, Callie's exquisite eyes and her fabulous smile took center stage; she looked youthful and sophisticated.

"This is a mistake," Callie said.

"Let me see." Professor Lenton leaned forward and took the check from Callie. She glanced at it and said, "No, that's about right."

"But it's too much. This is almost twice as much as the average work study student gets."

Lenton nodded. "You're twice as good Callie, worth every penny."

"Thank you," Callie said to her mentor. Once she began working for Lenton, the two of them quickly surpassed the typical instructor/ research assistant roles. Callie was more legally adept than Professor Lenton had realized, and Callie found a heart beneath Lenton's steely exterior. They worked well together and found that they shared many of the same opinions and values. Callie wasn't the first student to be invited into Lenton's home, but she was the only one the professor talked to about personal things—like how she felt about being almost fifty and never married. Callie told Lenton about her dad and about Omar. Lenton didn't like Omar; he seemed to be a brother who was always looking for an angle, but she didn't tell Callie that.

"So, what do I have to do to earn this kind of money?" Callie casually asked.

Lenton turned serious. "I've revised my reading schedule for my property and oil and gas classes. I need for you to cross-reference the assignments to the midterm exams and make sure that I won't be testing them on something that I haven't assigned as reading."

"Okay. Where are the exams?"

"In my computer. I'll print them for you before I take off."

Callie smoothly switched from business to teasing. "Albuquerque, I presume?"

Lenton's face opened up. There was no steel, no shark's teeth. She'd met a nice guy who lived in Albuquerque, a high school music teacher.

"Anyway," Lenton said, not bothering to answer Callie, "I'm leaving today, right after my last class. I'll leave the reading schedules and midterms in a sealed envelope inside my desk drawer."

Callie glanced at her watch. "I've got to get to my next class. I promise to have everything finished by Monday morning." She headed out, looked back at Lenton and winked. "Have a good weekend."

As she walked to her locker, Callie returned the smiles and hellos of people walking past her, some of whom she didn't know. Since Washton's trial it seemed like everyone knew her. Not to say that they necessarily liked the outcome of the trial; it sparked a major women's rights debate, but they respected her abilities. Callie hummed a little upbeat Mary J. Blige as she walked, "*share my world, won't you stay with me...*"

Tanisha and Omar were at his locker. Omar spotted Callie from a distance, but she didn't know it. As Callie got closer, Omar, pretending not to see her, said to Tanisha, "I love you. See you tonight." It sounded like an announcement for the whole damn hallway. He kissed the girl and sent her on her way.

"Hello, Omar." Callie spoke. Southerners do, no matter what. Omar didn't respond. Callie retrieved the books for her next two classes, and was careful not to slam her locker door when she shut it.

She walked away, still humming Mary J., but this time it was something different, *"gotta face reality, there can never be anymore us."*

ONE OF THE BEST-KEPT secrets about Dallas is that in January and February, many beautiful, spring-like days are sandwiched between blustery winter days. The first Friday of the spring semester was such a day, as fine as any day in April. After classes Callie felt like doing something, and she didn't want to be alone. Her pay raise was burning a hole in her jeans, yelling Cantina de Carlos like crazy. The sight of Omar and Tanisha unnerved Callie, but not as much as it would have five or six days before. Callie felt good about that. When she thought about their encounter at the lockers, Callie realized that Omar deliberately tried to hurt her. Every time she thought about it, which was often (you can't help thinking about a man, it's the acting on those thoughts that causes trouble), her anger elbowed her shame a little further out of the way. Callie went to her locker to get the things that she would take home for the weekend. She didn't care one way or the other about running into Omar and his girl. She was getting used to it.

Callie was shoving her Commercial Law book into her locker when she sensed someone behind her. Her heart started to go south, stopped midway, and resumed its natural rhythm.

"Hey, what's up?" It was Raven.

"Not much." Callie's reply was flat. She'd kept her distance from Raven since Raven's, "have you heard the good news?" performance.

"Girl, where have you been? I called you as soon as I got back from San Diego, the day after New Year's," Raven said. "I wanted to give you your Christmas present."

"I've been around."

"Well." Raven couldn't think of anything to say. Too bad she didn't have Callie's gift with her. In Raven's world, an expensive gift could clear up just about any misunderstanding.

"Want to grab some dinner?" Raven asked.

"Let me ask you something," Callie said. She'd been talking to Keith a lot. She told him about Raven, about how she loved her friend, but didn't understand her. Keith didn't have much to say about Raven, but he did advise Callie, "She's supposed to be your friend, ask her straight up what's going on."

So Callie did. "Why did you tell me about Omar and Tanisha the way you did? Were you trying to hurt my feelings?"

Of course I wanted to hurt you, you moron. Raven's eyes welled and she said, "Can we talk about it over dinner?"

By now the staff at Cantina de Carlos knew to keep the margaritas flowing and the chips and salsa coming for Callie and Raven. The women drove to the restaurant in separate cars, and by the time they arrived, Raven had crafted an explanation. It pissed her to no end that Callie confronted her, put it on her shoulders to maintain their friendship.

"I didn't know that you still cared for him," Raven lied. "You're so strong Callie, honestly, if I'd realized that you loved the guy, I wouldn't have told you, at least not the way that I did."

"I didn't know that I was such a good actor," Callie said. Raven's explanation satisfied Callie only because she needed to talk about her feelings for Omar, just the way she'd needed to talk about Sonny. There was only so much that she could confide to Keith or to her mother. Raven was the only one.

"Let me tell you how much I love Omar." Callie told Raven what happened the last time that she and Omar were together. She didn't give her the sanitized version that she'd given Keith. Raven got every detail.

"Damn. I can't believe he said that!" Not only did Raven believe it, she knew all about it. Omar called San Diego to tell her.

Callie idly twirled a chip in the salsa. It would be too soggy to taste good. "It was messed up, Raven. I was messed up, you should've seen me."

"At least you're okay now." Raven spoke the truth. Callie looked fit and relaxed. Omar didn't leave behind the carnage he intended.

"Keith's helped. He and Omar don't hang the way they used to." Callie said. Raven, her mouth filled with chips, nodded that she understood. This was getting interesting. Keith, the original Mr. Aloof, getting tight with Callie. *What's this all about?*

Callie kept going. "Keith reminded me that it's just a breakup, you know? It hurts like hell, but six months from now, it won't." Callie backtracked; she had to be real, for her own sake. "If I really loved Omar, and I know that I did—still do, I'll be feeling him for a while, but at least not as much."

"I could'a told you that."

"But you didn't. You made it worse, telling me about the engagement," Callie retorted. On the way to Cantina de Carlos, Callie decided not to let Raven slide. Cordelia always said to accept people as you find them. In Raven's case that meant accepting the fact that she could be amazingly kind and generous one moment and hard as stone the next. Because she could be hard, Raven didn't understand that things that didn't faze her could easily hurt someone else's feelings. That's what Callie thought. Even though she forgave Raven, Callie wasn't about to let Raven front like she'd tried to help.

"Well," Raven said and hung her head for half a beat. *If she wants me to say that I'm sorry, she's dumber than I suspected*, Raven thought. "Is that all it took, for Keith to tell you that you'll get over it?"

"No, he's been a real friend. We've always talked a lot, because of Set, but now it's more personal." Callie smiled to herself, unaware that Raven studied her every gesture.

"Keith reminds me that Omar isn't the only man I'll ever love."

No wonder Callie looks so good. Raven thought. *Keith slid between the sheets before they had a chance to get cold.* Raven couldn't wait to tell Omar.

Their waiter came to the table and leaned toward Callie. "Ms. Stephens, telephone for you."

Neither woman should've been surprised. The cantina was central station for their social lives. Everyone knew that if they couldn't be found at Reese's or the library, they were probably at Cantina de Carlos.

But Callie was surprised; she just didn't let it show. The only person who ever called her at the cantina was Omar. For all her talk about getting over him, she felt a nervous excitement as she answered the phone.

"Hello."

"Callie, I'm glad I found you! This is Adel!" the professor shouted. She insisted that Callie call her by her first name when they were not on campus. "Can you hear me? I'm on Lester's cellular phone."

"Yes!" Callie shouted back. She lowered her voice. "I hear you fine, Adel."

"Have you been to my office yet?"

"Not yet." Callie planned on picking up the exams and reading schedules on Saturday morning.

"Good. I forgot to print the exams before I left. I need to tell you where to find my password card so that you can get into my computer."

"Just tell me the password. I won't forget it," Callie said.

Lenton giggled. Actually giggled. "I can't remember my password! I've never been good at remembering stuff like that. I don't even have an ATM card. One time—"

"Adel," Callie cut her off. She couldn't believe how airy Lenton became when she was with Lester. "Tell me where your password card is."

"It's in my desk drawer, right hand corner, all the way in back," Lenton said. Suddenly she was all business. "You'll probably want to start cross-referencing the documents first thing tomorrow, it's tedious stuff, but I've got to have it Monday morning."

"No problem."

"One more thing. Get the password yourself. I don't want anyone else to know where it's kept."

Although she'd had two drinks, Callie was wide awake, not the best state of being for a jilted woman on a Friday night. She decided to get to work on Lenton's project right away.

Callie told Raven that she needed to drop by the law school. "It's too late for you to go alone. I'll follow you," Raven offered.

Monroe's silent halls seemed like a foreign place. The only sounds were the hum of copiers left running overnight and the women's own muffled steps. Graduates from years past, their earnest faces captured in class photographs, smiled down on Callie and Raven. The two took their time. Raven paused in front of the photo of Joseph's class. "This one is my favorite," she whispered, though they were alone. "Michael says members of his class are all over the world—Africa, Europe, Asia. Monroe produces the best."

Callie looked down the still corridor. She could feel the spirit of Monroe, the scholarship and dedication. It had become a part of the building itself. "I love this place."

Raven turned from the photo. "So do I. Being here is special." Raven was sincere. She added, "The friends that I've made, especially you Callie, that's what's special."

My friend. Callie once again forgave Raven her moods and thoughtless words.

"Wait here," Callie told Raven. "I've got to go to Lenton's office."

For all her scheming it turned out that Raven stumbled upon her chance to bring Callie down. Raven knew that they returned to the school so that Callie could get something from Professor Lenton's office, but she didn't know what.

Raven wandered from one class photo to the next until she found herself standing in front of Professor Lenton's office. She reached to open the door, Callie's name on the tip of her tongue, yet something inside Raven made her slow her moves and do things the Raven way. She twisted the doorknob slowly and pushed the door open just enough to peep inside. Raven watched Callie sit down and turn on the professor's computer. "Good evening," the machine said.

"Oh!" Raven startled by the sound of the computerized voice, let out a teeny cry and bumped into the door. Callie looked up. *Empty buildings make the weirdest sounds.*

The computer commanded, "Please enter your pass code." Raven watched Callie look at something laying to the right of the keyboard while she typed. "Thank you," the inanimate voice intoned. Callie looked through Lenton's directory until she found what she wanted. The printer whined to life. Callie looked briefly at what she'd printed and then logged off the computer. Raven watch Callie place the little card in Professor Lenton's desk drawer.

By the time Callie emerged from Professor Lenton's office, Raven was patiently seated on a leather seat halfway down the hallway. So patient that she'd fallen asleep.

"Hey, wake up," Callie said as she approached. "Sorry it took so long."

"That's all right," Raven said. She made a feline stretch. "That's just what I needed."

Poor Callie thought Raven meant the nap.

IT'S HARD TO get next to a lawyer, you can curse, threaten to kill yourself, threaten to kill the lawyer for that matter, and you'll get nothing for your trouble. But imply that a good lawyer is dishonest, threaten to do something about *that* and watch what happens. Lawyers hate their ambulance-chaser image so much that they take a test to prove how honest they are.

The multistate professional responsibility examination is an ethics test. All law students have to pass it before they are unleashed onto the general public. The PR exam, as it's called, isn't considered a big deal. It's easy—tons of questions about right and wrong. Law students give it scant attention and pass in droves.

Callie took Professors Lenton's advice and studied for the exam. Raven knew that the revised exam was supposed to be tougher, but she didn't sweat it. She was Raven Holloway, Valedictorian To Be.

Monroe students received their PR exam results by mail on the Thursday before Spring Break. Rumors flew like trash in a tornado: one student flunked and one made a perfect score. Raven didn't come to classes on Friday and was missing in action during Spring Break. She told Callie that she'd been sick. Raven never got sick. No one knew it, but Raven was the student who flunked the PR exam—ethics was a topic beyond her comprehension.

Callie, word leaked, was the one to make a perfect score.

Omar did fine on the test, made a good, high score, but he wasn't happy. Why did Callie have to come out on top again? Plus, she walked around campus like losing him didn't bother her. Callie looked like a woman starting a romance instead of finishing one.

He'd dogged her, but she bounced back. Omar wondered what it would take to bring Callie to her knees for good.

Raven knew. "I think that Callie cheated," she told Omar during a late night rendezvous at Reese's.

"Why would you think that? She's smart enough to do well on something as easy as PR," Omar grudgingly admitted.

"Smart enough to do well, sure, but a perfect score?" Raven said. She sank her teeth into a Godiva bar. Nothing like chocolate after sex. "Besides," she added, dabbing at the corners of her mouth with her pinkie, "I know how she did it."

"You're talking crazy." As much as Omar disliked Callie, he couldn't conceive that she would cheat at anything.

"She got the exam off Lenton's computer." Raven saw that she had Omar's attention. He knew that Lenton helped to revise the nationally administered PR exam.

Raven pressed. "Callie knows where Lenton keeps her computer password. She doesn't know that I saw her use it to get into Lenton's computer."

"You actually saw her steal the exam?"

"Yep. At the time I didn't know what was up, then, *boom*, a perfect score."

"Ain't that some shit," Omar declared. Still he wasn't quite there. "Raven, you know how I feel about Callie, but I gotta say, she's honest to a fault. I can't see it."

Raven slid across the sofa to the end where Omar sprawled; they never cuddled after doing it. "Damn right you can't see. She cheated on you with Keith for the longest, right under your nose, and you couldn't see it. If she'll cheat on a man like you, she'll cheat on anything."

Omar looked stricken. "Raven, you're such a liar!"

"Hey," she made a gesture of surrender. "Don't get mad at me. I didn't say anything before now because I didn't want to hurt you."

"Since when have you been worried about hurting anybody?"

Raven summoned her most exasperated expression, "Since we've been doing this Omar!"

"Yeah. You're full of shit!" Omar grabbed his keys and headed for the door.

"Don't believe me, check it out for yourself!" Raven shouted after him. She kicked back, ripped open a bag of Kraft Caramels, and relaxed.

The next day Omar did check it out. What he saw made him want to kill them both. Callie and Keith standing close (too close) to each other sharing a private joke. Callie had on a short babydoll dress. *If a stiff breeze blew through here, her butt would be all out. Slut.* Keith reached out and touched Callie's shoulder.

Omar ducked into a nearby classroom. He bent at the waist, hands on his knees and took slow, deep breaths until his head stopped spinning. Omar walked over to the table at the front of the class and stared at the small wooden podium that sat atop it. He grunted and gave a mean karate kick to the podium, moaned and kicked again, harder. After a time he walked out, leaving little more than splinters littering the floor.

✿   ✿   ✿

"We know that she cheated," Raven told Omar over the phone that night, "but she probably covered her tracks. I know how we can bust her. Meet me at the law school in twenty minutes."

Omar slid out of bed. He slipped on his usual jeans and T-shirt. He looked back at his bed where all he could see was beautiful, wild hair sticking out from beneath the comforter. He took two steps toward Tanisha, changed his mind and left.

Omar watched Raven pick the lock to Lenton's office. He wasn't surprised that she was adept at breaking and entering because Omar realized that, above all else, Raven was about getting what Raven wanted, no matter the obstacles. A person with an attitude like that developed a multitude of skills over time. May as well let her be in charge once they were inside.

"There." Raven twisted the knob, her ear to the lock until she heard it click.

"Don't," Raven said. She grasped Omar's arm as he went for the light switch. "I won't need it."

Raven moved around the pitch black room as though it were her own home. Omar heard Lenton's desk drawer open. He wiped the sweat from his forehead, but it didn't do much good because his hands were as sweaty as his face. He listened anxiously but heard nothing else.

"Raven?" he whispered.

Fingers clamped down on Omar's forearm. "Aahh!" He jumped in spite of himself.

"Come on choirboy," Raven said. She let go of his arm and slapped him lightly on the cheek. "Let's go to Reese's. I need to burn some energy."

Tanisha heard the door open. She looked at the clock, not that she needed to. She'd been awake since Omar slipped out without so much as a good-bye kiss or an explanation. It had been midnight then. Now it was four-thirty. Feigning sleep, Tanisha watched Omar. He placed his keys and something else on the dresser. Omar lay down, then got up again. Tanisha watched him pick up an object lay-ing next to his keys. He looked at it for a moment then laid it down again. Omar returned to bed and with his back to his fiancée, fell asleep.

Once his breathing became steady, Tanisha tiptoed to the dresser. She picked up the key card, examined it, then went back to bed.

*T*HE NEXT DAY it was Omar's turn to do his part. Although Raven and Callie had become friends again, they no longer studied together. Callie now used her library study carrel all the time. Raven told Omar that Callie was always there between nine and ten in the morning. Omar had Wills and Trusts at nine o'clock, but he skipped it. First things first.

Callie sat as she had the first time that Omar really noticed her: chair pushed way back, heels atop her desk. He looked at her and his throat constricted. Callie was beautiful even with the short hair. He imagined himself kissing her long brown legs and from there moving north or south, whichever suited his palate. *Too bad for her that she fucked around on me with wimpy assed Keith.* The thought fortified Omar.

Callie could pass Omar in the hallways, run into him at their lockers and not miss a step. Having him inside her small study carrel was another matter.

"Hi," his voice was mellow, Omar-style.

"Hi." An uncomfortable pause. "What's up?"

"Not much. It's been a while since we've spoken. That's all."

"It's been a while since you've spoken. I say hello every time I see you, Omar." If he was going to talk to her, Callie decided, Omar would have to be straight.

She always was a mouthy bitch. Omar kept smiling. He was ready to get this over with. "You've been looking good, Cal."

Callie got to her feet. "I don't want to—"

"I've been thinking we might get together, you know, like last time."

Callie stared at Omar. How had she fallen for him? He didn't deserve to be within her circle of friends, period, let alone be her lover.

"You're sick," she spat at him. Omar winced on the inside, but on the outside he was as cool as ever. He reached for Callie. "Come on, you know you want me."

"This is all you're getting from me," she shot him the finger. "I'm done dealing with trash." Callie stormed out.

Omar knew that Callie wouldn't stand around and be insulted by him. He stooped and placed Lenton's key card in a far corner underneath the desk.

❦   ❦   ❦

The next evening Raven arranged a private meeting with Professor Noah Small. When she walked into his office wearing a tight little sweater and jeans the old guy took one look at her exposed belly button and got so excited that he almost upped his lunch.

"It's about the Honor court," Raven purred. She sat down and leaned across the professor's desk. Her sweater was skimpy at the top, too.

Professor Small, his eyes never leaving Raven's luscious globes, purred back, "How can I help you?"

"I have information that a student cheated on the multistate PR exam."

This got the professor's attention. Cheating on a national examination could damage Monroe's reputation. "We'd better get Dean Burthood in on this." He reached for his telephone.

Raven stopped his fingers with her own. "No, we can't handle this through normal channels. You have the authority to bring charges without a full investigation. Just do it."

"Why the rush?"

"Because the evidence backing up this charge might disappear if we don't do something right now."

The professor considered this. He normally would've insisted on more, but, well, he was dealing with Raven Holloway.

"Okay. Why the secrecy?"

"No one can know that I'm the source of the charges," Raven said. Tears welled in her eyes. "The person who cheated is my best friend."

Professor Small thought about it. If things were left up to him, Ms. Holloway's word would be enough. But Burthood would want more, the entire Honor Court would. This case wouldn't get anywhere without a witness because the penalty for cheating was too serious to impose based upon a rumor. Small knew that the charges had to be true, seeing that they came from Ms. Holloway, but inside the courtroom, hard evidence counted more than the accuser's reputation.

"I believe you," Professor Small told Raven, and she was sure that he did. "But we can't proceed with a case like this without a witness."

Raven leaned forward just a little more. "Professor we can't just ignore this. There are folks out there looking for any opportunity they can get to knock Monroe's reputation. We've got to handle this ourselves, before it gets out." Professor Small didn't look convinced, so Raven went on. "The judges probably wouldn't believe me anyway; they'd think she and I were into some sort of cat fight."

The cat fight thing didn't make must sense to Small, but then, he didn't understand women. Even if Ms. Holloway was right about that, it made no difference.

"I'm sorry Ms. Holloway, but if you don't have a witness, there is no case."

By the time Professor Small said this, Raven had come up with a solution. "There is another person. I didn't want to bring him into this, but he saw exactly what happened. I'm sure that he'll be willing to testify."

ALTHOUGH EVERYONE KNEW it was going to happen, pandemonium still broke out when Omar took the witness stand. Callie sat calmly and tried to block out the craziness taking place around her and inside her head. She was blown away when she found out about the charges against her. But when she found out that her accuser was Omar? There are no words for how she felt. Disbelief. Shock. She felt those things, but that was the surface stuff. For the past three weeks, Callie had functioned in a nightmare world; her everyday routine and the people surrounding her at Monroe suddenly seemed alien and very dangerous. Students stared. Professors looked away. Callie shut out everyone around her, except for Lenton, Keith and Raven.

She didn't do it out of weakness. Callie knew that she needed to store up all the fight within her to beat Omar. He was her true foe, not the Honor Court. She decided not to waste her energy playing the public relations game in Monroe hallways. Friendly, outgoing Callie became aloof.

Much of the Monroe family took Callie's change as a sign of guilt, but Raven knew what was going on. She hadn't known that Callie could be tough when she needed to, and it pissed her off to no end.

So while Omar was being sworn in to testify, Raven was thinking, *he'd better be damn good if he expects to knock this bitch on her ass.*

Omar was Omar, so of course he was good. Wendell Roberts was the prosecuting student attorney. He took Omar through the facts at a brisk, almost upbeat pace. Omar acted like a reluctant witness, but he didn't go overboard and come across as fake. Roberts asked him about his relationship with Callie.

"Isn't it true that you and Ms. Stephens were romantically involved?" Roberts asked.

Omar looked over at Callie. Keith sat next to her, she'd chosen him to be her co-counsel. Instead of looking at Omar, Callie was busy scribbling a note to Keith.

Omar knew how to get her attention. "We were involved, yes. But it was more sexual than romantic."

That made Callie and Keith turn away from their notes. Just about all of their fellow 2-Ls knew that Omar and Callie had been an item, but who knew what the professors on the Honor Court thought? Relationships that were strictly stress-busting sex sessions were normal in law school, so what Omar said may not have hurt Callie, but it sure didn't help.

Roberts asked Omar whether his relationship with Callie affected his testimony.

"The fact that I know Callie, that she and I are friends, makes me reluctant to testify." Omar replied. He sat silently for a moment, then looked to the Honor Court. "I don't want to do this, but I have to tell what I saw. As fond as I am of Ms. Stephens, Monroe's reputation is more important."

Raven was the first justice on the Honor Court to ask Omar a question. "What did you see?"

Omar looked at Callie again. Why hadn't she had sense enough to be satisfied with being his woman? Why was she forcing him to put her in her place? It didn't have to come to this. When Raven first asked Omar to testify, he said no. Now, looking at Callie sitting next to her new bed partner, Omar knew that he was right to listen to Raven. He began his tale.

"Let me begin by saying that Ms. Stephens and I don't see each other any more."

Callie was immediately on her feet. "Objection. Non-responsive and not relevant your honor."

Lockhart Dees, chief justice of the Honor Court, was impressed. As a student who knew all about who was boning whom and whether it was for real or for fun, he knew that Omar was trying to embarrass Callie and cause her to lose focus. Even though she was under attack on a personal level, Callie went directly into lawyer mode.

Dees and Dean Burthood were the two highest ranking members of the court, and usually one of them responded to the objections. Dees took this one.

"Mr. Roberts, the witness' testimony is clearly non-responsive. Justice Holloway asked him a question and his answer was off base. Care to take a stab at the relevance issue?"

Roberts responded. "Your honor, Mr. Faxton is merely trying to let the court know from the outset where he's coming from. Because he's already stated that they did have a relationship, the court needs to be able to put his testimony in the proper context. It's relevant that the relationship no longer exists."

Dees leaned back in his chair and uttered tired words known to lawyers everywhere, "I'll let it in for what it's worth." Dees was already learning the art of being a fence straddling judge.

Roberts repeated the question. "Mr. Faxton, what did you see?"

"I saw the PR exam master answer sheet in Ms. Stephen's study carrel."

At that bit of information, Dees had to bang his gavel for quiet. Lying about sex, even under oath, was understandable, hell the president did it. But this was something altogether different. Dees couldn't imagine Omar putting his law school career on the line by lying to the Honor Court about whether Callie cheated on the exam. Dees looked at Callie. For the first time he allowed himself to consider that maybe the charges were valid.

Callie couldn't do anything but listen to Omar spew lies. Unless Roberts or Omar said something objectionable, Callie wouldn't be allowed to interrupt, she had to wait and repair the damage on cross-examination. She looked poised, but beneath the counsel table, her left hand gripped Keith's thigh like a vise.

"When did you see the exam answer sheet?"

Callie shot to her feet. "Objection, your honor. Foundation. Mr. Roberts hasn't established that what the witness saw was the master exam sheet, yet he's questioning him as though it's an established fact."

Dees didn't say anything, just looked at Roberts. "Your honor," Roberts began, "I need a little leeway, here. The question of *when* is a part of the foundation, just like where he saw it was, and how he came to see it will be."

Dees frowned, he knew what Roberts was trying to say, but Roberts was speaking in tongues! Sometimes, out of nervousness, perfectly articulate lawyers became babbling idiots. Roberts knew that he was having one of those moments. He rushed to correct himself before Dees sustained Callie's objection.

"Your honor, establishing when this act took place is a part of the foundation. I'm laying this out so that it will be easy for the court to follow the chain of events. With just a few more questions, I'll establish how Mr. Faxton knows that what he saw was the master answer sheet."

Good save. Dees overruled Callie's objection. Callie took her seat. When she moved to sink her fingernails back into Keith's quadriceps, he grabbed her hand and held it. That was better for both of them.

In the back of his mind Omar knew that everyone was focused on him. He'd always craved being the center of attention, but for once, it didn't matter. He was fixated on Callie and Keith. Omar saw Callie's left hand go beneath the table. Keith seemed momentarily startled, then he looked at Callie. Omar saw Callie give Keith a look that he'd seen dozens of times before. What a whore. Although her education was on the line, Callie still found time to give Keith a little hand action.

Omar started talking before Roberts could repeat the question. "I saw the master answer sheet about two weeks after the exam took place. I know that it was the master because it was different from the answer sheet that the students later received."

"What–" Roberts began, but Omar talked right over him. Raven had told him exactly how the master sheet looked (he didn't even ask how she found that out) and Omar fed the specifics to the Honor Court. "Across the top of the sheet was written in all caps, 'PROFESSIONAL RESPONSIBILITY EXAMINATION ANSWER SHEET. NOT FOR DISSEMINATION.' The sheet showed the correct answers and gave an explanation of why the answers were correct. At the bottom of the page, there were instructions telling the instructors how to confirm that they had received the sheet."

Professor Lenton's haughty expression faltered. She was embarrassed that her key card had come up missing, and now she found out, at the same time as all of Monroe, that someone really did steal the exam. How had Omar known this? She knew that he was lying about Callie, and didn't doubt her innocence, but that was because she knew Callie. The rest of the court, except for Raven, didn't realize that Callie could never cheat. Their decision would be made based on the facts, and right now, the facts were definitely not in Callie's favor.

Roberts had the court mark a document for identification. He showed it to Callie and then gave it to Omar.

"Mr. Faxton, I've just given you what's been marked as 'prosecution's exhibit A.' Can you identify it?"

"Yes." Omar sounded almost sad. He spoke softly. "It's the document that I just described seeing in Ms. Stephen's study carrel, the PR exam master answer sheet."

Roberts took the document from Omar and handed it to Professor Lenton. "Professor?"

By now Lenton had readjusted her face into a mask of bored composure.

"Yes counsel," she flipped the paper toward Roberts, "what the witness described is a copy of the PR exam answer sheet." Burthood looked at Lenton. She added, "the MASTER answer sheet."

Roberts had the answer sheet admitted into evidence and moved on to his next question. He asked Omar, "How did you happen to see the sheet?"

"This is where it becomes relevant that Ms. Stephens and I aren't seeing each other anymore," was the first thing the Omar said. He looked at Callie while he testified.

"You see, I met someone else, someone special, so I stopped seeing other women, Callie included. I told her in a nice way, you know, but she kept hounding me, wanting to hook up." As he spoke, Omar thought about all that he'd done for Callie, all that he gave to their relationship. He vowed not to leave the witness box until he got his.

"Callie lost it. She started calling my place at all hours, disrespecting my fiancée and so forth. Every time I went to my locker she was there. I hate to say it, but she was stalking me."

Callie was so angry that her hands started to shake. She stood and clasped them behind her back so that no one would notice. "Objection. Relevance." Her voice was steady, cold.

But Omar had established himself with the court by knowing about the master answer sheet. They were willing to give him room to make his point.

"Overruled. Counsel, get your witness to move along," Dean Burthood said.

Omar said that he went to Callie's study carrel to ask her to stop calling his place. "I wanted her to come out, those carrels are so small, but she said that we could talk better inside. Here I am, trying to hold a conversation, and she's wanting to do something else." Omar waved his hand, "But that's beside the point. The point is, I caught a glimpse of the answer sheet. She tried to cover it up with some other papers, but a corner of it was still sticking out."

Roberts asked him, "If you saw only a corner of the document, how were you able to know everything that it said, even the parts at the bottom?"

"I figured out a way to see the whole thing." Omar bowed his head. "I led her on, kissed her, that sort of thing. I told her to go to the ladies room and freshen up, then we could do what she wanted. When she left I pulled the sheet out and looked at it."

"When she came back, did you ask her about it?"

"No, once I knew for sure what it was, I left. I wasn't there when she got back."

Roberts ended his examination smoothly. "Since you didn't talk to her about it, what makes you think that Ms. Stephens cheated? Maybe she had an explanation."

"Ms. Stephens is a bright woman, and she makes good grades. But I knew that she cheated when I found out that she made a perfect score on the exam. I tutored her a bit during first-year, and I have to say, as smart as she is, Callie isn't one to perfect anything."

For months Callie had felt that she didn't know the real Omar. But at that moment she did. Callie saw a magnificent shell that housed a wounded, weak, petty soul, and she didn't give a damn. Callie had moved beyond the point where Omar could shake her by labeling her an easy lay. If he wanted to play rough, so be it.

Callie moved from behind the counsel table and directly into Omar's face. "Who do you study with, Mr. Faxton?"

"I mostly stay to myself, but sometimes with Brett Milstead and Keith Dawson."

Since Callie knew that Omar's direct testimony was a big lie, she was free to commit the cardinal sin and ask questions that she didn't, as a fact, know the answers to.

"You didn't tell your study partners that you saw the master answer sheet in my carrel, did you?"

"No."

"You didn't tell your fiancée."

"Didn't want her to know that I was there."

"The sheet that Mr. Roberts showed you isn't the sheet from my study carrel, is it?

"I wouldn't know."

"Why not?" Callie turned sarcastic, "You the king of civil procedure and evidence. You didn't take the sheet with you, to back up your story, did you?"

"I didn't want to be seen with it." Despite everything, Callie fascinated Omar. His story was pretty tight, but she was blasting away at it, just the same. Callie was so sexy when the fire blazed. Omar enjoyed a fair fight, as long as he was on top.

Callie turned away and walked back toward the counsel table. She thought about Omar coming to her study carrel and her storming out. If any students studying in the basement saw that, they would think that Omar's story was true. She couldn't ask him whether anyone witnessed his visit. Omar was also right about Callie not being a perfectionist. Her score on the PR exam was the only perfect score that she'd made since her sophomore year as an undergrad.

Callie decided to skip all that and cut straight to the core. Omar set her up and he probably didn't act alone. Time to expose him and find out who the other bastard was.

"Who did you tell?" Callie asked.

Omar and Raven hadn't covered this. Their only plan had been to make sure that their conspiracy wasn't discovered. Each had assumed that Callie would be too blown away by Omar's direct testimony to do a quality cross-examination.

"I didn't tell anyone." Too late he saw the trap.

"Sure you did." Callie smiled at Omar and put a little spice on it. She was about to nail Omar, and it felt good. "You made the complaint to the Honor Court, right?"

They locked eyes. Callie's said, *I've won. Again.*

Omar's eyes answered, *no, not this time.* He knew where to go to hurt Callie, to get her off his back. Omar shook his head, as though he regretted having to say what he said next. "My God, Callie. Stop this. You don't need to act this way."

"Excuse me?" Callie hadn't known what to expect, but she figured that Omar would tell a lie related to her question. *What was this about?*

"The way you're looking at me, flirting, while your career falls apart."

"Answer my—"

But Omar cut her off, no way could he say that he wasn't the one to file the complaint. He had to derail Callie, and quickly.

"Just because your father didn't get help for his sexual deviance, doesn't mean that you have to follow in his footsteps."

"OBJECTION!" Callie shouted.

"The fact that he committed suicide–"

"OBJECTION, YOUR HONOR, PLEASE INSTRUCT THE WIT-NESS–"

Dees had been banging his gavel throughout their exchange and now he also started to shout. "Mr. Faxton, that's enough!"

Callie tried to think of what to do next, but her brain wouldn't cooperate, it kept replaying Omar's words. She never thought that Omar would tell her most intimate secret to anyone, that was too low even for him. Callie gained a few extra moments when a 1-L student who assisted the Honor Court interrupted the hearing. The student whispered something to Dees, who then declared a five minute recess.

During the recess Keith told Callie, "Let me take it from here—you've done a great job Callie, but Omar's down in the dirt now. I'd love to go there with him, I owe it to him."

Even amidst the chaos, Callie couldn't help but be amazed at the change in Keith. She'd never seen his calculated, coldly menacing side. She could tell by the set of his jaw that if she just said the word, Keith would decimate Omar when the trial resumed.

"No, Keith," Callie told him. "This is my fight. I've got to finish it."

When the hearing resumed, it was Dean Burthood, not Dees, who spoke. "Professor Lenton's computer password card has just been found." The entire room leaned forward to hear the rest. "It was in the study carrel used exclusively by Callie Stephens."

Omar sat back in his chair. He was finished.

"FAXTON RESIDENCE," TANISHA said. She and Omar had an unspoken agreement—Tanisha wasn't to answer his telephone. But this was the fourth time it rang in the last half hour and Omar wasn't at home. Maybe he was the one calling.

"Is he there?" No polite hello. That was Raven's way with insignificant people.

"No. Is there a message?" Tanisha was too well bred to be rude.

"Tell him that Raven Hollow–"

"Hold on Raven, he just walked in." Tanisha extended the receiver. "For you." She walked away.

Tanisha couldn't believe that she'd held on to Omar for so long. She worried nonstop that someone would come along and whisper into his ear: *You can do better.* If Raven had her eye on Omar there wasn't a thing that Tanisha could do. At least she'd lost out to the best, she consoled herself as she tried to get cozy on Omar's unyielding leather sofa.

"You don't have to worry about your girl, anymore," Raven announced.

"What happened?" Omar spent all evening dreading Raven's inevitable call. He'd left the law school immediately after he testified. Having satiated his anger, Omar had time to think about what his world would be like if Callie was kicked out of Monroe. Seeing Callie everyday angered him, made him explode inside, but her presence also soothed him. If he went too long without seeing her, Omar felt anxious and empty. He'd scan the hallways for a glimpse of Callie, even though seeing her meant a sure wound to the heart, every single time. Omar didn't want to think about how thrown off he'd feel without Callie around to hate, and to love.

After the hearing Omar went over and over his rationale, just as he had from the moment he decided to set Callie up. At one point, he convinced himself that things weren't so bad. In fact they were quite good. He finally paid Callie back, in front of everybody, for disrespecting him during Moot Court and for dealing with Keith. Callie wasn't leaving Monroe, she'd find a way to make things right. He would still be able to see her in classes, and after a while, he'd start to talk to her again. Callie would be happy to have him in her life again.

Omar braced for whatever Raven had to say. Suddenly he didn't feel so good.

"Omar, after you left, it was too good! I wish you could have been a fly on the wall. Callie finally broke!"

"Broke? What do you mean, broke?"

"I mean, your girl cracked up!" Raven cackled. Omar held the receiver away from his ear.

"Raven tell me exactly what happened," Omar calmly asked.

"Callie held it together until everybody was gone, I'll give her that. Anyway I was snooping around, you know, trying to see what she and Keith were cooking up for tomorrow. Callie goes into the restroom, and she's in there forever. I guess Keith started to get worried, so when Lenton came through, he asked her to step in, check on Callie. That bitch Lenton's supposed to be impartial, but I know she's going to vote in Callie's favor, no matter what the evidence shows. Can you believe that?"

"Get to the point, Raven."

"So Lenton goes in, then she rushes right back out and makes Keith go in!"

Omar's heart felt heavy. He didn't interrupt.

"After Keith went inside, I opened the door and slipped inside. They couldn't see me. Callie was sitting on the floor, shaking like she had a disease. She looked like a mental patient and Lenton couldn't get her to stand up, so Keith had to pick her up and practically carry her to his car."

Omar was stunned. Callie wasn't crazy. She was all backbone, the last person he'd ever predict to have a breakdown.

"Did Callie say anything?" Omar asked.

"The bitch was crying for her daddy."

Omar hung up on Raven. Without a word to Tanisha, he rushed out.

         🍁   🍁   🍁

"What else do you want? More soup? How about some hot tea?"

Callie grabbed Keith's hand. "I don't need anything else. I'm fine, just tired is all."

She pulled the quilt up to her chin. "After I rest a while, I'll be fine."

"You're no where near sleep."

"Yes, I am."

"Callie you've got to face what's happened; you've got to get ready for trial," Keith said. Callie tried to avert her eyes, but he wouldn't let her.

Callie sat up. Silent tears ran from the corners of her eyes. "Keith, how could this happen to me?"

"Your emotions gave way. It could happen to anyone."

"It didn't happen to anyone! It happened to me!" Callie put her arms around Keith and buried her face in his chest. "My dad had to be crazy. Sane people don't commit suicide," she said. "I don't want to be like him, but I know that I am, and it scares me."

Keith told Callie, "When I offered to finish Omar's cross-examination, you told me that this was your fight. You're right Callie, it is yours, and it isn't just about law school and Omar. It's about laying down your father's problems. It's about moving on."

❦   ❦   ❦

Omar was glad that he knew the code to get into Callie's apartment complex. Cordelia was probably with her, and there was no way that she would let him in. After the breakup, Omar took a chance and called Cordelia. His exuberant, "Mama C!" was met with a restrained, "Hello, Omar. What can I do for you?" Cordelia normally called him baby, sugar pie or some other sweet nonsense. She didn't know the details, but she knew that Omar messed over her baby girl. Omar mumbled something about a lost sweater and quickly ended the call. He was surprised by how much he missed Cordelia.

"Too bad, she'll just have to deal with me today," Omar said aloud as he rang Callie's doorbell. You could have sold him for a dime when Keith answered the door.

"What do you want?" Instead of stepping aside for Omar to enter, Keith came outside and pulled the door to behind him.

"Is she all right?" Omar asked.

"No." That was a lie. Callie was on her way to being just fine, but as far as Keith was concerned, Omar didn't deserve to know that. Keith thought he'd wanted to hurt Omar over Set Shot, but that didn't even come close to the way he felt about how Omar treated Callie. The only reason he didn't kick Omar's ass was because Callie didn't need any more drama.

Omar knew that Keith was killing mad, but he didn't care. Keith saw something behind Omar's eyes crumple. *He still loves her.* Jealously and panic struck Keith's heart. Omar, for his part, felt like an outsider watching the scene from a distance. He saw himself still loving Callie, and he saw Keith loving her just as much. Omar felt no anger, no competitiveness. If Keith loved her, even if Callie loved Keith back, Omar could deal with it. Suddenly, all he cared about was that she be happy, safe and well.

"Tell me what happened, Keith."

"With all that's happened in the past months, no, in the past two years, her father's suicide, you, Tanisha, being accused, what you did to her the last time you were together, what you did today–" Keith paused, fully expecting Omar to react. But Omar showed no shame, no anger, just caring. Keith thought: *He loves her and he's already forgiven himself for what went wrong in the past.* For that, Keith envied Omar.

"Everything finally caught up with her, and she freaked out," Keith continued.

"Do you think that she'll get kicked out of Monroe?" Omar wanted to know.

"After your performance today, and the deal with the computer card, how can they let her stay?"

Omar peeked past Keith's shoulder into the darkened apartment. "Probably not a good idea for me to see her now, huh?"

"Probably not."

"Is Mama C—Cordelia—is she here?"

"No. Just me." Keith didn't mince words. "I'm going to be here, day and night, for as long as Callie needs me."

Omar rubbed his temples, clearing the cobwebs.

"What's next?" he asked.

"Burthood recessed the hearing until Monday after next, but according to Lenton, it's pretty much over. The computer card settled everything. Even though she's been given more than a week before the hearing resumes, Callie's not going to be able to come up with anything to overcome the computer card."

Omar shook his head. He was a grown man. Why had he been so weak, so vengeful? He had to fix things.

"Keith, don't let Cal give up. She's not going to get kicked out, I promise you that."

"Okay." There was nothing more for Keith to say. He moved to re-enter the apartment.

"Keith?" Omar said as stopped him. The men looked eye to eye for a moment. "Tell Cal that I love her." He stared past Keith for a moment and then directly into his eyes. "I know you and I won't be kickin' it no more, but you'll always be my boy."

Keith embraced his friend. "Take care."

"**Y**OU TAKE IT," Set Shot told Callie.

"I'm gonna be sick," Callie said as she reached for the last slice of pizza.

Keith rubbed the nape of her neck, "You might be," he teased, "but it's good to see you eat again. This is the most you've had in four days.

"Longer," Callie said as she savored a mushroom.

Set Shot, Keith and Callie sat on the floor around Callie's coffee table. It was Wednesday, a regular tutorial night. Keith called and canceled the session for the previous Saturday morning. When he sent word by Brett on Wednesday afternoon that he wouldn't be able to play ball or tutor Set Shot, the boy took action. At six o'clock Callie's doorbell rang. She opened it to find Set Shot, with a Super Deluxe pizza balanced on top of his books.

"I have to say this is the sorriest tutorial session I've ever had," Set said. "I'm thinking about firing y'all." The trio looked at Set's unopened books. Keith laughed first, and the sound was so booming, so carefree, that it set the boy off. Callie, who hadn't so much as cracked a genuine smile since she first learned of the charges against her, laughed until tears ran down her face.

"Aaah," Keith sighed as he settled down. "Everyone deserves a break sometimes Set, even you." He spoke to his protégée, but his words were also for Callie.

Set Shot stood up. "My mom should be downstairs any minute. I'll see you guys later. Next Saturday morning?"

"Wouldn't miss it," Callie said. She wanted to get up to see him to the door, but Keith was still massaging her neck. She felt too comfortable to move and Set Shot noticed.

"I can see my way out," he said as he picked up his books.

Set Shot had been around Callie and Keith for so long that they had forgotten that he could be shy. When he turned to them, speaking low, his eyes downcast, they were caught off guard. "I wondered how long it would take y'all to see that you belong together for more than just tutoring me." His eyes stopped roaming the walls, and he looked at them and produced a magnificent smile. "I'm glad to see that it finally happened." And he was gone.

Neither Callie nor Keith moved. After a time, Keith, his hands still kneading Callie's neck, said, "Set Shot's right, Callie. At least he speaks for the way I feel."

"Keith I—"

"Before you say anything, I need to tell you something. Omar was here. On Friday evening, after Lenton left."

Callie moved away from Keith's hands and leaned back against her sofa. "I guess he couldn't wait to rub my nose in it."

"You're wrong. He was concerned." Keith paused and rubbed his chin, "Concerned isn't the right word. Omar was worried about you. He still loves you, Callie."

"Yeah right. If what he did on the witness stand was love…well." Callie shook her head.

"No, I saw it. He loves you and he's already gotten past the bad things that happened between you."

Callie sneered, she felt herself tense. "No bad stuff happened *between us*, Keith, all the bad stuff happened to *me*! Excuse me if I'm not elated that Omar's forgiven Omar."

Keith touched Callie's arm, urging her to look at him. "Putting the past behind you is a big deal, sometimes. It's what you need to do. It's what I need to do. Neither one of us can go on until we do."

"I know, and I'm going to start by making the trip to Huntsville, to see Jason. I may not be a lawyer yet, but I know enough to look over his case and see whether there's something we can do."

"We?"

"You're going with me. I trust you Keith, and I know you. The visit's going to be hard for me, and for Jason. I need your support."

"You've got it. I have to tell you I'm not necessarily the trustworthy guy that you think that I am. I talk about Omar, but I'm no better, I've done some bad things to women, too."

Keith told Callie the details about Vicki and Adrienne. Keith searched her face for signs of disgust, but, whatever she felt, Callie kept hidden.

When he finished, Callie said, "I can't pretend what you said doesn't bother me—it does, because it's so much like what my father did. All I know is that the man you describe isn't the man you are today. You've grown Keith, and sounds like everyone but you can see it."

Callie took Keith's hand. "You could have told me about your past a long time ago. We're friends, Keith, you can tell me anything."

"In that case, I have one more thing to say," Keith leaned close to Callie. "I'm putting my past behind me, because I'm in love with you."

O N THURSDAY EVENING John Reese visited Callie.

"Well, well," was all that Reese said when he saw that Keith was there.

"Keith's just being nice Mr. Reese, he's just here to–," Callie stammered.

Reese cut her off, "The man's where he should be Callie, no need to explain."

Reese had never been to Callie's apartment before. He stood patiently while the couple recovered their composure and offered him a seat. He chose a straight-back chair, while Keith and Callie sat close to each other on the sofa.

"I've heard some rumors about what you're going through, so I asked Senator Joseph about it. He told me the whole story," Reese said. In his tone Callie heard an unasked question: *Why didn't you come to me?*

"Mr. Reese, I didn't want to bother you with this. Frankly I thought that I could handle it, but some things happened…" Callie said, stopping abruptly because she didn't know how to go on.

Keith sensing her hesitance, picked up the story, saying, "Things should have gone smoothly, but there was some unexpected testimony from Omar. There's also some evidence, a computer card, that really hurts Callie's case."

"Because of those two things, I'm in a tough spot, Mr. Reese," Callie admitted.

Reese cleared his throat and said, "There's a third factor that works against you and it's probably the most dangerous of all. It's Raven."

"Raven?" Callie repeated. She'd noted that Raven hadn't called her or come to see her during the hearing. Callie had heard from all her other friends; Brett and Janna stopped by after church on Sunday and Senator Joseph sent her flowers. Callie thought that maybe Raven kept her distance because as a member of the Honor Court, she didn't want seem biased. On the other hand, Raven normally didn't care about keeping up appearances.

"I should have told you about her a long time ago, Callie. I regret that I didn't," Reese said. "I have a friend who knows Raven from when she lived in D.C. The things he told me about her are almost unbelievable."

Reese paused. He knew that Raven's involvement in Dr. Vakar's death was so much speculation. He was reluctant to accuse Raven of anything specific, but he wanted Callie to be aware of the lengths Raven would go to in order to have her way.

"Callie, to put it mildly, Raven isn't your friend. She envies you and when Raven envies a person, she does all that she can to destroy them," Reese said.

"I'm not following," Callie said. "What do you know that Raven's done in the past and more importantly, why would she envy me?"

"There was a doctor, back in D.C. who was about to get something that Raven wanted. Raven destroyed the doctor and her family. The doctor's now dead," Reese explained. "And look at what she's doing to Senator Joseph, she's about to destroy his family and his career too."

Keith remarked, "I don't know about the situation with the senator. It takes two."

"That's true," admitted Reese. "But my wife talked to Grace, Senator Joseph's wife, about a week ago. Raven has Grace scared to death, and not about losing her husband. Raven's made some threats against Grace and the boys that Grace believes she won't hesitate to carry out. Grace plans to walk away from everything, their home, all their savings and investments, just to keep her children safe."

Callie was stunned. She knew that Raven would connive and cheat to get what she wanted, but to actually threaten someone? "I still don't see why she would want to hurt me. Besides, we already know who's behind the charges against me."

Reese regretted what he needed to tell Callie. But looking at her with Keith, he knew that Callie was prepared to hear the truth.

"Omar is behind the charges against you, but I doubt that he came up with the idea on his own. Raven helped him."

Callie laughed and said, "Omar and Raven despise each other. No way they're working together against me."

"They may despise each other, but they're also lovers," said Mr. Reese. "Raven wants *all* that you have Callie. She took that piece of man you had, and now she's trying to take away your reputation and your future. She'd take your very skin if she could. Don't let her get away with it."

Omar looked at the dish that Tanisha sat before him. She'd fixed crawfish etoufee for him half a dozen times; they always ate seafood on Fridays, and each time he'd scarfed it down. Delicious stuff. Tonight the little reddish lumps smothered in a rich brown sauce made his stomach churn. He thought about what a police diver told him once: go down to retrieve a body and you have to fight off the crawfish. They go at it like ants to a piece of bread.

It wasn't the diver's tale that made Omar push his plate away. All week he hadn't had an appetite for anything. On Monday the Honor Court would reconvene. Omar tried to think of a way to save Callie without giving up Raven and himself. He wasn't worried about getting kicked out, but he knew that Callie would never forgive him if she found out that he was the one who set her up. She suspected him, he knew, but when Callie found out the details of his betrayal, he'd be out of her world forever.

"What's wrong, honey? Too much garlic?" Tanisha asked. Crawfish etoufee was her best dish. She wondered whether she'd cooked it too often.

Omar reached across the table and grasped her hand. Tanisha was a good girl. When he first took up with her it was strictly for the money, but she turned out to be more woman than he'd expected. As soon as Callie's hearing was over, Omar planned to tell Callie that he wanted another chance. If she said no, (more like *when* she said no), he'd try to make it work with Tanisha. But he wouldn't string Tanisha along; he'd be straight up about the situation and let her make up her own mind.

"No, babe, it tastes fine, I'm not hungry right now. Save it for me?" He got up from the table, sprawled out on his sofa, and with remote control in hand, flipped through the Friday night offerings.

Raven threw a tantrum when he told her that he intended to exonerate Callie. "I'm *not* getting myself into trouble just because Little Miss Perfect can't take the heat!" she'd shouted. Omar and Raven argued all week. She refused to help, but Omar didn't care and by Friday he'd made up his mind. He left a message on Raven's voice mail. "I'm going to the hearing Monday morning. I'll try to keep you out of it, but I'm not going to let Callie pay for something that she didn't do."

Tanisha snuggled up next to Omar. She nibbled at his ear, hoping that this time she'd get a response. He turned to her and kissed her. For the past week they, or at least Omar, hadn't been able to get past the kissing stage. Their three to four times a week love sessions dwindled down to zero. Tanisha pressed herself to him; she felt something. *Well all right.* Just then the telephone rang.

Omar squirmed from beneath Tanisha and reached for the receiver. "Hello."

"Okay, Omar you win. Come on over, and I'll help you find a way to get Callie out of this mess."

"I'm on my way." Omar hung up the phone and reached for his jacket, which lay across the opposite arm of the sofa. "I'm headed out for a minute," he said, and without so much as a parting kiss, he was gone.

Tanisha sat there, alone, fighting back tears. She fingered her engagement ring (she loaned Omar the down payment and so far had made every monthly payment herself except for the first one) and wondered how long it would be before Omar broke things off.

Tanisha was roused from her depressing daydream by the door-bell. *Must have forgotten his keys.* Maybe he changed his mind and wants to make a dramatic entrance. She wiped her tears and answered the door.

Greenish-gray eyes met blue ones.

"Who are you?" the women asked each other at the same time.

Then again, in unison, "I'm Omar's fiancée."

SHELLY WAS SURPRISED at how calm she felt, sitting and talking to Tanisha. She supposed that she had no energy left for anger or jealousy. Ever since he entered law school, dealing with Omar had been nerve-racking for Shelly. Although she loved him, Shelly knew that once she and Tanisha compared notes, Omar would cease to be her life's focus. She felt relieved and ready to move on.

"I know about the woman with the Boxter convertible, but I didn't have a clue about you," Shelly told Tanisha.

"That would be Raven Holloway," Tanisha said. Unlike Shelly, Tanisha wasn't ready for the conversation. She cried throughout, in a sad, non-hysterical way. "How did you find out about her?"

"I've given Omar several of my credit cards. Law school is stressful enough without having to worry about money," Shelly explained. "But every month there would be a charge for a restaurant or some other entertainment that didn't make sense. It's not like we did those things together. It got so, he didn't even try to hide it; he'd charge lingerie, flowers, hotel rooms anything he wanted and I'd get to pay the bill." Shelly said. She smiled and added, "Or more precisely, my husband would pay the bill."

"You're married?" Tanisha asked.

"Yes. My husband is sweet, but he's the wrong man for me," Shelly admitted. "Instead of rectifying that mistake, I got involved with Omar. Mistake number two."

Tanisha thought about how much Omar wined and dined her when they first met. She was certain that she was the beneficiary of at least some of Omar's lavish spending, but she didn't tell Shelly that.

Instead she said, "At least you didn't have to pay his mortgage last month. He gave me the honor of doing that."

Shelly nodded and said, "I lied to myself for a long time. When I couldn't take it anymore, I hired a private investigator. That's how I found out about Raven."

"I'm still lying to myself, or at least I was until you showed up," Tanisha said.

"Don't beat yourself up about it," Shelly advised her.

Continuing her story, Shelly said, "Catching Omar was easy. My investigator saw him with Raven the very first night that he tailed him."

"When was that?" Tanisha asked.

"A few weeks ago. Funny thing is, it didn't sound at all romantic, at least not the first part. The investigator said they were sneaking around in the law school after dark. He said that if he didn't know better, he'd think they were doing some snooping of their own."

Tanisha stopped crying. "What else did they do?"

"They went to Reese's Bookstore. That's where I got the goods on Omar. The investigator took a picture on the parking lot of him and Raven kissing. That was about four fifteen in the morning. The investigator said that Omar returned home about four-thirty," Shelly told her.

OVER AT CALLIE'S place, she and Keith watched a *Martin* rerun. Keith slept on Callie's sofa every night that week. Keith could tell from the relaxed way that she laughed at Martin Payne's antics, that he could come off watch; it was time for him to go home.

"You okay about Monday?"

Callie sighed. "Sure. What choice do I have?" She and Keith had discussed her hearing at length. They couldn't think of any way to refute the evidence.

"Tell you what," Callie said, "if I'm going out, I'm going out fighting. What happened last week won't happen again."

"What will you do, if—you know—if you don't win?"

"I can get back into pharmaceutical sales for a while." Callie turned to Keith. "I will be a lawyer someday. Disbarred lawyers get to reapply after a while, so there must be some sort of provision for expelled students to reapply."

Keith couldn't help himself, though he'd promised to wait. He found himself kissing Callie in a way that made her forget about Monday and all the rest. Oh, to feel again! It was a marvelous thing.

"YOU HAVEN'T TOUCHED your wine," Raven said. The glass had been sitting there for over an hour and Omar hadn't so much as sniffed it. All he wanted to do was talk about Callie.

"You're down with this plan?" he wanted to know.

Raven did a left shoulder hair toss. "Of course, it's the easiest way. I've got two of the Honor Court justices in my pocket: Small and Jackson. Lenton and Burthood are just looking for an excuse to let Callie off the hook; they'll vote for her no matter what. Lockhart Dees is a straight arrow; I can't get his vote, but it won't matter." Raven took a sip of her own wine.

"You understand that if your plan doesn't work, I'm speaking up?" Omar said. Raven raised her glass to Omar, "Understood. One way or another your girl is off the hook."

She raised her glass, "A toast?"

Omar picked up his glass.

"To truth," he said as their glasses touched. He placed his glass back onto the table.

"What's wrong? Drink up!" Raven insisted.

"Not on an empty stomach, babe."

"That girl doesn't feed you?"

"Sure she does, I haven't had much of an appetite lately." He rubbed his growling stomach. "I think it's back."

Raven headed for her utilitarian kitchen. "I've got leftovers. Pork chops, collard greens and a baked potato suit your taste?"

Omar took a seat at Raven's dining room table. He looked out on the cool April night and felt content, free. Callie was going to be all right; everything else would fall into place.

Raven's pork chops were the best he'd ever tasted. The collard greens were heaven. The baked potato had an offbeat taste, good but unusual. The wine was a different story. "What's up with this wine?" he asked.

"Something new. Chilean, I think. Good, huh?"

Halfway through a slice of double-fudge chocolate cake that Raven just happened to have on hand, Omar dropped his fork and slapped his hand over his mouth. He moaned, stumbled toward the bathroom, but didn't make it. Vomit splashed across blonde hardwood. Omar, on hands and knees, valiantly tried to make his way through the slime. "Raven, please…."

Raven lay on the sofa, legs crossed and savored her chocolate cake. She made a mental note to leave the housekeeper an extra twenty on her tip.

WHEN CALLIE WALKED into the courtroom, her first impulse was to turn around and walk out, but Keith was beside her. He squeezed her arm, "You can do it," he leaned down and whispered. "Today I'll sit near the door, in case something turns up." Keith remembered Omar's parting promise. Callie didn't believe a word of it, especially after hearing about Raven and Omar, but Keith knew that if Omar could help Callie, he would.

Callie chose an emerald green suit. She would stand out today, look like the lawyer that she knew in her heart she would someday be. She looked across the aisle at the prosecutor, who looked embarrassed. Callie looked up at Lenton and smiled. She stared at Raven, deliberately keeping her eyes blank.

"Your Honor, I'm ready to proceed," Callie announced to Lockhart Dees.

Wendell Roberts called the librarian, Dr. Mary Ford, to the stand.

"Dr. Ford were you on duty a week ago last Friday?"

"Yes."

Roberts established that Dr. Ford's duties included assigning study carrels and that she remembered assigning a carrel to Callie. She checked her records before coming to the hearing and confirmed that Callie was given a carrel.

"Dr. Ford, who has keys to the study carrels?"

"The student assigned the carrel, of course. I have a master set; the dean has a master set."

"Where do you keep your study carrel keys?"

Dr. Ford answered that she kept them in a locked drawer that only she and Mr. Early, the assistant librarian, had access to. The dean also kept his set under lock and key.

Roberts continued painting a picture, using the librarian as his brush. "Did anything unusual happen on that day?"

"Yes. I received an anonymous phone call."

"Please explain."

Dr. Ford testified that she was working in her office about three in the afternoon, when her telephone rang. A woman, whose voice Ford didn't recognize, told her that Dr. Lenton's missing computer card could be found in study carrel number sixteen.

"What did you do?"

"I knew about this hearing," she looked at the judges and added, "everybody knows about it. So I checked the study carrel."

"Did you send someone else to search the study carrel?"

"No, I did it myself."

The prosecutor was given permission to approach the witness.

"Dr. Ford, I'm handing you Exhibit D. Can you identify the exhibit?"

"It's the computer card that I found in study carrel sixteen."

The spectators emitted a soft buzz.

"How do you know that it's the same one?"

"Because of the code on it M10T4."

"Thank you Dr. Ford." He took the computer card from her and walked back to the prosecution's table. He turned, and with all the dramatic flair that a third-year law student can display, said, "Oh, one last question. Who is assigned study carrel number sixteen?"

Dr. Ford looked toward the defense table. "Callie Stephens," she replied.

Callie asked Dr. Ford a few questions, to establish that no, she didn't know who the caller was, didn't know the person's motive and couldn't say with one hundred percent certainty that someone hadn't stolen the master keys, planted the computer card and returned the keys. Dr. Ford liked Callie, and she eagerly admitted that she didn't know anything beyond the bare facts that she stated on direct examination. Callie did a masterful job, but she knew, as did everyone else in the courtroom, that Dr. Ford's testimony hurt like hell.

Next, the prosecutor called Ronnie Zink, the law school's computer specialist. He testified that computer card M10T4 belonged to Professor Adel Lenton.

When her turn came, Callie stood and said, "No questions, your honor."

Callie felt law school slipping away. She looked behind her; a smile from Keith would go a long way about now, but his seat near the door was empty. It was her turn to put on evidence, but she had no witnesses. Still, she was determined to get through her ordeal with class.

"Your honor," she said to Lockhart Dees, "the prosecution has not proved its case by clear and convincing evidence. I request a directed verdict in favor of the defense."

Dees didn't even have to look at the other justices to answer that one.

"Denied. Call you first witness Ms. Stephens."

"Your honor I don't…" just then she felt a tap on her shoulder. It was Keith. He whispered, Callie frowned, and he whispered to her again. Callie called her witness.

When the witness walked in, the room went crazy. Dees got to use his gavel, "Order, order!" he shouted.

Raven spoke for the first time during the hearing. "Ms. Stephens, was this witness identified in your trial memorandum?"

"I didn't file one, your honor."

"Well, that puts opposing counsel at a disadvantage. I don't know if we can…"

Wendell Roberts interrupted her. His personal opinion was that Callie was set up, and if she could prove it, then this was one case he would be happy to lose.

"I have no objection to this witness testifying," Roberts said.

Callie approached her witness. They studied each other for the longest moment, then Callie plunged in.

"Please state your name for the record," Callie asked the witness.

"Tanisha Malveaux."

"Ms. MALVEAUX, DO you know me?" Callie began.

"I know who you are; we're not friends."

"Have we talked before today?"

"Never, except to say hello."

"Do I know what you have to say?"

"I doubt it."

Callie proceeded carefully. She had to establish that Tanisha's testimony, whatever it was, wasn't manufactured. Omar told Keith that he would come through for her. She wondered if he was making Tanisha testify, lie to the Court. Callie had to find out. She wouldn't save herself with a lie.

"Ms. Malveaux, did anyone ask you to testify on my behalf?"

"No."

"Is there any reason that you would lie for me?"

Tanisha leaned forward. *Time to start demanding the respect that I deserve,* Tanisha thought. "I wouldn't lie for you or anyone else," she said, her voice strong.

Callie took note. She didn't know Tanisha well, but clearly she wasn't the fawning female that Callie assumed her to be. She asked Tanisha to tell what she knew about the case.

Tanisha turned to the Honor Court. She told them that she was Omar Faxton's ex-fiancée. Raven smirked. Tanisha explained that two weeks before the hearing, Omar came home late, laid some things on the dresser and went to bed.

"Do you know what the objects were?" Callie asked.

"Yes," Tanisha said, "once he was asleep I got up. I saw his car keys and a card."

"Can you describe the card?"

"Yes. It looked like a credit card, but it was two-toned, green, with a gold stripe lengthwise across the middle." The justices looked at each other.

"Was there anything else distinctive about the card?"

Tanisha looked at her ring finger. She took her engagement ring off just before entering the hearing. She knew that her next words would extinguish any hope of marrying Omar.

"Yes. One corner of the card had ridges in it, like teeth. And there was a number on the card."

"Ms. Malveaux, you've seen computer cards before?" asked Raven.

"Yes."

"So you know they're all the same color, all have a ridge on one edge, that's no big deal." It wasn't a question and Raven wasn't at all smooth—her fangs showed.

"Right." Tanisha eyes flashed fire, but her voice was sure.

"If it was dark, how do you know there were numbers on the card?" Raven spat at the witness, who replied, "Moonlight, Ms. Holloway."

Callie was nearly floored by Raven's behavior. *Mr. Reese was right, she's the one, worse than Omar, even.*

Callie looked back at Keith. His expression was solemn. *I know it hurts, but you gotta finish.*

"Do you have anything more to say about the card, Ms. Malveaux?" Callie inquired.

"Just that I recall that the card number included a four and an M and a T," she had to raise her voice to be heard above the growing clamor, "I don't recall the order."

Raven sprang from her seat, "This is ludicrous! You expect this Court to believe that you memorized the code? How stupid do you think we are!"

Lockhart Dees had seen enough, "Justice Holloway sit down."

Raven turned her ranting on him, "But she…"

Dees banged his gavel. "I SAID SIT DOWN!"

Raven sat. She wiped her shiny face and tried to speak calmly. "Justice Dees, the witness has obviously committed perjury, her testimony isn't credible." She shot a hateful look at Tanisha. "She deserves to be brought up on charges herself."

Lenton looked like she wanted to throttle Raven. In her most professorial voice she addressed Lockhart Dees, "Mr. Chief Justice, may I?"

Professor Lenton said to Tanisha, "Ms. Malveaux, please tell us how you recall some portions of the computer card code."

Tanisha looked directly at her nemesis. No matter what happened, Tanisha knew that Raven wasn't even close to being the woman that Tanisha was. Raven had a hollow space where character should've been. "The T and the M, well, those are my initials. I have four siblings, so I remembered that." Tanisha spoke respectfully to Professor Lenton, "I'm good at puzzles, number games, that sort of thing."

Raven was so angry that she forgot to front it, "If this is true, then where the hell is Omar? Why isn't he here to get Callie off the hook himself? Why'd he send his little girlfriend in to do the dirty work?"

The gavel banged; the spectators went wild. Dean Burthood liked a lively trial, but Raven was out of control. Future valedictorian or not, he knew then that ultimately Raven would prove an embarrassment to Monroe. He held up one hand, more than enough to calm the room.

"Ms. Holloway, if you don't sit down and shut up," he said calmly, "and I mean right now, I'll have you escorted from the room."

Everyone except for Tanisha had forgotten that buried in Raven's outburst was a very important question. ""Dean Burthood? May I answer her question?"

"Please do," he replied.

Tanisha repeated the question. "You asked why Omar Faxton isn't here. I don't know why." She shifted her gaze from Dean Burthood to Raven and said, "I haven't seen Omar since Friday night, when he left home to meet you."

Now it was Callie's turn to smirk. *Stupid Raven. Didn't she know by now not to ask a question if she didn't know what the witness' answer would be?*

"This charade is over," Dean Burthood declared.

He looked at Raven, "Ms. Holloway, my office, in ten minutes." The justices filed out.

Callie walked over to her star witness. She reached for Tanisha's hand, changed her mind and embraced her, "Thank you. Thank you so much."

Tanisha wiped away a tear, "Hey, no big deal, glad I could help. And for what it's worth, after Omar testified at your hearing, he wasn't the same. In retrospect, I think that he was down because he'd hurt you. I believe in my heart that when he left home last Friday, he planned to do something to set things straight."

Tanisha wiped away another tear and looked directly toward Raven, who was headed their way. "Somehow she got in his way," she said, the hatred plain in her voice.

Callie gave Tanisha a final hug and turned to face Raven.

"I know what you must be thinking," Raven said. She was her old self, friendly, vivacious, and seemingly sincere. "I want you to know that no matter what, you'll always be my best friend."

"Raven you don't have any friends, and you never will." Callie replied. "You're pure evil, and you're going to pay for what you tried to do to me."

Callie thought of Omar. She felt the remnants of love and a wave of calm wash over her. In it's wake she was left with a resolve to remember only the good times and to forgive the rest. Because, in the end, Omar tried to set things straight, she decided to do the same for him.

"God help you if you've done something to hurt Omar. When I finish with you, you'll wish you were never born," she promised Raven.

Callie took Keith's hand and walked away.

Coming Soon

The Governor's Wife
Raven Holloway Returns!

*R*aven is back, only now she's Mrs. Raven Holloway Joseph, the sophisticated, accomplished wife of Governor Michael Joseph. Although her name and station in life have changed, Raven hasn't. She intends to live as she always has, taking life's pleasures at will and annihilating anyone with the audacity to get in her way.

Governor Joseph's oldest son, Jamal Joseph, is, like his step-mother, fearless in the pursuit of what he wants. And what he wants more than anything is to keep Raven from destroying his father.

For more information contact:
http://www.sheliadansbyharvey.com/

0-595-21535-1